PRAISE FOR

Raven's Fire

D1290559

"Join John Gubbins as he teaches you to never look at a raven in the same way again."

—Kenn Pitawanakwat,
Anishinaabe Special Language Instructor

"*Raven's Fire* is a story of life and death, a story that moves swiftly and relentlessly to a conclusion."

—Harry L. Peterson, President Emeritus,
Western State University of Colorado

"*Raven's Fire* [is] a new mythology at once oddly familiar and human and innovative and spectacular."

—Matthew Gavin Frank, Northern Michigan University,
assistant professor, author of *Barolo* and *Pot Farm*

RAVEN'S *Fire*

JOHN GUBBINS

SWEETWATER BOOKS
AN IMPRINT OF CEDAR FORT, INC.
SPRINGVILLE, UTAH

ISBN 13: 978-1-4621-1216-6

Published by Sweetwater Books, an imprint of Cedar Fort, Inc.
2373 W. 700 S., Springville, UT 84663
Distributed by Cedar Fort, Inc., www.cedarfort.com

LIBRARY OF CONGRESS CATALOGING-IN-PUBLICATION DATA

Gubbins, John (John L.), 1943-
Raven's fire / by John Gubbins.
    page cm
  ISBN 978-1-4621-1216-6 (pbk. : alk. paper)
  1. Marriage--Fiction. 2. Secrets--Fiction. [1. Family problems--Fiction.] I. Title.
PS3607.U235R39 2013
813'.6--dc23
                            2013017348

Cover design by Angela D. Olsen
Cover design © 2013 by Lyle Mortimer
Edited and typeset by Melissa J. Caldwell

Printed in the United States of America

10 9 8 7 6 5 4 3 2 1

To all the selfless people who do hospice work.

To my wife, Carol,
To my son Alexander and to Emily Kaney,
And to my son James and his sons, Gianni and Dominic.

Contents

Acknowledgments

BEVERLY MATHERNE, POETESS, FOR ALL THE WON-
drous changes she brought to Carol's and my life and the lives
of Alex and Emily.

Kenneth Pitawanakwat of the Department of Native Studies at
Northern Michigan University for his advice and direction. Kenn is
a master storyteller.

Pat McCreary and Joseph Bourgoine for generously reading an
early draft and providing valuable criticism. Joseph is an experienced
woodsman and skilled fly fisher.

Pat is a hospice volunteer serving this year as President Elect of
the Upper Peninsula District of the Michigan Association of Health
Care Advocates.

My sister Nora and my brother-in-law Jim Roderick, a true
brother, whose generous reading and comments on several early
drafts shaped many of the characters. Let it be known that Jim
would have killed Raven.

Eleanor Jackson, without whom none of this would have come
to pass.

My sisters Mary and Margaret, who have so lovingly supported
Carol and me.

Dr. Chet Defonso, friend, for all his encouragement.

Theo McCracken and his son Alexander for their encouragement, intelligent conversation, and the best brewed coffee in Marquette. A visit to Dead River Coffee is the best way to start any day.

The Northwoods Tale

THE NORTHWOODS TALE IS A PARTICULARLY AMERIcan sort of storytelling that was once popular but is now nearly extinct and so unfamiliar. The first tellers of the Northwoods Tale were an unlikely group. In the years following our Civil War, geologists, surveyors, engineers, and corporate emissaries searched the northern tier of the United States, looking for mineral deposits, principally copper and iron, and for stands of pine and hardwood trees—the pine for construction and the hardwoods for charcoal. During the day, they explored, keeping careful notes of their discoveries for the home office. During the evening, they relaxed around campfires, conversing with their native guides. Save for the skill of their guides, these urban professionals would not have survived in the woods. The native guides shuttled them from railheads and lake ports to the wild interior, and they set up and ran their wilderness camps. Travel was by canoe, and native guides were the premier navigators on northern rivers. They knew the rivers' courses and portages; they knew how to make and repair their birch bark canoes; and they knew where the mineral deposits lay and the densest timber stood. And most important, they knew how to get there and back alive.

For evening recreation, the native guides and their clients shared stories around their campfires. The last thought on their minds was inventing a new sort of storytelling. The Northwoods Tale is the offspring of progressive science and native tribal tradition. University trained in scientific observation, the clients described their forest experiences shorn of feeling, as they might recite laboratory notes. They recapped their day, inquiring about white-water rapids, arresting rock formations, deep lakes, strange noises, bears, drownings, weather shifts, moose, red squirrels, and so many other curiosities spawned by a day in the forest. Addressing their clients' inquiries, the native guides provided the meaning of the forest. The guides added the indispensable element of any good Northwoods Tale: a spiritual dimension derived from the guides' own tribal lore and storytelling traditions. The guides taught their clients the meaning of true wilderness. This same magical and frightening message captivated the newcomers as it had earlier captivated Henry Wadsworth Longfellow, who retold Anishinaabe tribal stories in his *Song of Hiawatha*. And these corporate emissaries brought the Northwoods Tale home with them when they returned to their offices and factories.

The Northwoods Tale matured during the era of the native guide, a brief period, hardly more than a generation. It began when the Civil War ended, and it ended when large-scale logging began. By then, logging and mining companies were laying out roads and towns. Signposts were planted, and the ticket offices of railroad depots opened for business. The guides were no longer needed. With the disappearance of the forests, the smoke of the guides' fires disappeared also. Nonetheless, in that short period, the Northwoods Tale became a literary fixture.

The heart of all true Northwoods Tales is the spirit world of the forest. For the guides, spirits inhabited rivers and lakes; they determined the behavior and destinies of animals; and these same spirits lived on after the animals died. Tribal legends were full of stories of both good and evil spirits, but it is the evil spirits that dominate the Northwoods Tale. For instance, among the evil spirits inhabiting the forests of the Upper Peninsula of Michigan, my home, are the man-eating *Windigo*, the northern Bigfoot, the *Puckwijinni*, and the underwater panther, the *Mischibizhii*. Campfire stories of evil spirits and stories of threatening animals, such as bears, wolves, and cougars, told in the middle of a dark and trackless forest terrified even the most skeptical listeners as they faced the prospect of bedding down for the night, a time when wild animals prowled for a meal and humans slept in their tents, protected by nothing more than a thin wall of canvas. The mark of a superior Northwoods Tale is the terror it awakens in its listeners, a terror that follows them to their cots and invades their dreams.

The direct descendant of the Northwoods Tale is the ghost stories told by parents and Scout leaders around fire pits dug in subdivided campgrounds. These stories include bloodthirsty bears, marauding wolves, and crouching cougars ready to pounce on an unsuspecting child looking for a drink of water in the dark. For today's wide-eyed urban children gathered about a bonfire, other stories have been added, stories of witches and warlocks, vampires and werewolves, the devil himself, or urban legend horror figures such as the vanishing hitchhiker, the spider bite, and the hook man.

A few novelists have written Northwoods Tales. James Dickey adapted the tradition for his river adventure, *Deliverance*. Edgar Rice Burroughs exported it to Africa for his *Tarzan* stories. Both Dickey and Burroughs captured its principle element, the sense of remoteness found only in wilderness. In a crowded world, plausible remoteness is hard to establish, but, once achieved, the listener necessarily falls victim to the general, faceless fears occasioned by being in wild places. The more threatening and faceless the fears, the better the story.

Not surprisingly, Stephen King is the most faithful adherent of the Northwoods Tale. He successfully employed it in his *The Girl Who Loved Tom Gordon*. In this short novel, a nine-year-old girl named Trisha McFarland accidentally wanders off the Appalachian Trail, becoming lost in Maine's boreal forest. She has little food and almost no resources, principally a poncho and a transistor radio. At night she listens to Boston Red Sox games and the exploits of Tom Gordon, their ace relief pitcher. Gordon's triumphs give Trisha strength to confront the evil spirits of the forest. She encounters all the common dangers of remote wilderness: impassable swamps, starvation, cold, wet, wasps, and a bear that she believed to be the God of the Lost. She survives, but true to the genre, King never exorcises her terror of the woods.

Finally, the greatest virtue of the Northwoods Tale is placing people of different religions, political viewpoints, and economic circumstances in proximity, talking openly with each other for hours. It is a gift of Victorian democracy, and it began around the campfire where urban professionals conversed openly with their native guides on equal footing. In *Superior Country*, Robert Roosevelt, Teddy's uncle, shared his campsites and his thoughts on Lake Superior's North Shore with Hudson Bay Company clerks, Anishinaabe guides, and their wives and children; not always to Roosevelt's delight, the locals reciprocated. In *Trouting on the Brule River*, Chicago lawyers and businessmen sat captivated by the tribal stories of their Anishinaabe guides, and they heard not only the tales of native legend but also of the white man's treachery. A great Northwoods Tale puts in dialogue residents of gated communities and trailer parks, the eastern elite and western ranchers, or as is the case in the following story, cosmopolitan billionaires and struggling rural people.

The story you are about to hear is a true Northwoods Tale. Time and place are temporarily suspended, leaving a remote venue dominated by forest spirits. Taking a lead from the Anishinaabe, the ever-hospitable and eloquent people residing in the lands surrounding Lake Superior, the characters in the story include an Anishinaabe native spirit, an Anishinaabe trickster, bloodthirsty wild animals, a forest fire, and the brutal Escanaba River. At every turn they threaten the lives of the human intruders. Also, there is a canoe, the one vehicle that appeared in all original Northwoods Tales. In the Upper Midwest, the Anishinaabe were masters of the canoe, and the rivers of the Upper Peninsula of Michigan have not seen any canoeists since to match their skill.

One disclaimer. My forest spirits, Raven and Pauguck, were suggested by the Schoolcraft translations of Anishinaabe stories and by Longfellow's *Song of Hiawatha*. My own experiences of ravens and my conversations with hospice volunteers have led me to make modifications to these two characters. The Anishinaabe people and their tribal members and elders are authentically in touch with the spirits inhabiting the lands surrounding Lake Superior. I make no pretense of knowing what they know.

THE
Beginning

CAROL

A SECRET STRAINED OUR MARRIAGE. MY HUSBAND, Joe, planted and nurtured the secret during what I call our "lost years." These were the years he attended engineering school and worked engineering jobs in the Southwest. About seven years in all. I was not part of his life then. Before the "lost years," I was very much a part of his life. We were high school students together in Marquette, Michigan. Close friends. Then, without discussion, he left for college, and I did not hear from him for seven years. When he returned, I was working as a nurse at a Marquette hospital, where he sought me out and became part of my life again. Joe never told me about the "lost years," and I never pressed him.

Early in our marriage, I learned the "lost years" held a secret. One evening while reminiscing warmly about a fraternity brother (one who referred him a job that day), Joe talked openly about college, but in the midst of telling the story, he caught himself and paused, fearful. Then embarrassed, he laughed and abruptly changed subjects. It had happened several times since. I knew enough not to prompt him, for in those moments I felt his fear and his shame, and I was reluctant to have him confess his secret, what could only be his disgrace, out loud.

I put off demanding disclosure. When side-dressing rhubarb or asparagus, a gardener tentatively turns over soil to skirt the hidden roots, careful not to damage them. So for thirty years, I skirted Joe's secret, choosing instead to share wholeheartedly in our experiences in marriage, asking nothing more. I never spaded up the hidden root that germinated so long ago.

I knew the risks. They did not include my feelings changing toward Joe. I loved him. Nothing in his past could erode my respect for him, a respect built on thirty years of living together, of knowing each other intimately. The real risks went deeper. He clung to his secret because he was certain I would cease loving him once I learned it. When his secret came out and my love did not die, the surprise would force Joe to reassess. That I did fear. He would realize our marriage has been based, at least on his part, on an unreality, his own unreality, years in the keeping. So many wasted years. A new shame would follow and with it regret and disillusionment. It was the shame of not knowing how deeply I loved him. And he would know that I knew it. So I did not press him. I did not dig deeper.

At first Joe's secret stood on the periphery of our marriage. As we came to know each other better and our life together admitted fewer and fewer surprises, the secret broke its mooring lines and called attention to itself. It became the fascinating unknown, one of the few surprises left to us. With the secret, Joe's fears also migrated and were followed by his rage. He kept them trussed, hidden with more and more work as the years passed.

Joe was resigned to concealing his secret, honoring the compact he worked out with it long ago: silence for stifled fear. Joe's compact was an illusion. Lately he grew more irritable, a sign I read as proof the compact was unraveling. I was certain there would come a day when the secret would slip the knots binding it, leaving Joe and our marriage vulnerable. Then Joe would take up residence alone in his unreality, be lost forever, and speak monosyllabically when prompted. Nothing to report. Nothing to feel.

Joe knew I was aware he guarded a secret. He tensed when I probed too close, so I backed off, compliant. Thankful, he noted my retreats. I did bring up his rages, and he would apologize for them, but his apologies were not enough. As a nurse, I faulted myself. It was a matter of health that Joe confronted his secret and quelled the rage feeding off it. He must see it for what it is, an imaginary threat speeding his heart and exhausting his adrenaline. High blood pressure, shortness of breath, fatigue. He was wearing out before my eyes. He said, "It's old age." I knew better and told him so. More frequently, his moments of irritability were followed by lengthening silences between us. I was certain having Joe talk about his rages was not enough. I needed to precipitate his confrontation with his secret and thereby help Joe live more comfortably with himself.

Lately my work days were taken up with Frank Talbot, a wealthy man—a man, like Joe, of rages. I was his supervising nurse. Talbot was a diabetic and his extremities lost vitality each day. He had only one foot, the left; it was loosely bandaged and bound up in a hospital boot. Talbot's right foot was gone, the stump covered with a sock. Next week Mayo would take his left foot. And the surgery would never truly heal. Frank Talbot was twice rich. He made his first fortune in Silicon Valley before the bubble burst. And his second on Wall Street before the crash. He kept both fortunes. But neither could buy a real scab.

Talbot did buy a nineteen-room lodge set on a point jutting into Lake Superior. The lodge apes Durant's great Adirondack lodges: lengthy, matching pine logs perfectly fitted together, a cedar shake roof, huge exposed log beams, and large stone fireplaces blazing even during summer to keep Talbot's legs warm. The access road is a half-mile long, and on the back lawn is a heliport. A broad porch punctuated with cedar posts encircles the whole of the downstairs. On stormy days, waves beat against the rocky shore, mount thirty feet high, and crash onto the lawn. It has been featured in home magazines. Talbot called it, "Ill Gotten Gains." The name dripped from his mouth when he said it.

The lodge was drafty and the smell of cedar carried throughout. Most days Talbot positioned his wheelchair near the massive fireplace in his study. His uniformed staff attended him there—the maids in black dresses, lace aprons, and caps, and the male servants in black formal wear, starched shirts, and pressed pants. His meals were served in a cavernous dining room, two stories high. Sometimes he and his wife, Meredith, ate together; more often than not Talbot ate alone. When Meredith dined with him, the staff was dismissed to the kitchen, and the Talbots testily discussed business. On those occasions, I sought the porch, the dangerous serenity of the lake a welcome break.

Talbot was a difficult patient. He spent his day playing games with everyone on his payroll. There was his pick-up game. He dropped books, spoons, tissues, and cups by his wheelchair, forcing anyone nearby to stoop down to pick them up, bowing and groveling before him. He took his greatest delight forcing his female attendants, me included, on their knees in front of him. His ruse was claiming one of his contact lenses dropped out. Everyone nearby got down on their hands and knees to search the floor in front of him. Most days we found nothing but humiliation. Then there was the phantom pain game, his favorite game for me. He would report a pain in one of his legs, and I would kneel down, probing the leg upward and asking him where it hurt. After fifteen minutes of this, he would laugh and say the pain is gone. "It's your magic fingers, sweetie." Because he paid well and because I report to a medical group that prizes a patient who pays promptly, I played his games.

Talbot's rages were another matter. They bore real consequences. One Hispanic maid, tired of the pick-up game, muttered to me, "Who does he think he is? The president?" I murmured patience. Later that day when Talbot dropped a pen, she went for a broom, swept up the pen, and deposited it in a wastebasket. Talbot cursed her and rang for his chief of staff, but before he could fire her, she spat out her resignation. "Get a new peon," she said. With that she ripped off her lace cap, threw it on the floor, and stomped on it.

We had ten minutes of grace before the games started again. Still seething, he grunted, "Replace my sock." I told myself, *It's the disease talking*. On my knees again before his wheelchair footrests, I gingerly lifted his stump, stripped off a sock no more than an hour old, and snugged up a fresh one. Before I could stand up, he leered and said, "I have a pain in my upper thigh. Hop to it."

"You know the rules, Mr. Talbot. I will call Meredith." It was his wife's rule.

"Forget the rules. I need your magic fingers."

I told myself again, *It is the disease talking.* Out loud I said, "Where would we be without rules?"

As I left to call Meredith, Talbot shouted, enraged again, and pounded on his wheelchair armrests. "She's the last person I want to see!"

A few days ago, the frequency of the games increased. A cold, gray mist hung over the lake, and Talbot's surgery was several days off. *Reason enough for anxiety*, I thought. That morning, I smelled gun solvent in Talbot's study. It was that day Talbot started talking about one last outing. He reminisced, sounding pathetic, about brook trout fishing. He asked about fishing the Escanaba, but I put him off, "The Escanaba is too rugged for someone in your condition."

Meredith joined us. "A fishing trip, yes. It may be Frank's last. Getting out would do him good, clear his mind before the surgery."

"Have you considered wheelchair accessible piers? Marquette has several."

"I want to fly-fish for brook trout from a canoe," Talbot said, no longer pathetic.

"Your doctors will not allow it."

"There are other doctors. Once I remind your group that they have competition, they'll buy in." Talbot read his doctors correctly.

So it was decided. Talbot would fly-fish the Escanaba River. Meredith took me aside and told me they wanted Joe as his guide. "Everyone at the club tells me he knows the Escanaba best." This was all foolishness.

My first thought was to tell the Talbots that Joe refused because he was not licensed. But the more I thought about Joe and Talbot together in a canoe for a few hours, I too began to buy in. Talbot helped me. That day, there were no pick-up games, no phantom pains. Talbot talked all the while of how he would like to meet Joe. "I want to meet the lucky man who married you," he kept saying. He was patently insincere, playing a new game. I did not mind because I decided to play a game of my own. Doing nothing about Joe's secret was no longer an option for me.

In my game, the goal was for Joe to see his future in Talbot's present ill-health. He would look into the mirror of Talbot and see his own reflection ten years hence. Joe would see what happens when his hypertension climbed to high blood pressure; he would see what follows when his high blood pressure defies medication; and finally he would see the lingering death sentence of diabetes and the gradual decline, dimming eyesight, slowing circulation, gangrene, and tortuous death. Suffering Talbot for a few hours might force Joe to look within and lead him to unearth his secret and slay it.

To trick Joe into playing a game was new for me. In our marriage, I shunned games. But I believed putting Joe in a canoe with Talbot was no worse than distracting a child with a lollipop before vaccinating it. For Talbot, Joe and I were no more than tokens to move about at will. I decided to play the gullible token because I saw Talbot as a token in my game. In both our games, Joe and Talbot spent a few hours together on the Escanaba. The question was, who would win? I was not sure what the goal of Talbot's game was, a great disadvantage. And I also knew that Talbot was more skilled than Joe at manipulating people, shepherding them to his own ends. But I knew too that Talbot was arrogant, a blindness affecting his planning. He was confident he knew Joe and the Escanaba. He did not. That flaw would give me victory. Or so I told myself.

Gaining Joe's cooperation would not be easy. Joe had personal reasons not to guide Talbot. Years before, Talbot had cheated Joe's father. But in the end, I had no doubt Joe would ignore his personal feelings and agree to guide Talbot. He would do it for my sake. I felt justified trading a few hours of Joe's discomfort for his release from fear and rage.

RAVEN

I COULD HAVE KILLED THE FIRE.
  Perched in a scrawny spruce, I watched it snake like a slow fuse through a clear-cut.

At any point I could have flown down and snuffed it out with one beat of my black wings.

I chose not to.

The Anishinaabe were the first to notice me,
And they named me,
Kahgahgee.
In their day, I robbed for a living, pillaging corn fields and birds' nests.
For me, it was a time of frequent famine.
I dined most days on what others left unattended.
Very little.
In winter the weak among us froze.
When the white loggers and miners came,
the Anishinaabe left for L'Anse, the Keweenaw, and the Soo.
The whites renamed me Raven,
A strong name . . . a name I like.
But that was not all. My diet changed.

Opening roads through the forests, the whites leave dead deer, raccoons, porcupines, and skunks alongside the road daily.

The whites call it roadkill.

I call it tribute.

I no longer live like a robber.

I live like a chief.

The week when winter turns to spring is best. The snow melts, and the bodies of winterkill emerge from drifts. So tender from the freezing and the thawing.

I start with the eyes.

The large brown eyes of deer and the black eyes of skunk are best.

This spring, after the melt, I had my fill of brown and black eyes.

So now I let the fire burn.

It will bring me something new.

It will bring me other colors.

I crave blue eyes . . . for a change.

Yes, blue eyes.

And there is more.

The fire will bring Pauguck. I miss him,

The ghost who collects the souls of the dead.

He takes the shape of an Anishinaabe hunter, more form than flesh,

A wraith emitting the rustle of his own footfalls and the fragrance of death.

I learned his talk from the smell of his words,

The soughing wind fluttering among birch leaves, the sigh of a swaying white pine canopy, and the plunk of dropping cones, escaping like a faint fetid breeze through death's door.

Pauguck and I are at odds.

I overload him with work.

When I take the eyes of the dead, they cannot find their way to Ponemah, the Land of the Spirits, on their own. Instead, they wander blindly, crashing about the forest.

It falls to Pauguck to lead them out.

One day, Pauguck shouted at me angrily, "I must introduce myself to each sightless soul and, with soothing talk, win their confidence! Only then can I lead them quietly to the great Silver Lake and its Blessed Isles. A four-day trip into the shades. I cannot afford the time!"

I shook out my wings and made ready to fly off.

But Pauguck was not finished. "You leave so many confused spirits. And worse, without their eyes, they will never enjoy the beauty of the Blessed Isles. All I can do is guide them to the level shores of Silver Lake where they kneel and splash cool water on their empty sockets. It is pathetic. You, Kahgahgee, waste my time."

"Aren't they grateful to you?" I asked innocently.

"Yes, I will give you that. They are most grateful. But you blind so many. Let up for a while . . . at least until I can clear the woods."

"I do not see them," I said.

Impatient, he shouted back, "They are all about you!"

Then he shook his fist at me.

It will be good to see Pauguck again.

Until Pauguck appears, I will patrol the Escanaba River.

Rising twenty miles south of the Great Lake in a ring of low mountains

Near the city white men call Marquette,

The Escanaba collects, as in a stoneware bowl,

Water from rain, melting snow, and a thousand seeps and springs.

This sodden tangle of bogs and marshes,

Charges the river,

Offers security to bear and moose,

And isolates the few humans who build camps on the hummocks of sand,

Barely rising above the damp and wet.

Here the river is rust colored,

With cedar, tamarack, and spruce crowding its banks.

Olive-tinted aspen flourish here also,

And gnarled tag alders
Root in the river's shallows, choking its tributaries.
From its first trickle, the Escanaba slides purposefully south
Toward the road called Highway 41.
There, the bowl begins to tip.
The river concentrates, gaining breadth and energy,
Swelling,
Confident in its newfound power,
Battering south against waves of three-billion-year-old bedrock,
Raised seams of basalt and granite,
Pinching the river, dropping it precipitously
Onto foaming pools and boulder-strewn rapids below.
Falls . . . the falls of the Escanaba . . .
So many falls . . .
Each one is different;
Each one has killed.
I have fed at the bottom of each one.

On patrol above the Escanaba's First Falls, I came across four white people this morning.
Among them was the green-eyed woman.
Pauguck favors her.
An able-bodied man was helping the green-eyed woman settle a one-footed man in an old aluminum canoe.
Many years ago, I found the green-eyed woman's father in a snow bank, dead.
All I could scavenge were his fingers, blue with cold.
I do not favor the green-eyed woman.
It would have been better if she had died with her father.
As with her father, she sits besides the dying,
Reading to them, listening to them, whispering quietly in their ear as they weaken.
How often I wished she would leave their side,
Just for ten minutes.
She has denied me many meals.

JOE

I NEVER LIKED MONEY. AND THE MORE I MADE, THE more I disliked it. But that was not my thought as I pushed a scarred Starcraft canoe into the Escanaba River. That thought came later.

Just then, my thought was to steady the canoe in the current. In the bow sat Frank Talbot, athletically trim, sixty years old, gray haired, and of medium height. He was a distinguished-looking man, even in his green plaid shirt and khaki pants, a man designed to stand out in a boardroom. But here, bouncing on the Escanaba's currents, he looked out of place clinging stiffly to the Starcraft's gunwales, all his muscles fully occupied keeping his balance.

Talbot looked out of place from the moment his Range Rover pulled in. Meredith, his wife, was driving, and she, with my wife, Carol, transferred him to a wheelchair and pushed him. They jostled down the muddy, rutted landing to the canoe. In creased slacks and a starched blouse, Meredith was a tall, crisp blonde, muscular from Pilates. My green-eyed wife, Carol, was in her scrubs. She was shorter and grayer next to Meredith but was more muscular, strength won from carrying and shifting patients over thirty years of nursing. A month ago, she drew supervision of Talbot's home care assignment.

We shifted Talbot to the canoe, and Carol introduced me. "This is my husband, Joseph McCartney. He knows this river and is the one man I trust to guide you."

"I'll call you Joe," Talbot said with a quick appraising glance. He reached out a hand. I smiled and took it. His grip was cold. Carol had warned me to pay attention to his fingertips and lips. "Check while you're out to see if they are turning blue. Cyanosis," she said. "That's when not enough arterial blood is getting to his extremities. One of the first signs a diabetic is in serious trouble." The day was warm. I did not expect that problem.

"You're huskier than I thought," he said.

"It's the logging," I said. "Just finished two weeks with a crew clearing forty acres of red pine."

"That accounts for the navy blue sweats," he said with disdain.

"First thing I put on in the morning," I said.

Talbot looked down at his necrotic foot. Anxious, Carol and Meredith looked at me, and Meredith said, "Bring him back in one piece."

"Yes," Carol said, concerned. "I filled and recalibrated your insulin pump this morning, Mr. Talbot." She then asked, "Do you have your power bars?"

Talbot patted a pants pocket and gruffly ordered, "No more questions."

"Carol is only worried about you," Meredith said.

Carol turned to me and asked, "Do you have the candy bars I gave you this morning?"

"Yes." I smiled again and pushed off. "See you in a few hours."

Once we were out in the current, as if opening a board meeting, Talbot spread his arms wide, looked up at the heavens, and intoned, "This is a good day to die."

I laughed. Meredith muttered about "Frank's vile sense of humor." Appalled, Carol stared and then called to me, "Remember Val's arriving this afternoon!" Val is our son, who's taking a break from graduate work at the University of Wisconsin. She broke into a smile. "Don't stop off anywhere on the way home, you two."

Yesterday, Carol asked me to take Talbot fishing. "I have a

demanding patient," she began. "Difficult to please. He wants to trout fish before undergoing surgery at Mayo's."

"Be happy to help," I said, jumping in before she finished.

"Just listen, Joe. This is no little favor. You don't like this man."

"Who is he?"

"He bought Lundine and ran it into the ground," she said. Lundine employed my father for twenty years, and I had worked there several summers during college. A solid balance sheet when Talbot purchased it, Lundine declared bankruptcy a few years later without Talbot ever leaving his office in New York.

I hesitated in disbelief, "Talbot . . . Frank Talbot."

"Yes."

"Someone else can guide him," I said, fighting the urge to utter an abrupt refusal and end the conversation. Sneering, I said instead, "He has all the money in the world. There isn't a guide up here he couldn't buy."

"He and his wife, Meredith, are emphatic. They want you," Carol said soothingly.

"I'm not a real guide."

"You know the Escanaba better than anyone I know."

"It doesn't matter," I shot back. "Any decent guide can put him on fish . . . if not on the Escanaba, then on the Fox or the Paint."

"He wants to fish the Escanaba above the First Falls, and he wants you to guide him, Joe," Carol said, adding, "It would be good for you."

My eyes narrowed. "No. He can't buy me."

"You'll see what's become of him," she said, laying a hand on my arm. "He has diabetes, and it's killing him." She looked imploringly at me with her earnest green eyes. "The worst part is that he's now in despair watching his body die cell by cell each day."

"He deserves it," I said without feeling.

Carol looked through me and said sternly, "He's my patient."

Relenting, I said, "Can't the doctors do something for him?"

"Nothing but amputate as his arteries slow," she said. She then repeated carefully, "It would be good for you to see him up close."

I was about to ask, "How could it be good for me?" when I caught myself. The question would begin a discussion I have avoided for years. I resented Talbot from the day he bought Lundine. While others touted his legendary wealth and argued that his interest in Marquette was good for local business, I distrusted him. When he drove Lundine into bankruptcy, Marquette stopped talking about the wealthy Mr. Talbot. Instead they spoke of the ruthless Mr. Talbot. Lundine limped on, just a shell of itself, after court reorganization. About then, my resentment against Talbot turned to rage, a silent rage allied with so many other of my silent rages. Carol thought them unhealthy. She pressed me to talk about then, but I shut her out.

Talbot remained a remote figure in Marquette, visiting infrequently during the summer. With his absence, I dealt with my rage by strangling it. In my mind, I pronounced Talbot dead, plotted the contours of his grave, and sealed it over. Forever, I believed. I did not care to blow new life into his memory just to please Carol. She would ask the hard question. How could I dislike him even before Lundine? It was a question I had indeed asked myself, but it was a question I refused to think through. There was no simple answer. Wasn't it enough that I was the first to see the danger? If I now disinterred Talbot for discussion, there was no telling what words would pass between us. Words I would later brood over and perhaps regret. What I knew, and what Carol did not know, was that I had buried Talbot in a mass grave with so many other murderous feelings. His burial was just the latest, although it was his name I inscribed on the lone headstone.

I pursed my lips and asked in an even voice, "What will I see?"

"You'll see what little shreds of a human being are left after a lifetime of rage," she said. "Talbot's diabetes is hastened by his uncontrollable high blood pressure. Even now, on medication, he can become volcanically angry with only the slightest provocation."

Carol was talking of Talbot, but she was also talking of me. We both knew it. I sighed and partly in jest asked, "What's the care plan?"

"Agree with him no matter how outrageous his insults."

Seeing Talbot up close would nettle me, but I could not refuse her. "I won't take a fee," I huffed.

"Joe, you should charge him the maximum. We need the money."

"I want nothing from that man."

"When will you get your pay from last month's logging?"

"Once the broker settles up."

"When?"

"Within the next ten days."

"Okay, but think about charging Talbot something. He expects to pay."

"No!" My anger punctuated the end of the discussion.

Carol paused. Her eyes searched my face. The discussion was over. "Okay, Joe," she said, disappointed. Another failed attempt to put away a little money for retirement. Another failed attempt to have me talk about my rage.

She beat a retreat. "It'll only be for a few hours," she said. "I wouldn't ask any more of you."

"A few hours," I mused. "I can do just about anything for a few hours."

"I wouldn't trust you two together for more than that," Carol said, giving me a hug. "Talbot has a way of needling . . . Just ignore him. Remember he's dying, and his will be an unpleasant death." I resolved to be patient when Carol added, "It's important to me. More assignments like Talbot will put us ahead. And he has many friends."

"For your sake, I will be patient with him," I said, although I did not believe we would ever get ahead. We were both in our late fifties. Unlike Carol who still believed retirement was possible, I believed I would be working until my death. But I did not want to discourage her. Nursing was beginning to take its toll: Carol felt the strain of tired feet, aching arms, and a sprained back. She was hoping to move out of her practice gradually, sleep late a few mornings a week, and take a few weeks off south during the winter. My plan was to take more ibuprofen.

"I know you will, Joe."

"Don't worry. Talbot will catch fish and be home in a few hours . . . contented."

For Carol, I could keep my feelings in check for a few hours. What I did not foresee was how soon my patience would be tested.

I paddled a few strokes downstream, and the canoe floated free, out of earshot. Talbot relaxed. "What rod did you bring for me?"

I handed him an eight-foot, four-weight fly rod. Mine. He took it and checked the butt section for the manufacturer's name. "Don't tell me, Joe," he said sarcastically, "homemade."

"Yes," I said, stung. I was about to add that it threw a straight line but thought better of it. This would be a day of long silences.

Talbot sighed, the disappointed chairman of the board.

"What can I expect?" he asked. "Trout?"

"Yes, brook trout," I said, more hopeful. "You can expect a few eight- to ten-inchers. Maybe a thirteen-incher if you're lucky," I said cheerily.

Looking absently at the passing shoreline, Talbot announced as if delivering a corporate press release, "A low-end leaky canoe, a no-name rod, and a so-so trout stream." He paused, then added, "What could be better?"

"You picked this stretch," I said hesitantly.

"Yes," he replied irritated. "Was I misinformed?"

It was not a question he expected me to answer, more a challenge. I should not have contradicted him.

"No," I said humbly. "Sorry, Mr. Talbot, I didn't mean to upset you."

Talbot drew back, looked at me coldly, and said, "People like you cannot upset people like me."

Collecting myself with a few strokes of the paddle, I let it pass. The lowly guide put back in his place. Not the first time for me. Talbot relaxed again. "Do you have a plan?"

"Yes," I said.

"Let's have it," he said.

"I propose . . . ," I began.

"Oh, you propose," he said mockingly. "Don't pretend to manage me. Just tell me the plan."

Nothing humorous or polite came to mind, so I recalled the fact that Talbot was dying. I waited until his shoulders relaxed and the rage drained from his face, then said, "The plan is as follows. Most feeding fish at this time of day are in the riffles or at the head of pools. We will work downstream, stopping at the top of each riffle. I will get out and hold the canoe in place while you cast. You should hook a few."

"Let's go," he said, satisfied with his subordinate's report.

A few minutes later, as I stepped out to hold the canoe in the current above a riffle, Talbot turned slightly and said over his shoulder, "I planned it this way." Then he turned back quickly, not inviting any questions.

We fished for an hour and a half. Talbot was an experienced fly fisherman. He knew where to place his fly, and he cast precisely, hitting the likeliest holds every time. He threw time after time under tag alder bushes bordering the river without getting hung up once in their branches. Six nice brook trout were his reward, and he knew enough to play them to the canoe where he took hold of the fly and shook the fish off, never touching them.

As we worked our way downstream, the wind increased in strength. Gusting, it brought whitecaps and the hint of wood smoke. *Someone firing up a sauna*, I thought. Casting became more difficult, and Talbot started missing his spots even though he made his loops tighter and tighter.

"Mr. Talbot, the wind's against us, and we're nearing our take-out point," I warned.

"The wind's no problem." Facing me, he became the chairman of the board again. "I'm fishing the First Falls." He waited for my reaction.

I hesitated. "The First Falls is past our take-out, and it's dangerous. It is certainly too dangerous today in this wind."

"The First Falls," he said firmly. The matter was settled. And as Talbot would say, I was on board.

I decided to wait until we came up on my take-out point to push the issue and ignite his rage.

CAROL

*O*N OUR WAY BACK TO TALBOT'S LODGE, MEREDITH driving, the smell of gun solvent in Talbot's study came back to me. "Meredith, was Frank cleaning his guns a few days ago?"

Slow to respond, Meredith gave me a quick glance and read a simple question on my face. "No. Why do you ask?"

"I smelled gun solvent in his study."

"You must be mistaken."

"No, the study was reeking of it. I needed to open a window."

"Probably one of the maids spilled it," she said. "They're always going through Frank's desk."

"You're probably right," I replied, unconvinced. We rode in silence the rest of the way. Meredith dropped me off at the lodge and drove to her club. Before getting in my car for the drive home, I made one last turn about Talbot's study. There were no stains in the carpets near his desk, and none of the drawers smelled of solvent. I turned this fact over in my mind. Talbot was playing a new game, a game with which I was unfamiliar. What was new about this game was that Meredith was a willing partner, encouraging her husband.

I thought about the game I set loose. And I thought back to bad diagnoses and the poor courses of treatment that followed. A few patients died, but most lived because nurses were at their sides, persistent nurses who read the vital signs, and when they faltered, the nurses followed their healing instincts. Cold compresses, cups of water, quiet, a fluffed pillow, a hand on the forehead, a lullaby sung to a child—those little signs told patients that someone cared for them. And the patients fought through and lived. I saw this happen many times. If I was wrong now in my diagnosis, I would not be there to help Joe fight through.

On the river, Talbot would play his game with Joe. Talbot knew the advantages of momentum, pressing and pressing until the opponent is swept from the field. Talbot's favorite opponent was Meredith only because she had no taste for staying stubborn, pushing back. He provoked arguments about the color of her car, the style of her hair, the height of her heels—stupid arguments designed to teach her she was no match for him. With a laugh, Meredith left the field, went to the club or shopped, rang up more bills, had more colors done to irritate Talbot, knowing that another inning of combat lay ahead. Meredith never admitted defeat. She hung on the edge of engagement, toying with Talbot. For her, the game ended when Talbot's heart stopped—and that wasn't too far off. She grew more confident by the day, and Talbot resented her mounting cheer, grimly playing on as if there were no time clock.

Joe did not have Meredith's experience. When the crisis came, when the momentum against him gained speed, Joe needed to look beyond Talbot's taunts. I was sure Joe could do that in the short time they would be out. He could put Talbot's insults and humiliations on hold for a few hours. If it went much longer, I was not sure, because the fear sealing Joe's secret sapped his mental resilience. Joe was a divided being—one part hiding and the other helping it hide. More and more when facing difficult decisions, his gaze looked inward for a measure of courage. Only after dipping into his reserves and refreshing his resolve did his eyes hold steady. Talbot noted all such hesitations, saw them as indecision, and exploited them. When his quarry reflected, Talbot was on them, driving them into confusion, routing them before they could form a plan.

Joe was stubborn about keeping to his thoughts. This is where Talbot and Joe would spar. Talbot would rush Joe, hurrying him to act thoughtlessly. Talbot was the master of the broken play. Relentlessly, Talbot would crowd in on Joe, hoping to shred his composure and leave him casting about for temporary solutions. Talbot wanted to put Joe out in the open where quickness alone counted. There was no quicker wit than Talbot. At the lodge, I could fall back on the rules. On the river, Talbot and Joe would be making their own rules. Joe's first instinct, his first rule, was to reflect, to plan. If he held to that, Joe would survive Talbot's rushes.

It was then I thought back to the last time I listened to Talbot's heart. Through my stethoscope, I heard an unfamiliar sound: the beat of wings, a dark bird caged within Talbot's ribs, fluttering for its freedom. I pulled away and checked the earpieces. Another reading and the fluttering was gone, and I heard only the beat of his merciless heart.

Although Talbot was smarter than Joe, I believed Talbot would fail because Joe would hold to his thinking and come back better for the experience. I believed in Joe.

THE
First Falls

JOE

*E*ARLIER THAT AFTERNOON, I PARKED MY TRUCK ON A SINGLE-
track dirt road three hundred yards above the First Falls. A safe
margin. I respect the First Falls. It drops fifty feet. After the river crosses
a broad ledge, granite berms crowd the Escanaba, funneling it into
a narrow trough. Briefly pent up, the river escapes, springing in one
single, narrow, shimmering column to a two-acre pool below. Where it
strikes the pool, the river is deep, a dozen feet or more, but after a violent
upwelling, it rotates out gently into a large, endlessly circling eddy. A
pond within the river's flow. The Escanaba's great eddy. It's not deep; in
some places it's six feet, but more often it's shallower. The eddy's bottom
is mainly silt and sand sifted for millennia out of the river's burden.

The sound of the falls dominates all. It announces itself first with
a muffled thunder; closer in, the thunder becomes a relentless din.
Minute by minute, tons of water drop fifty feet onto the anvil of
more tons of water. There is no polite conversation in its presence.

The hundred yards above the falls is barely wadeable rapids. By
the time the angler gets to the broad granite ledge leading to the lip,
there is no turning back. Thousands of years of sliding sand have
polished the ledge, and once an angler is in its grips, there is only the
terrifying skate to the lip with a long plunge to follow.

When Talbot and I came opposite the truck, the wind was driving foot-high whitecaps and throwing spray from the rapids five feet

into the air. I was braking with the paddle so that Talbot could work side-arm casts under the powerful gusts. Picking spots was useless. He was now fishing the river blindly.

"Mr. Talbot, this is the end of the line!" I shouted over the wind and roar of the falls. The wood fire smell was stronger now. I looked back upriver and saw a line of smoke scudding across the horizon. A forest fire, burning on a broad front, south of the river. I comforted myself with the thought the take-out and my truck were north of it.

"You're wrong!" he bellowed. "I planned a few casts on the lip of the falls." He hesitated and then pled, "Just one good fish."

"No!" I shouted. "There will be other days after Mayo's." Not looking at Talbot, I swung my legs out of the canoe and grabbed the stern's painter. Pulling hard against the wind and the current, I started leading the canoe across to the shore.

"I'm fishing the falls!" Talbot shouted, his voice imperious.

I turned to confront him. After taking in his flushed face, I said firmly and evenly, "To go any nearer the falls in this wind is fool-hardy." Pointing to the smoke upstream, I yelled, "There's a forest fire coming our way." Talbot did not even look. I said firmly, "We need to get to my truck and outrun it."

With that, he slashed at me with the fly rod. The first swipe he aimed at my head. Dropping the painter, my hands came up to catch the rod tip. I missed. Talbot kept slashing at me until a powerful gust of wind caught the canoe and lifted it toward the falls. I fumbled in the water for the painter and came up empty-handed. Lunging for the canoe's stern, I caught the paddle handle with its lanyard instead and then slipped, falling face-first into the river. By then, the current had captured the canoe, and it sped toward the brink of the falls.

In the bow, Talbot sat still, facing me in triumph. And when the knotted painter caught in a rock crevasse, tethering the canoe just above the lip of the falls, he rolled out and disappeared in the spray and roar below.

Crossing the river, I made it down the granite slope to the edge of the First Falls' plunge pool. A raven flew just above my head and croaked. I looked up into one of its sparkling black eyes. It croaked again. Perhaps it was a warning.

RAVEN

Soon, everyone from the nearby forest will be
here.

Right here, just below my roost, this old, wind-sculpted white pine
standing beside the falls.

I see it all.

I see the white smoke from the forest fire.

I see the sinuous blue course of the ever-rushing Escanaba.

And I see below me the passage across the river away from the
fire.

It is the only passage for miles.

It runs through an eddy,

The Escanaba's great eddy,

A large revolving pool below the First Falls,

Fully two hundred yards across.

The way down to the great eddy is gentle. A timeless threshold of
pink granite billows, a front stoop, sloping from billow to billow, it
descends by shallow steps to the water's edge.

Opposite the billows, directly across the great eddy, is a notch.

An ancient cleavage, the notch beckons all who risk crossing the
eddy.

A wedge-shaped ramp, fifty yards across at its widest, is near the
river's edge. Lightly forested with paper birch, a few fir, and green

grass, it ascends up and away from the river, narrowing as it climbs. It is kind to all who pull themselves from the water, for the slope is gradual, an easy walk out.

All else about the eddy is sheer gray granite cliffs as high as the First Falls itself, a forbidding escarpment.

Together, the granite billows, the great eddy, and the notch navigate the river in as sure a straight line as any surveyed road.

All in the forest know this.

And they remember that in the past, this road offered safe passage.

But today, their memories will mislead them.

For today, this escape route leads only to death.

All believe the fire will stop at the great eddy.

This fire will not.

Instead, it will stride onto the pink billows and, in a giant leap, clear the great eddy, all two hundred yards, and land in the notch beyond.

I have seen such a fire before.

I am the only one here today who has seen such a fire before.

The heat, the leading edge of the fire, will do most of the killing. With a high wind and four years of drought, the fire will reach two thousand degrees. The heat moves forward as a pulsing, swirling, colorless wall, extending skyward a hundred feet or more. This wall is, even now, driving through and over the tops of the tallest trees, torching them scarlet and orange before they begin to smoke.

It will scorch and blister all life in the forest today.

And when it jumps the great eddy,

It will pounce on the forest's refugees crowding the notch, incinerating them with its breath.

I see too the white men.

They, like the others, underestimate the fire.

And they, like the others, will place their trust in the great eddy.

One thing I know for sure.

The two white men will not leave this river alive.

The one-footed man will die, for all with one foot soon die in the forest.

And the able-bodied man will die trying to save him.

In the end, the able-bodied man will weary, and his judgment will falter.

In the end, the able-bodied man will chance the impossible.

For in the end, the only option left is the impossible.

And both will die.

Yes, I have grown fat on men who chanced the impossible.

But before I fly to wait by the Great Lake, the lake white men call Superior, I have one piece of business left.

I must find out the color of the able-bodied man's eyes.

I know the color of the one-footed man's eyes. Blue. He is lying face up in the eddy. When he tumbled over the falls, he caught on a protruding rock barb twenty feet down, and after hanging there for a moment, he struggled and fell again, this time cart wheeling and landing on his back, too dazed to move. Now he bobs about, staring into the sky, feebly moving his arms. His stump and his foot ooze puss and blood.

Dropping off my roost, I hover just above the able-bodied man. He is running with the paddle below me toward the granite billows, the way down to the one-footed man. The running man is not looking up, so I croak, and he looks up at me.

Blue eyes.

I croak again, pleased.

I will return for the white men once the fire relents.

More work for Pauguck.

JOE

*A*NGRILY, I KICKED OFF MY HIP BOOTS, PULLED THE belt out of its loops, and picked up the paddle. The belt I fastened around my waist and the paddle's lanyard I slung over my head and tucked under my right arm. Sliding into the river, I swam hard past the upwelling from the plunge pool. The driving wind and the eddy current helped. Coming up on Talbot, I took hold of his shirt, lifting his head above the white caps. I saw his hospital boot was missing, well downstream by now.

The chop was more than a foot high. Talbot coughed up water and then vomited his breakfast. His breath stank when he yelled above the roar of the falls, "I get my way!"

"You were lucky!" I shouted in his face.

"I get my way," he repeated. "This will go smoothly when you understand that fact."

"Talbot, we must make for the other side of the river." He was not listening. Instead, he was looking up at the canoe stuck on the lip of the falls. I followed his eyes. "Forget the canoe, Talbot. We need to swim for the far shore. Do you see the birch trees? The grass? That's where we need to go now."

Talbot did not look. "We'll wait for the canoe to come to us," he commanded. Then he shouted, "There's something wrong with my back!"

"Probably a sprain," I shouted. "The canoe isn't coming."

"I get my way," he said with finality. "Do you understand?"

"Yes," I said to quiet him.

I wound the wader belt around Talbot's chest, just under his armpits, and began to pull him toward the notch. He tried to wiggle out. I pulled it tighter and swam harder.

"Talbot, this water's sixty degrees. Every minute you're in it, your body temperature drops and your circulation slows . . . Your arms and legs receive less and less oxygen . . . You will begin to die," I said between strokes.

"I pay *real* doctors to worry about my circulation," he said.

I grabbed one of his hands and held it out of the water so that he could see it. "Look at your fingernails! They're turning blue."

Without looking, he shook off my hand. "I belong out here."

I continued pulling him toward the notch. We were a hundred and fifty yards away. "Talbot, help yourself and start swimming!" I yelled. "We don't have much time."

Talbot struck out. I avoided his fist, and it splashed harmlessly into the river. "Talbot, we need to get to my truck. Above the birch notch is a road that circles back to it," I shouted over the wind and pounding of the falls. "It's simple. We make the notch, walk up to the road, and get back to my truck," I said. "You'll be home in an hour."

"This is entirely your fault," he said sternly.

I let it pass. "Start swimming."

Talbot lay limp. "No!" he yelled, his eyes twitching with anger. "This is your fault."

I let it pass and continued to pull him toward the notch.

Talbot went quiet. But, shortly, I felt a sawing on the wading belt. I pulled up Talbot's right arm. A knife flashed, and in a sweeping arc, he tried for my throat. I caught his right wrist and twisted it behind his back. Taking the knife, a five-inch Buck, I closed and pocketed it. Then I slapped him. Hard. It felt good.

Shocked, Talbot cried, "You'll pay for that!"

"Maybe . . . if we live through this," I replied.

I felt through his pockets. A thin wallet and power bars. I replaced them as Talbot squirmed and then cried in pain. He grabbed my head and tried to push me under.

I shook him off and said vehemently, "You'll kill us both."

Talbot looked me straight in the eye and was about to say something but shifted his gaze downriver.

"If you hadn't pulled this stunt, I'd be unloading you at your place right now," I said.

I continued to swim for the shore. It was then the first deer hit the eddy. Turning, I saw more, tails erect and twitching, leaping down the pink granite billows. One after another, they plunged into the eddy and began swimming toward us. Behind them were more deer, frantic red squirrels, and running coyotes sliding and leaping down to the eddy, panic in their every step. Talbot hardly noticed. He was fighting against the belt. I tightened it again.

"I want my knife back," he hissed.

"I'll give it to Meredith when I get you home," I said. "For now, I will keep it. Help me, Talbot!" I shouted, expecting none. "These deer will swamp us."

He didn't move.

I swung Talbot toward the center of the eddy. Treading water while holding his head above the wash, I watched the line of deer and coyote pass. Talbot reached out for one of the coyote, and it snapped at his hand. I menaced it with the paddle, and it turned aside to continue toward the notch. Talbot smiled smugly.

Keeping Talbot's head above water was tiring. Turning about to look up through the spray, I saw the canoe still sitting on the fall's rim. My eyes traced the escarpment. Bent double with the wind, fir, larch, and pine limbs started breaking off and flying over our heads like green kites. The smell of smoke grew stronger, and so did the sulfur smell of skunk.

"Come on, Talbot!" I shouted above the noise. "This is no time to give up."

"I'll do as I please," he said.

I felt his foot. It was cold. When he kicked back, I let go. "Don't say anything," he said.

"Have it your way," I replied.

"I will," he muttered.

At that moment, a mother bear with two fat, glossy cubs climbed out onto the pink billows. Briefly surveying the panic, she loped down to the water's edge. The cubs followed. All gave them wide berth. The mother barked at the cubs. Stubbornly, they sat down, bawling. The mother swatted one into the water, and the other, after a quick glance up, dove in. She rolled into the water behind them, barked again, and all three paddled furiously for the notch.

Raccoon, hare, squirrels, and more deer, this time with spotted fawns, stampeded down the billows. Splash followed splash, and heads appeared above the water: bedraggled raccoon heads; the slim, elegant heads of the deer; and the fragile heads of fawns, all rhythmically jerking toward the far shore. None looked back. All eyes fixed on the notch.

It was then that the largest cat I had ever seen sprinted onto the billows. It snarled at all below, and frantic deer and fawn scattered with this new fear, some slipping into the plunge pool, others running back up the slope to flee along the forest parapet skirting the sheer cliffs. One lost its footing and fell the full fifty feet into the water. Its limp body surfaced and began to circle the eddy, inert as a discarded knapsack. The cat snarled again, and in a great tawny leap, it cleared the pink granite and dove beyond the upwelling.

The mother bear barked again, and the cubs stopped paddling. All three turned, absolutely composed, to confront the great cat. As the cat neared, the mother bear snapped her jaws and then roared. The cat stopped swimming. Looking first to the right and then to the left, it changed course. A tentative swimmer, more concerned with keeping its head dry, the cat slowed as it circled just out of reach of the bears. Then, as if challenging the mother bear, the big cat stopped a dozen feet away from her and coyly lapped some water. The mother was not intimidated. The cat's head shot up. Staring intently into the water, it lapped again, looked up, and began searching the eddy deliberately with its large yellow eyes.

Almost immediately, the cat saw us. It stared. Forgetting the bears, the cat slid forward into the revolving thread of current carrying Talbot and me. The eddy was shallower here, no more than four feet. The cat held steady, waiting all the while, its great yellow eyes fixed on us. I swam harder against the current, pulling Talbot toward the bears. "Talbot!" I shouted. "Start swimming. We need to put the bears between us and the cat." Getting no help, I stroked harder.

"Let me go!" he shouted back.

Within a dozen feet of the trio, the mother bear started snapping her jaws at us. I looked back at the cat. It was paddling closer.

Just then, the eddy flashed scarlet. The fire had arrived. Its herald, a turkey with tail and flight feathers ablaze, screeching a fanfare of death, soared, tumbled, and then splashed immobile into the water. At that moment, all the pines above the pink billows exploded. Firebrands and great sparks arced out over us like rockets. The huge white pine beside the falls exploded with them; its severed top fell flaming end over end onto the canoe, crushing it instantly. Hesitating for a moment on the rim, the two went over the falls locked together, a single flaming mass. The canoe never came up. The blackened treetop did. Still smoking, it began to circle the eddy.

The heat was intense. Whorls like raindrops pattered across the pool. Beginning at the foot of the pink granite, they advanced like a squall line toward the notch, knocking down the whitecaps. Then I felt the brunt of the heat. It knocked the breath out of me. Ducking under water, I pulled Talbot down with me. He struggled back to the surface, taking me with him.

We were nose to nose. "Talbot!" I shouted. "Stay down."

He shook his head.

"The heat will kill your lungs," I said.

As I pulled him underwater again, I looked toward the far shore. Immediately, with a great whoosh like the concussion from a cannon, the notch and surrounding woods burst into flames. And above the roar of the fire and the thunder of the falls, I could hear the animals that had gained the notch screaming for an instant. Just an instant. And then their voices went silent. The smell of singed fur, urine, and roasting flesh was all they left behind. Talbot flailed and rose up coughing, but I pulled him down again dragging him underwater several yards behind the bears. For the moment, the cat was stymied.

From the well of the great eddy, I saw a landscape I had never seen before. Looking up through the swirling water, past the heat whorls and the flaming debris, I could only make out distended shapes of swirling orange and scarlet, eighty and ninety feet high, engulfing the parapets. And I saw below the flames the gray of the sheer granite walls. And that was all I saw. Granite and flame.

In the eddy, a truce was called. The terrible first heat passed. And we all circled in place. Bears, cat, raccoon, rabbits, squirrels, deer, coyotes, and men. Heads, large and small, bobbed and migrated about the eddy at a stately pace. A slow pavane in a crimson ballroom with each dancer alone and watchful.

At one point, the pine treetop floated by us. I caught it, pulled it over, and rolled Talbot onto it. He was lighter than I thought, and the tree trunk hardly shifted. It was then I saw that his soaked pants draped over bony legs, legs with muscles atrophied from sitting in a wheelchair for years. Laid out prone, he did not protest, although he fought me vaguely at first. "Stay put!" I yelled into his ear. Talbot did not look at me.

All, even Talbot, watched the fiery rim in silence. At one point, the gas tank of my truck blew in a geyser of flame. I looked over at Talbot. His eyes flickered, and I knew he understood. Then regularly from downriver, we heard the booms of propane tanks and more trucks and cars. Once from a nearby camp, a column of ignited propane jetted upward like an accusing finger pointing angrily at the sky. The explosions marked the progress of the fire. I counted off the propane tanks. Every camp downriver was hit. There was no hope for us.

About then the wind fell and the smoke lowered, hanging just above our heads. The great eddy dimmed as at dusk, and white ash began to fall like snow. Stretched out and unmoving on the pine treetop, Talbot turned as white as any alabaster effigy. He started to cough violently. I cleared his mouth and placed a flap of shirt over his face.

The ash that fell in the water turned black, joining the black mass of smoldering trees and exploded embers as well as the charred bodies of the dead. The black froth grew thicker with each rotation. And just above the froth were the eyes of the survivors searching the shoreline and the Escanaba downstream, planning an escape . . . and their next meal. A patch of green grass to nibble, pine boughs with pine cones and nuts, or the weak young and the slow old, the maimed, and the confused.

The truce was nearing an end. Ever so gradually, the fire lost its fury. Crackling and popping, it clung to anything it could consume and fed unhurriedly, reducing trees and the cluttered forest floor to ash and rock.

The din of the falls returned. And with the return of that old sound, the old order of predator and prey stirred among the eddy's survivors.

I looked over at the large cat. It returned my gaze, unblinking.

CAROL

*T*HE FIRE EMERGENCY BULLETIN INTERRUPTED A
Mozart symphony. Turning in our driveway, I sat and listened
for details. Spotter planes were up. The fire was burning north,
jumping every road and firebreak in its path. It had already jumped
the Escanaba. Fire crews were called out and roadblocks were being
set up. The road where Joe parked his truck fell within the fire zone.
The most ominous news was the absence of any estimate on contain-
ment. The car radio warned against anyone, even landowners, entering the fire zone, for the forest was still ablaze.

Over the telephone, a maid told me Mr. Talbot was not home.
"Please call me when he shows up."

"Of course. He is with your husband?"

"Yes. I need to go now."

As the teakettle heated, I heard reports that southerly winds were
strengthening, some gusts topping sixty miles an hour. The wind
would blow all night. The radio said that a checkpoint was set up
on the Highway 480 bridge, a bottleneck for all traffic south, always
the first roadblock set up after a forest fire in our area. There were no
other bridges for miles. Then my mind went out to the Escanaba, and
I saw myself looking downriver from the First Falls. I was standing in
the riffles just above the chute, and I was shouting for Joe. My words
echoed and reechoed off the steep escarpment. No one answered.

The whistle of the teakettle brought me back. I took a cup out
to the front porch and watched the canopy of white pines surrounding our yard sway dangerously, cracking and moaning with each
gust. Siren after siren sang frantically on the wind. Branches snapped
and crashed in our woodlot, and yellow pine pollen and brown pine
needles blew onto the porch. Between sips, I covered my mug with
my hand, waiting for Val to arrive. Evening was not far off.

 As I sipped, I decided Joe and Talbot survived the fire. I made
this determination my starting point and would hold to it until I saw
their dead bodies. Instinctively, Joe would stay on the river, keeping
Talbot with him. The river held two dangers for them, the falls and
hypothermia. Joe would know the nearest help was waiting at the
Highway 480 bridge. By now, he and Talbot should be below the
First Falls. That left three falls. The Second and Third Falls could be
negotiated safely, assuming both were uninjured. I had fished both
falls with Joe. The unknown factors were the wreckage left by the fire
and the dark. Night was at hand, and everything on the river looked
different in the dark. Many years had passed since the last time Joe
and I fished the Escanaba at night. The Fourth Falls was the most
dangerous. It killed canoeists trying to shoot it in high water, and the
portage around lay over uneven ground, an ankle breaker.

 My tea cooled. I drank more deeply, thinking back to my father's
death. My mother phoned me at the Lansing hospital where I was
completing my clinical rotation. Her message was brief, told between
sobs. My father was missing. He was driving Highway 550 through
a snowstorm; he had visited a patient the night before. When he was
not home by morning, my mother believed he was waiting for snow-
plows before driving back, and she had gone about her day. She was
worried, but it had happened before.

 That day and the next, my mother sat waiting for news. I was
with her the day they found my father. He slid off Highway 550,
tumbled down a steep embankment, and came to rest in a drift.
Hours more of falling snow covered him and his car. It was the cold
that killed him. The searchers found him when they became curious
about a raven feeding in a snowdrift. By then, the raven had ripped

the flesh from my father's fingers and sprinkled the snow about with his blood.

My mother and I did not visit the scene of my father's death. We waited at home for word that his body was recovered. We waited with the undertaker to plan his funeral. Then we waited to greet the line of mourners, and we waited for days afterward for our new lives to take shape and become familiar. My mother's new life never took shape. Instead, she waited for death. She was not disappointed; it came a few years later. The neighbors said, "She died of a broken heart."

I believe waiting killed my mother. She faulted herself for not going out that night to find my father. If she had, she might have seen his car tracks going off the edge of Highway 550 before the snow covered them over. And she might have seen the snow slide down the side of the embankment. She told me later if she had gone out that morning, she could have saved him. That morning will never return. And the words I spoke to comfort her could not bring back that morning nor my father. My mother demanded admitting no less before she accepted any comfort.

"Where's Val?" My cup empty, I looked around the porch. The house will be Val's someday, and he will see the ghosts of his father and me in every board, every pot and pan, every jam jar, every flower, bush, and tree. When he came back from Iraq, we wanted him to come home to a place he could claim as his own. So we put him on the deed and gave him a stake in making new memories. Family dinners, the first snowfall, migrating birds flocking to the feeders, and times on the river would not replace his memories of Iraq, but with their growing bulk, they would in time take precedence in his mind. He would never forget Iraq, but we hoped his life at the house would diminish its importance.

Our house was a useful place, aesthetically unremarkable even for Marquette. Small at first, we kept adding to it because we found our life needed more room to flourish. The three of us saw it from the inside out—a collection of sites: a site for cooking, a site for storing fishing tackle and skis, a site for sewing, a site for our computers, and so on. Our front hall held waders, fishing rods, cross-country skis, and a tray for dripping LL Bean boots. The walls of our kitchen displayed cast iron skillets and sieves; its cupboards held a yard sale collection of dinnerware, canned tomatoes, corn, pasta, and dutch ovens.

There was a site for everything we did. And most of what we did was unfinished, dropped to make dinner, answer the front door, or take a telephone call. It was a house of promise. A place to pick up where you left off. We had no time for "neatening up." We had just a few minutes to snatch a fly rod walking out the door to the Escanaba, a few minutes to finish stitching up the hem started yesterday, and a few minutes to check emails.

The house was indelibly ours. Likely Val would use it as a summer place or maybe a retirement place. But whenever he was here, he would be living with our ghosts. He and his wife would be sleeping in our bed, and they would think of us whispering our love to each other in the dark. They would sit at our dinner table and see us and their children with bowed heads about them saying grace. Perhaps they would add more rooms. Perhaps they would use the sewing room for storage. There might be more computers and fewer bookcases with our books.

I heard tires crunching the gravel of our driveway. It was Val.

JOE

"TALBOT, BE READY TO MOVE!" I SHOUTED IN HIS EAR AS he lay on the pine treetop.

"We're staying here," Talbot replied without facing me.

"If we stay in this eddy much longer, your legs will lose all circulation," I said.

"I say we stay here," he said angrily and then screamed. "I own you, Joe!" I did not respond. So he screamed "I own you!" so loud that the walls of the eddy echoed with his words.

With little time for argument, I decided to humor him. "Why do you want to stay here?" I asked.

"Don't challenge me," he said imperiously. "I've made up my mind. That is all people like you need to know."

"That may have worked when I was a volunteer," I said. "But it lost its magic the moment you went over the falls."

"We'll stay here," Talbot said, lifting his head. We were nose to nose, and he tried to stare me down.

"Sorry, Talbot. It's very simple. There will be no help for a day or more!" I shouted into his face. "If we wait in this water, your feet and hands will die. Even now they are beginning to die."

"Right now, my company is organizing a rescue party. I know this. Helicopters and the best security people. They'll get us out," he said with authority.

44

"It takes time to organize a rescue. The very best, the type your company hires, are a long way off. Night will be here shortly. Even if a rescue party could be organized in a few hours, no helicopter pilot will put down in the middle of this fire. They certainly won't search the Escanaba at night.

"No, Talbot, I'm going downriver," I said firmly. "And you're coming with me." I reached for him.

"Don't touch me," he hissed.

"Talbot, if we follow the river, we can make the Highway 480 bridge tomorrow morning. It is fifteen river miles downstream, and there will be help there," I said.

"You're a simpleton," he said, refusing to look at me.

I took his hand, brushing off the ash. It was as cold as the river. His fingertips were faintly blue. He struggled to pull his hand away, but I held on, saying, "We must get you to a hospital as quickly as possible." I let go of his hand and checked his insulin pump display. A decent reading.

"We'll be rescued. Meredith will hire local people," he said. "I have enough money to buy everyone in Marquette."

"No, Talbot. I know the young men you need. They're now fighting this fire, and no amount of money will pull them away from the homes of their friends and family," I said. "They may help when the fire is contained, but even then, they'll be searching for anyone . . . anyone . . . who is missing."

"There will be a rescue," he said, looking at me steadily.

"I'm sure there will be," I said. "But it'll come too late for you."

"You're operating well beyond your competence," he huffed. "You're not even a certified guide."

"Be ready to move downriver," I repeated.

Talbot lay back down and announced, "The notch is the better route. We could walk out on the camp road. The rescuers will be coming that way."

"We have two and a half healthy legs between us and not one shoe. We won't make it out of the notch before our feet are so blistered we'll be crawling on our hands and knees the rest of the way.

An easy meal for any predator . . . And there will be hungry predators out there."

Angry, Talbot shouted, "You really enjoy pushing me around, don't you?"

"No, Talbot, but what I really would enjoy is unloading you at a hospital once we're out of here. We're going downriver."

Talbot turned his head away and said nothing.

I surveyed the eddy. No one had moved ashore yet. More important, the cat was still there, and the bear trio was still in place. Occasionally, a deer thrashed in the shallows. Otherwise the sound of the falls dominated all. With the paddle, I knocked a few red squirrels off the pine treetop. For my efforts, I received silence from Talbot and a lengthy scolding from the squirrels as they swam off like water beetles.

All of us continued to rotate in place. By then, thick black froth covered the whole eddy. I dipped my hand in it and smeared it on my face. And one of my father's baseball stories came to mind.

My father was a professional baseball player. A left-handed pitcher, he came up through college ball, impressed the scouts, and signed with the Chicago Cubs. One rainy night in Chicago two years later, a car weaving through traffic on a slick outer drive crushed one of his legs and ended his career. Toting a wooden leg, he convalesced, went to work, and raised a family.

My father never spoke about his professional career. But he did tell us stories of playing college ball at the University of Chicago. One story he told me more than once was the time, touring the west, the University of Chicago team was scheduled to play a local college on an alkali flat. Under a bright sun, with heat waves turning the outfield into a mirage, my father pitched flawless ball. No hits, no runs, no errors. Mostly strikeouts. The problem was that the pitcher on the other side had the same record. No one could see the white ball against the glare of the flats.

The batters rebelled. The game was heading to a no-hit tie. Even the umpire admitted he had a hard time reading balls and strikes. Although, according to my father, misreading balls and strikes was an endemic condition for umpires, he found it surprising that the umpire would admit it. He would laugh at this point in the story.

The solution was to make the white ball black. The umpire wet the ball and rolled it in the ashes of an old campfire, turning it black. The rest of the game was played with a black ball. My dad would laugh again and say he wished he could have played with a black ball more often. "It looked no bigger than a BB coming through the heat waves," he said. His team won by a run.

I must have been smiling to myself because Talbot broke the mood with a harsh, "What are you grinning about?"

I looked at him coldly. He drew back. "Moron," he said. I looked at him for a long moment and smiled again.

He grunted in disgust.

We rotated several more times. The flames ashore noticeably thinned, and a cool breeze swept the eddy. As if on signal, the squirrels, hare, and raccoons began to climb the notch. The coyotes followed at a distance. The deer were next, although they kept looking back at the big cat. The bear and cat left together, the bear to the billows, the cat to the notch. Above the thunder of the falls, I could hear the scrape of the cat's claws as it leaped upward and stopped, silhouetted at the top. There, it slowly turned and looked down at us.

Talbot waved. The cat stilled. His long tail froze in place, every muscle tensed. His great yellow eyes fixed on us, imperturbable. Talbot waved again.

Then he shouted to me, "He's my type of guy!"

"That's one way of looking at it," I said.

"He sees his equal in me," Talbot crowed.

"Whatever you say, Talbot."

"He's interested in me."

"Yes, he is," I said. "You're the only one bleeding."

Silent, Talbot stared and then dismissed me. "You know so little about me."

"I know you're dying," I said, thinking back to Carol's words. "That explains you to me."

Talbot narrowed his eyes, and something clicked behind them. He stared through me, and his eyes became dull and lifeless, like a snake sunning itself.

"We need to get moving," I said.

PAUGUCK

*K*AHGAHGEE HAS NOT YET RETURNED.

The ones the fire killed are happy to see me. I lift up the newly hatched chicks, throwing them skyward toward the Blessed Isles. They take wing, and their parents follow.

For the rest, I point out the right path.

I will clear the forest before Kahgahgee returns.

But what to do about the white men?

Their death will come soon. The great cat stalks them, and I have never known the cat to fail.

The cat gives me the best kind of work . . . clean kills. It attacks from above, waiting until its prey passes underneath. Then it jumps, knocking the unsuspecting victim to the ground. With one snap of its powerful jaws, it severs the victim's spinal cord, leaving the victim limp. The victim's brain is still working when the cat drags him off to its cache. The last sound the victim hears is the cat marking the victim as its own.

I do have one complaint about the big cat.

Walking with it is lonely, tedious work.

At the heart of the cat is silence.

It stalks silently.

It attacks silently.

It kills silently.

Right now, I know the cat meditates on killing the white men.
The two will fill its cache.

I know too it will follow them until it finds the place along the Escanaba where it can hide, crouching one short leap away.

There it will lay in ambush.

And it will wait silently.

CAROL

*M*Y WEDDING RING LAY ON THE SILL OF OUR KITCHEN window. Its gold glinted orange in the sunset. Slumping over the white porcelain sink with arms stiff, fingers splayed, and shoulders raised, I bow my head and wonder if this week my ring would rest forever with Joe's death certificate in the top drawer of my dresser. Lifting my head, I look out the window. A young lilac bush fills the frame, its violet and blue sprays swinging in the wind. Joe planted it. I think of him on the river, Talbot's plaything.

Val was upstairs moving around his room unpacking. I looked at my wedding ring again and thought of Joe and our marriage. After more than thirty years, we had sloughed off all pretenses of career and personality as airy affectations. We became to each other what time proved—our enduring strengths and weaknesses. The daily striving to balance the budget, meet the demands of our jobs, raise Val, and weather the emotional storms of loss and suspicion left us naked, gazing on each other without embarrassment as we might when undressing for bed to revisit quiet, dependable pleasures. No more talk of "trying something new" or "making a fresh start." Now we faced each other over dinner or lying together in the dark as we are, what our history together has left of us, without apology or shame. Our so very direct life together.

People believe I am a dedicated nurse. My mother and father

often praised my dedication, and that accolade motivated me at first. It was my patients who tested my dedication. I became attached to them and found myself whole-heartedly rooting for their recovery. My training warned me against such attachments, for they brought feelings not just of joy but also of loss. I ignored the warning and suffered for it. The deaths of the young, especially infants, left me empty of all conviction. They labored so hard for their next breath. Each intake was a triumph, often an empty triumph, for their small lungs never captured enough oxygen to bring them a future, and they died. The day after such deaths, I fought just as hard as they to inhale heart into my deflated dedication. But often enough I succumbed to grief. My self-discipline put me behind the wheel of my car, twisted the key in the ignition, and guided me to work. And I made it through the day, somber, drawing on hospital procedure for energy.

Sometimes I thought of doing as others counseled, spending less time with patients, or mentally transforming ailing persons into corporate consumers to whom I administered a unit of care. These tricks did distance me from the anguish of my patients' suffering and dying, but I could not in conscience maintain such attitudes for long. I was warned by my supervisors that I was too kind and needed to harden myself. And so I began to think of new careers.

Joe convinced me to stay in nursing. And he did not even know he was doing it. Joe saw few significant junctures in feeling and fewer in time. He did life at the quick step. This is not to say that he does not sympathize with my ups and downs, for he does, quietly taking in the stories of my losses. He would have a few questions and then give a tearful embrace. But Joe was never arrested by defeat. In his own life, he moved past defeats with dispatch, accepting them without remorse. Even now, he moved from drafting and inspecting construction sites to roofing, logging, and going back to his duties as an engineer year after year. Joe was always working or looking for work. There were fewer engineering projects now, so Joe supplemented our income with more logging. It was spotty work, but it paid well because of its hazards. Often he was the oldest man on site, but he never commented on it. He just kept pounding ahead.

Joe kept the relentless beat of my life. And through his firmness, I became a better nurse. I no longer needed to brace myself before taking a shift in the emergency room, or in the oncology or pediatrics departments. Instead, I thought of Joe. He was always there urging me on, and so I was always there urging my patients on. Yes, he refused to express his feelings about Talbot, and I sensed that he hid much more. But whatever his flaws, Joe's firm resolve drove the pace of my life.

It was dark now. I looked up to catch my reflection in the kitchen window. Instead, I saw Joe's mother as she looked in the days following Joe's father's death. With my mother and father both dead by then, I came to call her "Mother McCartney." She too was standing at the very sink on which I now rested, and she too was mourning an absent husband. With her husband gone, she followed the routines put in place over a lifetime with one exception. She sang more, as field workers once sang at harvest time. Sweeping, folding laundry, or dicing vegetables, she worked to the rhythm of her favorite hymns. She knew hundreds. When she completed a task, she would finish with a flourish on the last word of a refrain, bouncing her broom, smoothing the last creases out of a folded sheet, or doing a quick "chop, chop" to finish off a carrot for the pot. Nearby, I would chuckle, and she would join me until we were both laughing with tears in our eyes.

True to my memories of her, Mother McCartney was singing. And I listened to catch the words. She began on the simple truth,

"To everything there is a season under heaven . . . "

I started to join in but choked on the next line,

"A time to be born and a time to die . . ."

The cowardly sweetness of self-pity gently stroked my right hand. "There, there, dear. A cry will do you good." And before my eyes, it conjured the scene of Joe dead, an ugly mound of ash and blackened bone. "Your game is over," it whispered soothingly. "Surrender and call a sympathetic friend. Let it all out. You have so often been the shoulder to cry on. Now it's your turn."

Looking into the window, I trembled and said, "Mother McCartney, sing a new hymn."

"All right . . . How about . . . Let me see . . . Yes . . . 'Lead Kindly Light.' " And she began to sing, "Lead kindly light amid the encircling gloom."

"Thank you, Mother. Just the right note."

So often terminal patients like Talbot tell me they do not wish to linger longer than necessary. They see clearly the inevitable outcome of their disease, and they decide to meet it sooner rather than later. So often it is neither the pain nor the medical costs that puts them into this mind-set. Rather it is that they have lived beyond any meaning they ever took from their lives. They reach the point where they find no purpose in waking up to begin their day. Daily they ask themselves what purpose their existence serves. And they inventory their hours, and finding no deed of merit, they grow more and more impatient for the end. And in their impatience, they begin to entertain the unthinkable: a swift end of their own choosing, an end to medical bills and disruptions to their children's schedules, and, more important, an immediate end to the constant probing into why they were still alive, each probe refreshing the wound of their worthlessness.

A chill pierced me, and I quivered. This was Talbot's game. His delight at humiliating subordinates never allayed his fear of lingering on and becoming more and more helpless, dependent, and in time scorned. He knew those whom he humiliated throughout his life would retaliate by humiliating him as he died. And they would laugh at him. Thus, he wanted his end to come quickly, well before pain sets the agenda for the few hours left him. Well before he becomes the ward of those he humiliated. Of that I was certain. He had decided on a quick death. And then the smell of gun solvent came back to me. I thought of Joe and wished I could warn him.

Again I looked up into the kitchen window. This time, the reflection was of me, and I began to hum to myself, standing transfixed before the dark of the lilac bush. I thought again of Joe on the river and whispered aloud, "Amid th'encircling gloom; lead thou me on . . ."

Val came into the kitchen behind me. "Hi, Mom," he said, taking a seat at the old oak kitchen table scarred black from casserole dishes and pie tins pulled hot from the oven. When I turned, he sensed my distress. "Don't worry, Mom," he said. "Dad can take care of himself. He's up to a night on the Escanaba."

"He's up to the river, Val. I don't know if he's up to Frank Talbot," I replied, subdued.

"Dad will be fine. Who's Talbot?"

"One of my patients. A rich man who hurt a lot of people up here years ago. Your grandfather was one." I stared at my wedding ring again. "If anything happens, I'm to blame." I took a breath and said, "I asked your father to take Talbot fishing."

"Dad knew what he was getting into," Val replied.

"No," I said and let the remark fall into the silence between us.

Finally Val said quietly, "I don't follow you, Mom."

"Talbot pestered me. He wanted Joe and only Joe to guide him."

"Dad knows the river better than anyone else."

"Try to understand, Val. I was suspicious of Talbot, but he and his wife pestered me, and I found my own reason for doing what Talbot wanted." I brought my right fist up and placed it against my breastbone. "I'm afraid I became his accomplice against my own husband."

Val stood as I sat down. "Can I get you anything? Dinner? Some coffee?"

"No, I'm all right," I said, smiling up at him. "You're so like your father."

"How did it happen that Talbot and Dad went out today?"

"I asked your father to guide Talbot, a man your father hates. I sensed that Talbot did not really want to fish. I suspected that he had another agenda and that your father was part of it." I raised my head and said tonelessly, "The man is dying, and I thought your father could make peace with his feelings against him if he saw the despair the man was in." Shaking my head, I added, "It was too much to ask." I reached out a hand to my son. "Val, I've put your father in danger because I thought it would do him good."

"No, Mom, you did what you thought was best for Dad. You couldn't have foreseen the fire."

"Talbot is a dangerous man."

"Never count Dad out. I've seen him do amazing things."

I sat back and thought for a moment. "He holds a deep grudge against Talbot. You know your father's temper."

"It's never more than words and then it blows over," Val shot back. He didn't like the direction of my conversation.

"Talbot's insidious. I thought they would be together for a few hours at most, not enough time for him to infuriate your father. If they're alive . . ." I caught myself scrambling for composure, reminding myself of my starting point. Joe and Talbot were alive, and I began again, "I'm afraid Talbot will prod your father to the point where he'll kill him."

"That's silly talk, Mom."

"Listen to me! I think Talbot wants to die," I said. "He'll use every trick, and he knows a lot, to goad your father into doing it for him. He's a master at getting others to do his bidding without asking directly." Silent again I looked inward and said, "Look at me." I gazed down at my hands. "I did what he wanted even though I felt he was lying. Talbot has a way of reading people."

"Dad will be okay. You must believe that," Val said, but his voice was now cautious.

"I do believe in your father," I said.

Then he replied, "Let's check the road near the first falls. Maybe Dad's already made his way out and is waiting for us."

"I tried to drive out there before you arrived, but the sheriff set up a roadblock on Highway 581, and the deputies made me turn around."

The telephone rang from the next room. I motioned to Val to sit down, "I'll get it. The sheriff promised to call if he had any news." But it was not the sheriff on the line. Returning to the kitchen with the phone receiver, I said, "No, Meredith, I haven't heard anything."

I pointed to the phone while Meredith was speaking and silently mouthed the words, "Talbot's wife." Meredith wanted to begin her own search for Frank and Joe. "It's urgent we do something now," she said.

"It's just a matter of waiting until the firefighters move in tomorrow," I replied.

"I've spoken with the governor," Meredith said loudly, "and he agreed to have the locals coordinate with our security people. We'll be calling the shots."

I pulled the receiver away from my ear and said into the mouthpiece. "If you think it best, Meredith."

"This must be resolved immediately. Thousands of people, Wall Street, and pension fund managers will be affected should we not reach Frank in time to save his life . . . if he's still alive. Just agree to cover half the cost of the rescue. You want Joe back, don't you?"

I replied, "Of course we want Joe and Frank back as quickly as possible, but we can't afford to pay half the cost of your team. We have no choice but to wait for the Forest Service and the county to send their people in—"

I was about to say more when Meredith interrupted me. "I would think you would want to support the rescue of our husbands. It is after all Joe's fault that Frank is out there now."

Stunned, I said in response, "It's not Joe's fault. Frank wanted to go even after I and his doctors tried to talk him out of it. Joe was reluctant to take him."

Meredith spat out her words. "We'll see what the courts say. And then there's the matter of your license."

Too shocked to reply, I said, "The doctors and I tried talking Frank out of going. You were there . . . But I'm repeating myself."

"I don't remember that!" Meredith shouted.

Before she went on, I interjected, "We'll talk about this later when Frank and Joe are home."

Meredith screamed. "You're fired! Because of you and your husband, Frank will not be coming home alive. You saw the TV reports of the fire."

I began to repeat, "We will—" when Meredith screamed again. I held the phone out from my ear. Val grabbed the receiver from me.

"I don't know you, Meredith, but you're upsetting my mother," Val said.

"Your mother misled me," Meredith said.

"You're lying."

There was silence and then Meredith said softly, "I have never met you, but—"

Val interrupted, "Both you and your husband are liars."

"No one speaks to me that way."

Val continued, "I'll speak to you any way I want."

Val heard a click. I took the phone from his hand and went into the next room to return it to its charger. When I returned, I said, "The Talbots are very powerful."

"I won't let anyone talk to you that way, Mom."

Val and Joe were so alike. "Thank you, Val, but you should've let me handle it."

"I can't stand seeing you crawl to people like her. Why should you? You haven't done anything wrong."

"It doesn't matter. I take Meredith at her word. When she says she'll have my license, she will throw everything they have into it," I said patiently.

"But you haven't done anything wrong!"

"It doesn't matter. Meredith will hire a team of attorneys, and we won't be able to stand up to her money. They'll drain our savings dry in a week. Even my group couldn't support a full defense."

"There are other jobs," Val said, puzzled.

"No, not for me. Not up here," I said. "The U.P. is thinning out. You know that, Val. When you graduate, you'll have a hard time finding a good job up here."

"I know," he replied.

His stark confirmation struck deeply, and I paled. After graduation, the days of Val visiting home would become fewer and fewer. "Your father and I are growing older. Physically, I'm not up to a full schedule anymore. I was hoping if I did a good job for the Talbots, I could cut back on some of my other assignments. It's good money for a few hours of work. And there might be other work like it if they recommended me to their friends."

"Dad's working."

"Yes, but for how long? He can't go on logging. His engineering work has nearly all dried up. Not enough construction. Most schematics are popped out of CAD programs now."

"Is Dad thinking of retiring?" Val asked, shocked.

"No, and neither am I." I went silent, then said, "Truth be told, Val, we can't. Your Dad must give up his logging in the next few years. It's a young man's job. What other jobs are out there for him is unclear."

"In a few years, after I graduate, I can help." Val lapsed into silence and then said slowly, "I'm sorry. I didn't know."

"It isn't your fault. Dad and I didn't want you to know."

"I wish you had told me."

I went to the sink and stared out the kitchen window again. My wedding ring was in shadow. I looked back over my shoulder at Val. "This is our life. This is what we live with day after day." I paused. "I wish your father were here."

"Me too, Mom," Val said.

I reached out toward the windowsill, took my ring, and slid it onto my finger. Then looking down at my hand, I made a fist.

JOE

*T*ALBOT, NOW'S THE TIME," I SAID INTO HIS EAR. He ignored me. Below the great eddy, the Escanaba runs through canyon lands. It's a little more than a half mile of gray granite cliffs and white water throughout. No deer ever drank from the waters of the canyon lands. The only way down is a four-story drop, and the only way out is a long swim down a churning chute of white water. The chute is the portal to the river below.

Cinching the wading belt to bind us together, I pushed the treetop to a gravel shallows and broke off a few branches, leaving the rest to act as outriggers. Then, like a hospital attendant guiding a wheeled gurney, I walked Talbot downriver to the top of the chute.

Hesitating, I scanned the white water below, looking for a line through the boulders. I could see none.

A shadow slunk over us. Surprised, I looked up toward the rim. The rim is chancy. Loose sand and granite chips give way immediately to empty space. All in the forest avoid walking it. But there on the rim was the sure-footed cat, neon tawny in the flickering fire light. He was watching us.

Talbot saw the cat too. "My friend is following me," he said.

"Yes," I said.

"What do you plan to do about it . . . Joe?" He smirked as if he had just ordered a subordinate to have a forty-page report due on his desk the next morning.

"Avoid him," I said.

Talbot laughed. "What are the odds of that?"

"You're better at figuring odds."

"I calculate them as one hundred to one against you," he said. "We will be meeting that cat face-to-face before we leave the river."

Talbot's odds were about right. I fell silent and pulled up memories of every stretch of the Escanaba downstream. There were places where the cat would have the advantage on us. We could skirt some of those places. The pictures of the ones that could not be skirted, I filed away to study later.

Time to start our run. Once we were in the grip of the canyon lands, there was no turning back. The drop was steep and the river current relentless. I clung to the side of the tree as we went down the river. At times, there was no bottom; at times, boulders threatened to hang us up; and at times, they spun us around. All I could do was react by stabbing, kicking, pulling, or swimming. "Face forward," I kept saying to myself. "Face forward."

Once as we slid past a large boulder, I pulled Talbot into the quiet water on his backside. Breathing hard, I again surveyed the white water left. Dusk had crept up on us, cutting the light into the narrow canyon, always the first place on the Escanaba to go dark. Again I saw no line, caught my breath, and checked Talbot's foot. It was cold and dark with blood.

The rest of our run down the chute was a match to the start. Hidden boulders, errant logs, and granite walls. I worked the paddle, pushed and pulled the tree, and kicked off the chute walls. Reacting, reacting, reacting but keeping Talbot out of the river . . . for the most part.

I was exhausted, and my feet and ankles were in pain when the cool shadows of the canyon and the last of the white water gave way to the heat of blazing hardwoods and calm water below. Once flourishing mature maples and red oaks, the trees were now welcoming torches casting warmth and light. We passed two gutted camps. Rock foundations, crumpled cars, and smoking tires. And as far down the river as I could see, there were tranquil waters and steadily crackling fires.

As the current slowed, Talbot said, "Let's pull in. Nature calls." It was a shallow riffle, hardly a foot deep.

"Soon," I said. "There is a better spot a quarter mile down."

"I say we pull in now!" Talbot shouted angrily. His face flushed and he choked on his words. "I do not need your permission, Joe."

"Just a little farther," I said, unmoved. "We're too exposed here."

"My friend, the cat." Talbot laughed. "You're going to meet him face-to-face. Might as well be here. It will give me great pleasure to watch him tear you apart."

I let it pass.

At one point rounding a bend with a large exposed sand bank, I said, "We're almost at the pull-out."

Talbot remained wrapped in silence.

My destination was a large flat rock, about the size of a small bedroom. It divided the river's swift current almost evenly, and the two streams, skirting it, dug glides four feet deep. An adequate moat.

Behind the rock was a small spit of sand where I slid the log up. I released the belt, and Talbot relieved himself. Gently taking his arm, I said, "Let me help you up."

Talbot pulled away. He hopped and winced. I caught him before he fell. He again shrugged me off.

"I don't need your help," he growled.

I picked him up in my arms and placed him up onto the flat rock. His withered legs left him weighing hardly more than an average fifteen-year-old. I then climbed up beside him. The rock was warm from the fire. Talbot settled back, resting . . . thinking.

"This might hurt," I said as I began to unwrap the bandaging on his foot. I need not have warned Talbot because his foot was turning blue and seeping puss. His toes were worse, a dark gray-blue. The stump was no better. It showed traces of blue up to the knee and seeped blood. I laid the stump and his feet out on the rock. For once, he did not quarrel.

He needed a hospital. "Relax, Talbot," I said.

He fixed his gaze on me suspiciously. "Stop playing the Good Samaritan," he said dully.

"I promised Meredith and my wife I'd bring you back in one piece."

"No need," he said. "Meredith hates me."

"Things will look better when you get home," I said.

"Home?" he said. "I share a house with a woman who hates me. You call that a home? Meredith has hated me since my first billion."

"It couldn't have been the money," I said.

"No. I started having affairs." He puffed himself up, and his voice grew louder as he said proudly, "And I enjoyed each one of them."

"Forget the past," I said, trying to dampen his growing excitement.

Ignoring me, he quickly glanced over and said, "But it was not the affairs that made Meredith mean. No, she hoped I would be discreet . . . So her girlfriends would not find out. By then, she had embraced the role of the long-suffering wife." After a long pause, he stated, almost to himself, "I refused to be discreet, and she punished me by waiting . . . blameless."

"Forget Meredith for the moment," I said.

"She cut me out of her life."

"I can understand," I replied a little too quickly.

"You sanctimonious hick!" he screamed.

"Rest, Talbot, while we have the time. We need to make the Second Falls by dark. Then we'll be on schedule to make Highway 480 by dawn."

"She would have divorced me then, but there's too much money," he said reluctantly. "She only needed to wait. And Meredith got good at waiting." Talbot paused again and, with great effort, said, "She'll get it all and become the wealthiest woman in the world . . . probably." He stopped for a moment, then looked off, and said, "It all depends on the market the hours after my death is reported. Meredith believes it would be good if I died on a weekend. Then publicists will have time to get ahead of any damaging rumors."

"I'm sure you're right, Talbot," I said, trying to end his monologue.

He then looked up at me, smiling slyly. "When you get me back, I'll insist that your wife become my live-in nurse. She'd love the extra money." He leered at me.

Shocked, I tried not to show it, but my hands shook. I crossed my arms and put my hands under my armpits as if they were cold.

Talbot noticed and pushed on. "Yes, Carol can be bought. I sense it. She's probably worried about retirement. Not enough money in the till. You've certainly not done a good job providing for her."

I scanned Talbot's features. He was braced for another slap or maybe worse. He was riding me and plainly took delight in it, but there was something more. He was studying me . . . probing.

"The smell of money is an irresistible cologne," he said. Talbot looked over at me, waiting.

I replied, taking time to enunciate each word carefully. "Carol will do what, in her judgment, is best for your health."

Deflated, Talbot looked at his necrotic foot and stump. His shoulders shook, and he screamed, "Do you hear me? I'll keep your wife so busy you'll never see her again!"

I ignored him. As Carol would say, it was the disease talking. I just was not sure which disease was talking. It was then I thought of how Talbot was dying, and my resentment evaporated. And when it dried up, I first thought of how much I disliked money.

The fire damped down as the evening came on. Still heat and flame, but noticeably cooler. I pulled off my socks, checking my feet and ankles. Bruised but nothing broken. The socks were wool, and it occurred to me Talbot would be better off with them. Washing the blood off, I wrung them out and slipped them on him.

He sat up and said, "What are these for?"

"They'll keep your foot and stump warm," I said.

"They won't help," he stated authoritatively.

"Whatever you say," I replied. There was too much river ahead of us to waste time arguing. I caught the flash of the big cat's flank on a rock knob just below where we pulled in. That was what I needed to think about—the places where the cat could ambush us downriver. I started to run pictures of downstream.

"Whatever you say. Whatever you say," Talbot said, mimicking me.

"Whatever you say," I said, and then, added with emphasis, "Frank." I stared into his eyes. It was true he was dying, but how many more times would I need to tell myself this fact before we made the 480 bridge? The truth was we were all dying. Before long, I would need another reason to smother my anger, because I knew if I didn't, I could see myself with my hands around his throat, choking off his last breath. I had done it before with less provocation.

Talbot fought with himself, then relaxed. "I like it out here. It suits me. The big fish eat the little fish."

He looked over, expecting a reply, so I said, "You're not a fish."

"A philosopher." He laughed. "Let me amend what I said, Joe." Sitting up, he turned and said, "The big bad kitty cat will eat the stupid little fish." He paused and said more confidently, "Then again, you might be my little fish to eat." He fell back, silent, and stared into the growing dusk. His eyes closed, and his breathing grew regular. I checked his fingertips. They were pinking up.

I watched the river for the next half hour. Mayflies started to emerge above the glide. About size 16, they had wings of a deep gray and bodies of brilliant emerald. Like little sailboats, they floated past us on the water until their wings were strong enough to fly upward. Trout began to rise. Both brook and brown. Sloppy rises, at first, then steady, mechanical feeding on the mayflies coursing through the glide.

The last time I fished this stretch was with Carol. I saw her again as I had seen her that day, casting sixty feet with her favorite fly, the Adams. She had changed little over the years we knew each other. We met beneath a diving raft about the size of the rock Talbot and I were on. The raft was one of a half dozen sitting just off the sandy shoreline of Blue Lake, a popular Marquette camping spot. Summer after summer, the same families showed up, and the water games played along the lake bonded generations of children. My family had just moved to town, and my father insisted we spend a day there to meet our neighbors.

The day extended into the slanting shadows of evening. I joined a group playing hide-and-seek among the diving rafts. There was one rule. No player was allowed to leave the water. If you did, you were it. The most courageous hid among the fifty-five-gallon steel drums that buoyed the rafts. For them, they had to first swim under the raft, guess where to surface, and finally avoid the clinging spider webs and desiccated bug carcasses. When players found worse, bats and snakes, whoops and screams marked them for discovery.

Swimming under a raft, I came up too quickly in the dark and bumped my head on the side of a drum. The raft shook.

In the dark, I heard a gasp. "Are you all right?" a girl's voice whispered.

"Sure," I said. I felt for blood but found just the beginnings of a bump.

"Shh," came back through the dark.

I whispered, "Just a bump."

"Let me check it," she said.

"Where are you?"

"Just follow my voice," she said.

Feeling my way, I made small strokes toward her, the last brushing across her chest. I recoiled. "Sorry," I said.

"You didn't mean it," she said. "Turn around so I can check your scalp."

I did and felt her fingers search my skull. They found the bruise and gently felt around it. "You'll live." We couldn't have been more than a foot apart, and I felt her presence intensely as we tread water.

"Thank you," I said.

"What's your name?" she asked.

"Joseph McCartney."

"You're new," she said.

"Yes. My family just moved here," I said. "What's your name?"

"Carol Campbell," she said. "I grew up here. My mother is a teacher at the high school, and my father is a doctor."

Just then, I heard a splash alongside the raft, and a singsong voice bellowed the rhyme,

Joe and Carol
Sitting under a tree,
K-I-S-S-I-N-G
First comes love,
Then comes marriage,
Then comes Carol with a baby carriage.

High-pitched laughter erupted from under nearby rafts. Carol swam out to confront the spy. It was a classmate.

"We were not!" she shouted angrily. Just then, whoever was "it" caught her in the open. And her exasperation was complete.

She did not talk to me for the rest of that night. We did exchange polite words at school that fall.

"You're smiling again, Little Fish." It was Talbot. He was sitting up and grinning at me.

"Get some sleep, Frank. Let your arteries work," I said.

Talbot lay back down and said into the dark of a late afternoon sky, "You're hiding something."

Confused, I said hurriedly, "Not true." It was too quick. Even I heard the trace of fear in my voice.

"I'll find out what it is," he said.

"There's nothing to find out," I said slowly, each word a threat.

"You betray yourself, Little Fish. You'd never win at poker . . . or business. But you already know that." Talbot closed his eyes, shifted the stump of his amputated foot, and lay still.

Seeing Talbot's stump reminded me of August vacations with my father. He and my mother rented a cottage on Blue Lake for three weeks every August. For him, it was three weeks of fishing. For her, three weeks of reading.

Once every August, my father swam in Blue Lake. It was a private swim and among the happiest moments of his life. He would dress in bathing trunks and a bathrobe and, with my mother and me, take a rowboat out to an empty cove. There he removed his artificial leg, lowered himself in the water, and swam. He did not say much but smiled broadly as he paddled about.

July and August were especially hard on my father. The heat, the dust, and the uneven ground of the logging sites he inspected raised blisters on his stump. The cure was an evening Epsom salt bath. Night after night, I remember his first exhalations of relief when his stump slid into the warm water. My mother dedicated a white porcelain bowl solely for his relief. Pads of Dr. Shoal's plasters cluttered his bedroom stand, the first thing he put on in the morning. It was all guesswork predicting where his stump would rub that day. Many days his guesses were off, sometimes by just inches but enough for a blister to form. Deep into the summer, my father rarely spoke.

The swim in Blue Lake brought my father boyish joy for a few fleeting minutes. I still remember his first whoops when he hit the cold water of the lake. And I remember his sidestroke with his white stump pumping in the water. His August swim ended with a brief sprint and then a return to the boat, where we helped him crawl in. Once he strapped his leg back on, he stowed the smile and turned to chatting about shopping lists and evening fishing.

Talbot was snoring. Smoke from what was left of the forest ran upward in columns collecting overhead in gray pedestals. Enough fuel was left in the woods for a few more days—hot spots, as the firefighters called them. And there was always the chance the fire would go underground in some places and burn for months.

I slid down the rock and splashed water on my face. Then I climbed back up and lay out near Talbot, too anxious to nap. Looking up into the smoke filling the sky from horizon to horizon, I never felt so alone on the river.

The good days at Blue Lake relieved my days of pain also. I never had my father's athletic gifts. This showed up early in baseball. My mother sensed my frustration. One day, she and I were sitting, reading on our weathered cedar dock. It was a sunny day, and we were sipping cold root beers. The sky was a pale blue, and the lake sparkled. My father was napping before evening fishing.

My mother turned to me and said, "Joe, no matter what you do with your life, your Dad and I love you."

"I know, Mom. I always feel your love."

"Dad too."

"Yes," I said tentatively.

"Remember the words of the song, 'Do not wait to shed your light afar . . . Brighten the corner where you are,' " she sang softly.

"Of course, Mom."

"Every day you brighten the corner where we are."

"Thanks, Mom," I said, then sang the first line, "'Do not wait until some deed of greatness you may do,'" and my mother joined in. Laughing, we sang the first stanza and then the refrain together.

"Brighten the corner where you are.

Brighten the corner where you are.

Someone far from harbor you may guide across the bar.

Brighten the corner where you are."

Even with my mother's support, I found it difficult to accept my lack of athletic talent. Never better than a second string ball player, by junior year I stopped trying out for our high school baseball team. The few times I asked my father to coach me, he made suggestions that were beyond my abilities. When it became clear his advice was not helping my pitching, he told me, "You don't have the arm." He said it without malice as a child might say, "The sky is blue." At that moment, my interest in baseball wavered, and we never spoke of pitching again.

Even now, I returned to his words, "You don't have the arm." How was it that he, my own father, did have the arm, and I did not? I saw him on the mound in Wrigley field, his raised left arm, his kick, and the downward snap of the white ball against the green center field seats. High school biology gave me one explanation. The genes that blessed my father bypassed me. And as I grew older, I discovered more genes that bypassed me. I was a top student in high school, but at Michigan Tech where I enrolled for the engineering program, I was average. In every class, there were those who had better memories and math skills than I did. They took tests better, led our study groups, and received higher grades. The chaotic meeting of sperm and ova blessed them and spurned me.

Chance. The luck of the draw. These thoughts did not cool my resentment. High school and college run on contests. And without consulting me, life decreed once and for all that some would be more competitive than others, and those few were destined to beat the rest of us out. I kept score and found I was losing. A merely adequate engineer with only a few offers of work, I took a job with a second string firm after graduation. Just smart enough to make an impression but never superior to the rest of the field.

As children, we chose sides for baseball by kicking a bat. After the captains were chosen, usually the two best players started in gripping a bat hand over hand, going upward until only the knob on the handle was left. The captain who held his grip on the knob was given first pick from among the players, but only if he could hang onto it after the other captain was given the chance to kick the bat out of his hand. It all depended on the strength of the hand holding the bat and the strength of the leg kicking it. A clash of better genes. The rest of us were just observers. No one except me ever questioned it. That was the way the world ran. If the bat was dropped, the other captain won the right to choose first. And the selection proceeded until all the players were chosen, teams based on the accidental allocation of genes.

The better players were chosen first. They had a better batting eye and quicker reflexes. They were the faster and stronger among us. I was never among the first players picked, and each time I was passed over, a new wound opened. My resentment against the flux of my birth grew deeper and deeper. I refused to accept the way the world worked. And I saw myself objectively, as a collection of mediocre abilities. I was condemned without a hearing to struggle the rest of my life among the also-rans.

No matter how hard I worked to improve, there were the times those life favored worked just as hard and beat me out. Handily. My resentment pooled within me, a subterranean reservoir drowning my confidence. With each lost contest, this pool broadened and deepened, and my expectations for the future narrowed. For all my efforts and practice, I achieved little in high school baseball. I began to think of "personal bests" to distract myself from my failures. Triumphs of my personal best became an excuse for avoiding the judgment of my peers. The truth was, and I recognized it immediately, my personal best was not an argument winning me a starting position.

From the first time I heard Talbot's name, I knew the universe favored him as it favored few others. He was superior to the field, and I resented him for it. After Lundine slumped, my resentment turned to rage, because I saw that winning was not enough for Talbot. He could do that easily. His purpose was to make sure everyone feared him winning. Talbot always held onto the bat after others tried to kick it out of his hand. He always had first picks. And he made the most of them. For Talbot, there was no slaughter rule.

I needed a plan to endure Talbot's taunts. Outlasting him was my first thought. What little sports success I had in high school was on the cross-country team. For once, I excelled. I did it by never letting up. Our team won regionals in my senior year, and I judged myself and others by the grit we showed. All of life became the kick over the last three hundred yards, and I prided myself for running it in flat out every race. Finishing the job, giving it my best to the very end while others, some faster than me, slacked off. Even today, I see my mother and father clapping near the finish line, urging me on.

My classmates started calling me the Grinder. And that is who I became. Laying back on the rock with the Escanaba swirling past, I thought about the night ahead and the last miles down to Highway 480. This would be my hardest race, true cross-country. I felt Val and Carol urging me on. And I saw Talbot rooting against me. There would be no personal best over the next hours. There would be only finishing or dying.

So I reached down and took the temperature of the pool of resentment within me. I found it boiling. Hot enough to fuel one last kick, but mounting dangerously close to a scalding vapor dissolving the wrappings where I held my hatred of Talbot. My rage. My own necrotic limb. And so I stood on guard, fearing the moment the ancient wrappings parted and the necrotic bile gushed out, blinding me. Soon the vision of Talbot's painful last hours, blind and without legs, would not be enough to extinguish my rage against him. I needed to compose another vision, another excuse for mercy, one artful enough to push Talbot to the edge of my feelings, to cooler regions. Nothing came to mind. So I thought of Carol and Val.

The mayfly hatch petered out. My eyes followed a lone beaver, cruising upstream, when a low-flying raven caught my attention. Coming abreast of us, it fluttered its wings, spread its tail feathers, hung in place for an instant, and then gathered itself to continue downriver toward Highway 480.

RAVEN

*T*HE WHITE MEN DO NOT LOOK HAPPY TOGETHER. So much the better.

Pauguck was keeping pace with the big cat.

I croaked for his attention, asking, "How much longer, Pauguck?"

"The able-bodied man has not given the cat an opening yet. But that will change. Downriver, there are many openings."

"Call me when the cat kills them," I said.

"No," Pauguck said firmly.

"I am not—" I tried to argue.

"No," Pauguck repeated even more loudly.

"Just hear me out," I pleaded.

Pauguck grimaced. "Make it brief."

"I want to fly above the First Falls and rummage among the dead," I said. "It would be a great help if you could call me back when the cat makes the kill."

"No," he said again.

"You should be helping the cat end this," I said. "If you had helped the cat, I would not now be waiting."

"And why should I help you? You make my life difficult."

"We have talked of that," I said.

"Do you have any idea how hard it is to guide white people to the Silver Lake and the Blessed Isles?" Pauguck shot back.

"I do not see what that has to do with my problem," I said.

"Of course not. You see only your problems, Kahgahgee."

"I just want their eyes," I said.

"And I do not want you to have their eyes," Pauguck replied immediately.

"We are at an impasse," I said and waited. Pauguck nodded his head and continued to hike downstream with the cat. "All right, all right. Tell me your problem."

He turned and said, "Every white person believes a personal guide will meet them when they cross into the spirit world. They know the guide's name and have even studied pictures of their guide. Some names I hear over and over, but many names I do not recognize, and I do not have time to familiarize myself with all of them."

"I still do not understand your problem," I said.

"Kahgahgee, let me finish," Pauguck said impatiently.

"I am sorry," I said. "Take all the time you need."

"When I approach a white's spirit, the white keeps looking over my shoulder for someone else to show up. After meeting dead spirits for many years, I can say with absolute certainty that I am the last person whites expect to meet after their death. So now I just tell them I am the doorman or the conductor. It is easier when I use such a title. And I tell them their guide is just a little farther along." Pauguck paused. "And here is the point, Kahgahgee, so you won't miss it."

"I am paying attention," I said.

"Because they have their eyes, I need only point them toward the Land of the Spirits and the beautiful Silver Lake, and they see their path and make the four-day journey by themselves. Maybe they meet the guide they expected later. I do not know."

"I am beginning to understand," I said.

"Let me make it clear. When a dead white person loses his eyes to your beak, I spend four days on the trail with him. Do you know what that means?"

"No," I said.

"Four days of theological discussion. The whites expect me to explain how I fit within the grand scheme of life, death, and the divine. I do not know enough theology to spend four minutes discussing those topics. I have a job, and I do my job. That is all," he said. "Now do you see my problem, Kahgahgee?"

"I see," I said and fell to thinking. Pauguck waited.

Finally I looked up and said to him, "But I must have those blue eyes."

"It does no good arguing with you," Pauguck said disgustedly. "Why do I bother?"

"It is always good for us to discuss sore points," I said. "You feel more kindly toward me after our discussions."

Silent, Pauguck stared at me.

"So you will call me when the cat makes the kill?" I asked tentatively.

"No," Pauguck said, shaking his head. With that, he disappeared downriver.

I will fly up river. No telling what I might find. Then if all goes well, if I am lucky, I will get the white men's eyes while they are still breathing.

JOE

*T*HE LAST OF THE MAYFLY STRAGGLERS FLEW OFF.

"You're smiling again, Little Fish," Talbot said between bites of a power bar.

"For a moment, I'd forgotten you," I said.

"You couldn't have been thinking of the big cat. It must be the saintly Carol," he taunted.

"Time to start moving," I said.

"Whatever you say," he replied, finishing the bar and throwing the wrapper into the river.

I liked Talbot more when he was abusive. Helping him to the log, I seated him and shoved the log into the current. Holding onto one of the outriggers, I guided it downstream. Not far away was the Second Falls, and it would be close to dark when we arrived. I was counting on the dark. It gave us the best chance for safe passage.

Talbot was muttering to himself. Instead of listening, I turned my mind again to Carol. She was the one who talked baseball with my father. In high school, Carol fascinated me. Her pale skin, dark red hair, slim figure, and passionate interest in sports seized hold of my dreams. Agile and quick, she was all motion and heat on the ball field or basketball court. Afterward, she led enthusiastic *postmortem* discussions on every run . . . every basket. We became strong friends without thinking about it. After school, we did our homework together at my house, and she often stayed for dinner.

It was over the dinner table that Carol grew close to my father. As I look back now, it must have been obvious to all. I see how my mother even encouraged it by inviting Carol to family parties where, often enough, Carol would sit with my father, listening to his baseball stories and sharing reports of her team's latest games. Occasionally on summer weekends, they sat together in our den watching Tigers' games with my father predicting each pitch. They truly enjoyed each other's company and talked and laughed together for hours.

Occasionally, Carol and I did homework at her house. And her mother would invite me to stay for dinner. Our classmates saw us as going steady, and her mother, a high school English teacher, must have heard the gossip and approved the match, because she was always cordial.

Sitting at the Campbell's dining room table, I always felt Carol and her family ate in anticipation. Carol's father, the doctor, showed little interest in me. He attended dinner more out of the need for nourishment than for the company. He was hardly a presence, with Carol's mother proposing subjects for discussion one after another as though she were organizing one of her English classes.

In fact, what the Campbells were waiting for was the ring of the telephone. Carol's father was the last of Marquette's doctors to make house calls. Any request for Dr. Campbell, day or night, brought him out, no matter the weather. At the dinner table, he was usually haggard and always distant. The doctor didn't resent the ringing telephone. Once it rang, Carol and her mother glowed with admiration when the doctor announced he was needed, and they should not wait up for him.

From time to time, the telephone called not only the doctor away but Carol also. On those occasions, the doctor would say to his wife, "Don't wait up for us." And Carol would look over at me and say, "I'll see you tomorrow at school." This left me and Carol's mother to finish dinner alone. Mrs. Campbell asked me about my family and my school day. She seemed pleased to have the company. Once I finished my food, the evening was over, and Mrs. Campbell corrected papers and I went home.

I dreaded hearing the telephone at the Campbell's. One time after Carol left with her father, I asked, "Is Doctor Campbell training Carol to be a nurse?" I knew Carol had decided to attend Ferris State for a nursing degree.

"Yes," Mrs. Campbell said.

Unsatisfied with her one word answer, I asked again, "She helps him with his patients?"

"Yes, she does," she said and then fell silent.

I didn't press Mrs. Campbell that night. After Carol left with her father during our next dinner together, I asked Mrs. Campbell, "How does Carol help her father?"

Mrs. Campbell anticipated my question. "She comforts his patients by listening to them. They're usually older and have been forgotten by family and relatives for years. It takes a special person to work with the old, to make them feel important. Does that answer your question, Joe?"

There was a long period of silence between us. "Yes, Mrs. Campbell," I said, and the talk between us went elsewhere.

The spring of our senior year at the last dinner I ever had at the Campbells', the doctor and Carol were called out. And again I was left alone with Mrs. Campbell.

"Have you decided where you're going to college, Joe?" she asked.

I lied. "No, I have a few more weeks to make up my mind." In fact, I had made up my mind to attend Michigan Tech in Houghton.

Mrs. Campbell was suspicious.

"Could you answer a question about Carol?" I asked.

"Because you're so important to her, I'll try, Joe."

"Why is Carol so ready to help her father? Doesn't she have other things she'd rather be doing?"

Glancing down, Mrs. Campbell picked at her meal, thinking. After a few moments, she said, "Carol is dedicated."

"Yes, I see that," I said. I was jealous that my presence at the table never raised the slightest ambivalence in Carol when her father requested her help.

I believe Mrs. Campbell felt my distress. "She'll become a dedicated nurse," Mrs. Campbell said, almost as a warning.

"I believe you," I replied.

Finally, she looked up anxiously and added, "Joe, don't hold Carol's dedication against her."

Again I lied. "I won't, Mrs. Campbell." In fact, I did hold it against her, and I fell silent, thinking not of Carol, but of my father and his long conversations with her. The truth was I had been forgetting him, and she filled the place I vacated. I threw that memory down into my pool of resentments and heard it splash and sink, its ripples spreading out until they merged with all the others, indistinguishable.

"Little Fish, I'm talking to you," Talbot growled.

"Yes," I said. "I'm hanging on your every word."

"Don't patronize me," he said, raising his voice, "Answer my question!"

I was vaguely aware of Talbot muttering about the cat, so I said, "The cat will be there."

Talbot went silent. I saw a smile play on his lips, "That's not an answer to my question, but it's a good enough answer for a loser, so I'll take it."

I checked Talbot's fingers and the pump display. Decent, but he had lost ground. I decided his testiness was piqued at me for ignoring him, and I made the grave mistake of underestimating my adversary.

CAROL

A SQUIRREL SCAMPERED ACROSS OUR STEEL ROOF. I WENT to bed early, more for solitude than for rest. Sleep did not come. Looking up at the knotty pine tongue-in-groove ceiling of our bedroom, I remembered Joe on a ladder fitting the boards together one at a time, nailing each in place as he went. The fresh wood smelled sweet. For months, it felt like camping in a pine grove.

Staring at the ceiling, my breath caught. Perhaps I asked too much of Joe. He did the house and car repairs and much of the cooking and cleaning. He made the evening meetings with Val's teachers alone when I could not. And sometimes he had canceled evening appointments with prospective clients at the last minute to stay home with Val. Some clients never rescheduled. Coming home, I would apologize. "Sorry, a nurse called in sick." Or "The ER was a zoo." Or one of the hundreds of other reasons health care has for breaking schedules and lengthening shifts. "Don't worry. Val's sleeping." I fumbled for the box of Kleenex and heard the muffled rasp as I pulled one out.

So many years, he took it all on, smiling and saying, "Don't worry." That's what he would be telling me tonight, if he were here. And Joe meant it. He always meant it. He meant his kisses for me. He meant each hug when he pulled me or Val close. And he meant each word he sang with the choir at church services. Joe found significance in every moment, and he gripped them tightly.

Joe was always musing on our life together. His mother once described him as being too "mindy." She said college changed him into "a serious person" and "now he never stops brooding." I remember once after he came home after visiting an aged aunt nearing death, Joe hugged me in the front hall and said, "This is for real." We were both tired, but as he took my coat, he said, "This is not just a calibrated moment in the passing of our lives. Our love for each other is real." Then he hugged me again struggling to contain his feelings of grief. He could only repeat, "This now, this here, this love of ours is real. This very moment, our love tells us that we're alive. My aunt's loneliness and pain is all she has to remind herself that she's alive." Then he paused and stared off into space before turning sorrowfully to me. "Her struggle with pain is all we have of her. There was once so much more."

Joe stayed unflaggingly "mindy," living each moment intentionally. It was the way he lived every moment I tended the dying; it was the way he lived every moment of Val's deployment in Iraq. Others saw it as sincerity. People trusted Joe, although they did not enjoy his company. I heard often enough from neighbors that Joe should "lighten up." It was true Joe did not deal with bullies and hypocrites easily. Rather than just note their shortcomings, he condemned them to their face. Every day he fought for composure, and most days he succeeded. But on some days, at family parties, church events, hospital get-togethers, I glimpsed the rage. Advised to "go along, get along" or "you do what you have to do" or some such cynical remark, his eyes flashed, and he called out the speaker. "There's no excuse for doing what is wrong." I never questioned the targets of his anger, just the vehemence of his opinions. People avoided serious conversation with him. Luckily, he was known as someone who gave a full day's work. And he kept deadlines. Business people knew they could count on him to get a job done, yet they never invited him for a drink on Friday after the work week was done.

Without knowing it, Joe became a loner. Without comment,

I let it happen. He embraced his isolation and trout fished every opportunity, appreciating the solitude of fishing. The Escanaba was his favorite river, a short walk from the house, and he explored miles of it. Early on, I began to see what sustained him in his quarrels with himself. It was the beauty of the river. So often returning home exhausted in the evening, he spoke of the Escanaba's shows of nature: the darkening evening mists, the sparkling riffles midday, the deep silent pools reflecting the pale blue of the sky and the orange of sunset, the gray granite boulders on which he sat drinking his coffee, the looping swish of his casts, the rainbow spray of a jumping trout, and the liquid calls of robins and white-throated sparrows.

Before I knew Joe, I never fished. For my mother and father, fishing was a diversion in which others indulged. I grew up thinking of fishing as a waste of time, an innocuous waste of time, but a waste of time nonetheless. Joe invited me out to fish with him. At first I went along sitting on a nearby bank reading and swatting mosquitoes, the time on the river justified by what I learned from my books. Joe bought me waders, and on the promise of fewer mosquitoes, I waded along with him reading. The river running between and around my legs, the pressure of the water on my thighs and calves were new feelings. As the child of my parents, I justified my wading as a way to strengthen my legs and gain balance, but in fact I was swept away by the pleasure of walking through running water. Soon I stopped thinking of the river as useful. It became a delight.

I did learn to cast. Setting the rhythm of the fly line aloft was a further delight, a task I performed well. The back and forth of my cast became as graceful as the turn of day into night and the turn of spring into summer. It is the beauty of my well-timed cast I will remember when all else has passed. Cloudy days brought those moments when my cast started in shadow and finished in bright sunlight, the greased line flashing as it stretched out to reach a rising trout. Even the fishless days were of no account because my hours were spent blending my body and emotions into an elegant rhythm, graceful and airy, ignorant of gravity. I was a dancer springing forward fifty, sixty feet. After a few years of practice, Joe said I was a better caster than he. I pointed out he caught more fish.

In high school, I played baseball. Casting brought back those moments on the ball field when athleticism reached its climax, when muscle and tension and purpose united in the perfect throw. Many times casting I am reminded of throws I made from the outfield to the cutoff when runners were on base. If it was a fly out, I held back and then at the last moment rushed the ball and used my forward momentum for greater thrust. I remember that last moment when the ball was released, and I saw my hand coming down, pointing to the cutoff taking my throw. So it is with casting. I savor the rhythmic swinging of the rod and line back, the wait and then the pivot and downward snap of my rod propelling the line forward, looping out leader and fly. I loved when it rolled out straight, releasing more line until all was airborne, and my hand and rod pointing to the rising trout. The ultimate pleasure I felt when the cutoff made the perfect throw and the runner was called out comes back on the river when, after a perfect cast, a trout rises for my fly. Athleticism and sinew and determination married together for the perfect moment. I found so many perfect moments on the river.

Through it all, Joe was my mentor and guide. Beauty surrounded us each day. On the rainy days, we waited under fir trees for the squalls to pass over as we watched gathering drops of rain drip off the tips of branches to patter on leaf-matted forest floors. Then there were the days of long rains when the firs became soaked, and we reveled in the cascading water, running our hands over wet faces and burrowing further down into our chest waders. After the long waits, Joe always reminded us that the fish were always wet. So often on those days, the evening's cooling drafts chilled us, although we hardly noticed as we cast to leisurely risers in the backwaters.

The fullness of a river comes in May and June. It is then that water, fish, birds, and anglers harmonize. It is the days of the spring hatches, mayflies popping to the surface, floating like miniature sail boats waiting for their wings to dry, and then, once dry, flying upward, and at each juncture their flight to freedom interrupted by fish or dragonflies or birds. The air sounds of whirring and steady gulping.

On such days, the angler can be excused the mistaken belief that she is one with the river. To the river, the angler is, and always will be, an obstruction, no different than fallen trees losing bark and branches and then moldering away in its currents. No different than granite boulders growing smaller by millimeters year after year. Thousands of years from now, boulders I sat on will be sand shifting in the river's currents shooed downstream each spring to Lake Michigan.

The river makes no place for the angler. I feel ever the alien, wading pounding rapids and walking pools so deep they come up to the top of my waders. Each step can bring a slip, which can lead to waders punctured, knees lacerated, and even unconsciousness and drowning. When fishing a river, I remind myself that I will not find what I want as I slide into its waters. I can only take what the river offers. The unexpected. And that is enough. Whatever wounds Joe and Val and I felt when we stepped into the river, its currents healed us by the time we stepped out on the last gravel bar to make our way back to the truck.

In the morning, I would be on the Escanaba breaking the rules, not waiting on what the river had to give. If I waited, the river would give me corpses. I thought of the great black bird near my father's car and saw Joe's hand plucked clean. Fingering my starting point, I reminded myself Joe and Talbot were still alive. And I called up their faces and saw the rise and fall of their chests as they breathed. By daybreak, they should be at the Third Falls. And that was where I planned to meet them.

I heard the wind ruffling our birch. We needed a good rain. Val was up. The stairs creaked as he descended into the kitchen. I heard the refrigerator door open and close.

Joe's hardest time was during the months Val was in Iraq. After the invasion, he raged against the war and all who supported it, almost everybody we knew . . . at first. He had been right about the war as he had been right about Talbot. No one, not even I, gave him credit for it. So he withdrew, a brooding, belligerent presence at office meetings and lunch breaks in logging camps. People would whisper behind his back, "He has a son in Iraq. Don't bring it up."

Val was in Iraq for fourteen months and out of touch much of the time. Once Joe confided to me that he lived daily in fear of the "knock at the front door." He paled every time he heard the crunch of tires on our gravel driveway. And he hesitated to open our front door to greet unexpected visitors. He told me he had rehearsed in his own mind how he would handle it when the bad news came. He would be cordial to the messenger, a soldier under orders and as powerless as his own son, offer a cup of coffee, and remain silent to hear the soldier out. Then without recriminations, he would thank him or her and leave them with a "Take care."

Once a uniformed visitor drove down our driveway one dark evening, too dark to make out the agency of the vehicle. There was the knock at the door, and Joe opened it to a uniform, a deputy sheriff. He relaxed some, grateful to answer questions about a recent outbreak of teenage vandalism. Afterward, Joe sat in front of the television, his breathing ragged. An hour or so later, his eyes flickered, and he took a few deep breaths, made slow lisping exhalations, and sat inert, silent and dull, until he roused himself and informed me he was "turning in." I noticed the glint of tears on his cheeks as he stood up from his chair. And that was the end of it. That night, I again wondered, as I so often wondered, where he disposed of his rage. And I knew he would go fishing the next day.

Tonight, Joe was out on the river he loved. For years, he brought his anger to the Escanaba instead of to me. I accepted his choice, for the Escanaba brought him sure respite whenever he asked. For years, his rages lingered, stored in some reinforced inner compartment, but I never feared them because he never showed them to me. They were never an impediment to our love, our marriage. There was so much else to Joe, so much else to share. And if Joe was anything, he was generous in sharing himself with Val and me.

Once at a hospital Christmas party while Val was in Iraq, a hospital administrator praised the president for keeping America safe after 9/11. Standing in a nearby conversation group, Joe overheard and shouted at him, "The president is a war criminal!"

The administrator turned and said, "I'm sorry to offend you, Joe."

"You don't offend me. The president offends me. You're just his shill."

Flustered, the administrator colored and then turned back to conversing with his circle.

With mounting anger, Joe shouted at his back, "While we're standing about safe, enjoying ourselves, kids are dying. America is throwing away its youth."

The administrator remained silent, pretending to ignore Joe. The room fell still. I went over and drew him away before he shouted any more insults; we sat and talked for a few minutes in a corner. Slowly, blowing out cleansing breaths, he calmed down. "I'm sorry," he said contritely. "I see Val dead and all for a hollow cause."

"I worry also," I said, looking into his agitated eyes.

"Of course. Without you, I could not bear Val being over there."

After a long silence, I suggested we make the best of what was left of the party. Joe said, "My heart's not in it."

"Then give me a few minutes to stop by the ladies' room," I whispered.

On the way there, a friend, another nurse, fell in beside me. "You're husband's a real primitive," she said. "I worry about you."

"No need," I said, turning to face her. "Joe has deep feelings for Val. He worries about him."

"I understand," she said. "But he just lost it with our boss. What will that mean when you come to work tomorrow?"

"Joe sees little distinction between people."

"That's fine for him. He doesn't work here," she said, dismayed. "Aren't you the least bit embarrassed?"

"The least bit." I laughed. "But then I remind myself that there's a shortage of nurses."

"I'll give you that he's a good looking guy in a rugged way, and smart enough, but I worry he'll explode and take it out on you one day," she said earnestly.

"Joe loves me."

"Is that all you have to say?"

"There's nothing more that needs to be said."

I did not tell her that if I were forced to choose between a job at the hospital and my life with Joe, I would pick Joe. By then our day-to-day experiences together erased the borders of our selves. Even when I was away from Joe, I felt his presence. No matter where I was, I dwelt within the stockade of his person, that magnanimous person who spread himself generously well beyond the visible horizons of our life together. There was no beginning or end to us. And I know he felt the same, because he embraced every moment of my life, never checking boundary charts.

I felt just as fiercely about Val as Joe did. But I took a different approach, one I learned from my father. What I cannot control, I put out of my mind. I work with what I have, what my father as a doctor nurtured—life—no matter how tenuous. It is my foothold against the prospect of imminent death. This was hard while Val was overseas. The war, Iraq, Falluja—they became my portion as though recorded on a hospital chart at the foot of a patient's bed. It was where I started every morning as I looked for vital signs. I clung to life, Joe's life, Val's life, the life of my patients . . . the life all around me by the Escanaba. News reports of war casualties preceded the knock at the door by a few days, so I stopped watching television, the instant news from the front. It was then I started planting perennials in our yard.

In the dark, I blotted my eyes with a tissue. I will never find another like him. I will never make that search again. I had my man . . . if he was alive. If not . . . I had had my first, my only love. And in the absolute empty ether of the night, I heard the steady pumping of Joe's heart from downriver. And I felt my heart pick up the beat and tap out its response. "Hang on." My bedside clock read 12:30.

I flipped open my cell phone and scrolled to the hospital number. The charge nurse answered, and when I began to beg off my morning shift, she said, "Don't worry. We know Joe is missing, and we've already taken you off schedule."

"Thank you." I could think of nothing else to say.

"We're all praying for Joe."

"Thank you. You're so kind. I wish I could talk, but I have a lot on my mind."

"Of course."

"I'll call tomorrow if there is any news."

Laying back, I stared again at the knotty pine ceiling. Each board was different, each knot different. I thought back again to my days on the river with Joe. Each day was different, the weather unpredictable, the fish unpredictable. In early and late season, we fished sometimes in snow squalls. It was Joe who was never different. He was the unfraying thread binding my days together.

A maple branch ticked the bedroom window. A faint whiff of putrefying death filled my nose, the same stale fetid whiff I smelled in the rooms of the dying. Alert, I felt a presence in the room. I stood up and placed my outspread hand on the pane of glass the branch brushed. The ticking reminded me of Morse Code, although the patterns were different. I sensed an invitation, an end to worry. I withdrew my hand quickly, and the ticking stopped. Then in a few pounding heartbeats, the smell and presence dissipated. Another dimension to existence had opened and just as quickly closed. I was certain of it. I heard in my innermost ear the beckoning portal clang shut. Another world waiting for me. Uncertain when it would open again, I put my index finger to my wrist, checking my pulse, checking for life, and made the count. Coming down. How often had I sat by the dying and checked their pulse when breathing stopped? A few times I felt the last reedy thud as life passed. A privilege.

Val needed to cut back the maple branch.

So at first light I would be on the Escanaba. Meredith had her experts, but they did not know the river as well as I did. From the moment I was turned away from the roadblock on Highway 581, I decided not to wait. I would not wait for word from the sheriff. I would not wait at the emergency center for news. I would be on the river searching for Joe and Talbot.

JOE

*J*UST ABOVE THE SECOND FALLS LAY A SMALL, TEAR-shaped, gravel island. A perfect place from which to stage our plunge over the Second Falls. To get there, we needed to travel through several large, deep pools and long, boulder-strewn rapids. The pools were easy, just a swim. The rapids concerned me because they showed many faces. Tricky negotiating in the daylight. Much trickier in the dark. Some sections were shallow and manageable; others were white water battering head-high boulders, so closely clustered together they leave little room for passage. Tonight the stalking cat threatened the shallows close to the riverbank. The safest path lay through the white water. The only unknown was whether the log carrying Talbot could clear the boulders.

I hooked the wading belt onto one of Talbot's belt loops and drew it tight.

He looked up. "You're a fool to try this in the dark," he said.

"I've fished this section many times, so I'm familiar with it," I said.

"Rivers change," he replied.

"It will be different after the fire," I agreed. "But we have no choice."

"Little Fish decides to take a risk," Talbot taunted. "The cat will tidy up when Little Fish fails. You've been thinking of the cat, haven't you?"

89

"There's a small island downstream where we'll stop a few minutes before we shoot the Second Falls," I said. "Time to move."

The river was wider here and the pools placid. A slow swim brought us to the head of the rapids. There, I heard scrambling and dislodged rocks clattering to our left. As I waded into the rapids, more rocks clattered. The cat was tracking us step for step.

The white-water trail blazed scarlet in the dark. Light from the rising first quarter moon and burning forest revealed the worst of the boulders as well as new obstacles with fire-downed trees wedged among them. Talbot's gurney would never make it. Soon, he would be in the cold water, with slowing arteries starving his every cell.

"You're right, Frank. The river has changed," I said to warn him. "You might be swimming before we get out of here."

"Not me. That's why you're here, Joe." He laughed. "It's the Little Fish that swims hardest."

"Expect a swim," I said, taking hold of his belt.

It began benignly. We slid down the first hundred yards of white water without a mishap. But then the river began to play pinball with us. Trying to stay between Talbot and the worst of the boulders, I pushed off again and again with the paddle to avoid being crushed. Once the treetop slewed sideways and hung up across two boulders. I jimmied one end loose, and it straightened out for a quick fifty more yards.

The tear-shaped gravel island flashed out of the dark on our left. Distracted, I let Talbot and the treetop shoot forward to bury itself in a log jam. Trying to pull them out, I went under, wedged between the treetop and the largest of the boulders anchoring the jam. Squatting underwater and pushing outward with my legs, I was able to swim free, only to hear Talbot groan as he was thrown onto a jagged rock slab. Grabbing him by the waist, I draped him around my shoulders and, using the paddle as a staff, slogged toward the island, wrestling fast water and an uncertain bottom as I went.

Laying Talbot gently on the flat shore, I undid the wading belt and collapsed beside him, exhausted and breathing hard. I did not need to check Talbot for cyanosis. I knew I would find it. My feet bled in places.

"Frank, we have only a few minutes to rest," I said urgently. "Make the most of them."

"You mean lie here quietly," he said.

"Yes," I said.

"I heard my friend," he said, ignoring me.

"Yes, he's out there tracking us," I replied. "Rest easy, Frank. Your ally has not given up on you."

"You should take advantage of this time with me to find out my business methods," Talbot said. "At the very least, you could sell them to *Forbes*."

"I know your business methods," I said, shamming boredom to end conversation before it started.

"Really, Little Fish? Then how come you're so poor?" he said sarcastically.

"I don't like money," I said.

Talbot wouldn't be put off. "You're a liar. Everyone likes money."

Ignoring him, I said, "I saw your business methods up close. When I was a student at Michigan Tech, I worked summers at Lundine Wood Products."

"Lundine? Lundine?" Talbot mused. "Oh yes, Lundine. One of my better moments. One of the businesses that the Hamilton Group owned when I took it over."

"A good moment for you," I shot back. "But not for us in Marquette. You took a solid business, stripped out its cash reserves, siphoned off its cash flow, and then when it hit a rough patch, you put it in bankruptcy."

"Reorganization, Little Fish, reorganization." Talbot laughed. "You lost money, Little Fish."

"No. But people I knew lost their jobs, and the retirees lost their health benefits and most of their pension money," I said angrily.

"It was all perfectly legal," Talbot said. "I raced the retirees to the pension money. Not much of a race, really. Of course I won."

"The retirees never knew there was a race until it was too late," I replied.

"The bankruptcy court approved using the pension money to capitalize our reorganization," he said, enjoying himself.

"I believe you," I said.

"The big cat would have done it," he said.

I remained silent and thought there was more to his glee than gloating. He was not just boasting; he was testing me again, assessing my reactions. Blindly, I hoped.

"You've been holding out on me, Joe. Shame on you," Talbot said. "You researched me." In a mocking singsong, he recited, "Little Fish, Little Fish, what other secrets do you have?"

I let it pass.

Talbot would not let go. "You're a man of many secrets, Joe. I'll sniff them out," he said, pretending to sniff and wrinkling his nose like a cat on the hunt. "No matter, I have a new idea. Are you listening?"

I turned to look at him. "Yes," I said suspiciously.

"Leave me here and go for help," he said. "You'll make it alone."

"I'm not leaving you," I said.

"You'll be able to move more quickly without me," he argued. "Besides, I like it out here. I can sit around here and watch the sun come up. By then, you'll be back with help."

"No, Frank," I said.

"And why not?" Talbot asked. "Give me one good reason."

"You'll not be here by the time I get back," I said.

"You're worried about my compatriot out there in the rocks," he said.

"Yes, and the coyotes," I said. "If the coyotes find you first, we'll be searching the woods for your body parts."

"I can deal with them," he said, sounding as if he actually believed himself.

"What are you going to do when they find you?" I asked sarcastically. "Write a check?"

"I know how to deal with them," Talbot said, angry now.

"Tell me, Frank," I said. "How will you deal with them?"

"I can take care of myself," he said belligerently.

"No, Frank, you can't. Not out here," I said firmly. "You're not the equal of the cat. And let me tell you, the cat does not respect you. You're just a meal—"

"I can deal with the cat," he spat out.

"—an easy meal," I said.

Talbot leaned forward and sneered. "Is that what the saintly Carol told you to say?"

Jarred by his words, I said too quickly, "Leave my wife out of this. She has your best interest at heart."

"I pay her," Talbot barked.

"That's not why she works for you."

"You spend her money, don't you?" he asked. "You couldn't get along without it. People like you have budgets, I've heard. How quaint." Talbot leaned back. "Did you—how do you say it?—stay within your budget this month? I've heard you haven't always in the past."

Anger flared up like a struck match. I took a deep breath and snuffed it out. Focus on the task at hand. Think of the cat and what was needed. "We'll wait for your pants to dry before moving downstream. The time in the water after the log tipped slowed your circulation. Your legs need to warm up."

"Tell me something I don't know . . . I won that round, didn't I, Little Fish?" Talbot asked fatherly.

"Yes, Frank, you did." The admission cooled what was left of my anger.

Talbot looked toward the opposite shore, surveying the rock outcroppings.

"I don't see your friend," I said, following his eyes.

"He's there."

Before I could say, "Rest, Frank," he said, "Rest, Little Fish. You'll need all your strength to face the cat." Then he laughed and lay back.

Talbot was a quick study. The thought chilled me. He was getting to know me too well.

I looked across the river at the flickering flames and thought about my father. I don't believe my lack of athletic skills bothered him. What did bother him was my coldness toward his heroes. I could not match his deep commitment to his heroes, mostly churchmen and politicians. My father started a true believer and never veered off course throughout his life, no matter the news. I started life as a skeptic, looking for reasons to believe in his heroes, for reasons to deepen my allegiance, but rarely found any.

In discussions with my father, he would often test me with, "Senator Kelly is a true statesman," or "Trustee Maki puts the people's interest first," or "Pastor Brown is well read." I would respond with a halfhearted, "Yes, Dad," or "Of course, Dad." I never challenged his judgments, but he sensed I never accepted them fully either. I knew this disappointed him, but I justified my reluctance as clear-sighted honesty.

The truth was I saw no need for heroes in my life. I had my father. While he was alive, my loyalty was wholly fixed on him. And while he was alive, he so dominated my life. I lived unaware of the full extent of his influence on me. It was only after his death, after the thought of him waned, that I realized that fact. Ever since, the thought of my adolescent blindness leaves me with regret. I should have told him. So often I picture myself sitting with him saying, "Dad, you're the only hero I ever needed." But that picture is just a dream, and it is my regret that it will never be more than a dream. What is real is my regret.

My father's heroes did not deserve his loyalty. They disappointed him again and again. Nonetheless, my father never acknowledged to me or my mother any lessening of his belief in them, blaming instead a hostile media or their grasping political enemies. I stayed silent, more often believing his heroes deserved the bad publicity and some even prosecution. Watching this over time made me an expert on recognizing the early signs of corruption. I saw the inevitable progress between early innocent excuses for slight ethical lapses, and later full-blown instances of egregious wrongdoing ending political and church careers.

I catalogued the lapses, judging people by my final list. Sometimes harshly. I carefully parceled out my loyalty accordingly and withdrew it on the slightest deviance. Some classmates in high school and later at Tech believed I took on airs of superiority. Not so. Unsure, I remained aloof. I refused to be charmed because I believed trust was sacred. I dreaded the thought of placing the fulfillment of my dreams, no matter how small, in the hands of someone who might prove unreliable later. It was better to remain distant than to suffer the disappointments my father had.

It was hard to put my name on the full list of those who disappointed my father. But by my senior year in high school, I knew my name belonged there. My father and Carol had grown close. One Saturday afternoon when Carol was visiting, I walked in on her giving my father a neck massage. They were laughing and talking, and they did not stop to acknowledge my entrance. That incident, learning of Carol's dedication from Mrs. Campbell, and the interrupted dinners at Carol's house confirmed to me the decision to select a college without discussing it with her. She did not react when I simply announced my decision to attend Tech. She attended Ferris for nursing, and I went to Tech to study engineering, a nine-hour car trip from Ferris. Neither of us ever made the trip during the four years of college. Yet I missed Carol every day we were apart even though I metered out my resentment so it would last over the four years. My calculations were accurate to the decimal point.

When I was home, my father asked me for news about Carol. In high school, I had always given him a tidbit. But after she went downstate for nursing and then took a job in Lansing, I purposefully did not keep up with her. My mother came to the rescue and fed me news of Carol that I could share with my father. He was happy enough with the secondhand reports, but I sensed he wondered why I didn't visit her.

In the end, my father saw less and less of Carol . . . as I had planned. I justified forcing them apart by convincing myself that her dedication to nursing was ghoulish. That was the most face-saving explanation I could come up with. Even then, I knew I did not have the courage to put a more accurate name to it.

I felt Talbot's pants. They were dry. "Get ready. We're going, and we're going together."

"I look forward to it," Talbot said without looking at me.

As I went to hook the wading belt on Talbot, I looked up and saw a raven silhouetted against the half moon. It was flying toward the Second Falls.

RAVEN

*T*HE MOON STRIPED THE LENGTH OF THE ESCANABA. High up, tugged by the jet stream, I traced the river's silvery path down to Highway 480.

All along its banks, fires still burned, and hundreds of pillars of smoke rose into the night sky.

As my shadow swept over the river, Pauguck looked up.

"Get on with it!" I shouted down to him.

"I know my place, Kahgahgee!" he shouted back. "Why don't you come down and finish them off yourself?"

"I am just a scavenger," I croaked, descending.

"Modesty is a rare virtue for you," Pauguck said, surprised.

Ignoring the remark, I asked, "Why is it taking so long?"

"The able-bodied man is shrewd," Pauguck said. "He knows where the cat will be before the cat knows it."

"But in the end, the cat will win," I said.

"No doubt, for in the end the cat is more single-minded than any of its prey. In the end, the cat wants to kill more than the prey wants to live. Even now, the cat is more single-minded than the able-bodied man. He wants very much to live, but he is distracted by the one-footed man. The one-footed man wants the cat to win. It will come down to how much the able-bodied man wants to live," Pauguck said.

"The one-footed man has the stink of death about him," I said.

"True," he replied. "I have grown used to it, but when the cat is downwind from the one-footed man, it drools. Its eyes never leave him."

"So the cat and the one-footed man are linked," I concluded.

"Yes," Pauguck said.

"We must hurry this up. I want to search for bodies near the Great Lake," I said.

"Go ahead, Kahgahgee," Pauguck said, chuckling. "I will tell you all about it when you return."

Pauguck can be so infuriating. He broke off and started toward the Second Falls with the cat. I had no choice but to follow.

THE
Second Falls

RAVEN

*T*HE BIG CAT WILL AMBUSH THE WHITE MEN JUST BELOW the Second Falls.

There the Escanaba built a perfect hunting blind.

It took ages to carve.

It took as long to carve as it took the river to shape the Second Falls.

No more than a ten-foot drop, the Second Falls is the least of the Escanaba's falls.

When I first came here, the lip of the falls was smooth and sharp, and the Escanaba fell evenly in sheets to the long gravel run below. In those days along the north bank, slabs of granite as regular as blocks cut from limestone bordered the falls and the riffle below. Along the south bank, a vortex drilled relentlessly into the river bottom, leaving a generous ten-foot hole lined with clay.

This all changed over time.

It was the first of the Escanaba's falls to freeze in winter and the last to thaw in the spring. Decade by decade, I watched the sharp lip of the Second Falls shatter and retreat inch by inch until the sharp edge disappeared altogether.

Then during one long, hard winter, the heart of the falls—a panel of granite—erupted and shifted, casting a flare of white water toward the massive stone block face guarding its north bank.

For ages, the flare ate at the stone like a fire hose.

And it carved out an overhang.

Almost a tunnel.

Very little of the river does not feed the flare. This very little now wastes itself on the shattered rim of the Second Falls, rushing helter-skelter through cracks and crevices, over loose rock, and around small boulders to trickle into the riffle below.

A long time ago, the vortex died. And the pit it dug now serves as a beaver's winter storehouse, a calm spot in the current.

The flare's power promises the impatient quick passage downriver.

If the able-bodied man has put all thoughts out of his head except reaching Highway 480 quickly, he will meet the big cat face-to-face here and now.

All is in readiness.

The cat now crouches in the dark just beyond the overhang, where the flare dies in a knee-deep, gentle riffle, all open to the sky.

It needs but a short leap to catch the white men from behind. The back of their necks will be exposed. Their end will come quickly. He will take the able-bodied man first, and then leisurely kill the one-footed man in the riffle below.

I looked down at the hunting blind. There was movement.

"Where have you been, Pauguck?"

"To look in on a friend."

"And who would that be?"

"The green-eyed woman."

"The one who fishes with the able-bodied man?"

"You miss nothing, Kahgahgee."

"More important matters are at hand. Once the white men exit the flare, the cat will take them. Right, Pauguck?" I croaked.

Pauguck sat relaxing on the slope behind the cat. "If the able-bodied man decides to ride the flare," he said thoughtfully. "I say *if*."

"But once the white men shoot through the overhang, the cat will pounce," I said. "We know that it is quicker and stronger than the able-bodied man."

Pauguck said, "No doubt."

"Even if they get by the cat, it has a hundred yards of knee-deep riffle to run them down. No one can outrun the cat in that water," I said.

"True. And the one-footed man wants the cat to kill the able-bodied man. He will work to slow down the able-bodied man," Pauguck said.

"Then I will have their eyes here," I croaked.

"Do not be so sure," Pauguck mused. "I have seen the able-bodied man fishing here many times. He knows this river. The cat does not."

"No matter," I said.

"Have you considered that the able-bodied man may find another way downriver?" Pauguck asked.

"Briefly. For that, he will need luck," I said.

"I do not believe in luck," Pauguck said.

"What do you believe in?" I asked.

"I believe in what the able-bodied man knows," he said.

"What he knows will be no help to him. The cat is stronger and faster," I said. "I will have their eyes soon."

Pauguck shrugged. "There is no arguing with you." He was silent. "We will see how fast you are in the dark," he said, looking directly at me. "It is past your bedtime."

"No owls tonight." I shivered. "The fire has been a great help."

"*If* there is a kill, and I emphasize 'if,' it will be made in the water of the shallow riffle," Pauguck said. "Last time I checked, you had not sprouted webbed feet."

"Even so, for this prize, I will chance the river," I said, irritated.

JOE

I HELPED TALBOT INTO THE RIVER. WITH MY RIGHT arm about his waist and his left arm over my shoulders, he hopped with me into deeper water. Looking downriver to the flare of white water on the left, I asked, "All set?"

Following my eyes to the flare, Talbot said, "Looks like fun."

"We're not riding the white water," I said.

"It's the fastest way down," he said.

"It is," I replied. "We're taking the slower current to the right. Much safer for you." Reaching deeper water, I eased into the swim, keeping my arm around his waist. "Kick, Talbot," I whispered in his ear. "If you want to get to the Second Falls and your friend so badly, kick." Dodging rocks, Talbot kicked, and the two of us swam toward the falls.

The ceiling of smoke had cleared, and the first quarter moon was setting, its silvery light dying within a forest of orange flickering black shafts. There was still just enough light to see the whole falls, from bank to bank.

"Shouldn't we be more to the left?" Talbot asked.

"No. There's a crease in the middle of the falls," I said. "We're taking it down to the water below."

"I don't see it," Talbot said.

"It's there," I said. I found the crease one day casting streamers to the edge of the falls. A few fish always rested there.

"Then what?" he asked.

"We wait," I said.

"For my friend," he said gleefully.

"Yes . . . for the cat," I whispered.

Talbot started kicking harder. We made the crease and rode it to the edge of the falls, where I placed Talbot in front of me. Holding him firmly between my legs, we shuffled ahead as if starting a toboggan run until we were on the edge of the falls, and then with one backward thrust of the paddle, we were airborne, smacking down into the water below.

"This water is only a few feet deep!" Talbot cheered. "My friend will not mind it."

Standing up, I quickly dragged Talbot to the quiet water farther to the right. We were immediately swallowed up, no bottom beneath our feet. Talbot went under and came up choking and sputtering. Pulling him downstream a few more yards, I found footing on springy popple and alder branches, stockpiled by beaver as winter rations. One summer, I found this hole by blundering into it. I pulled Talbot against me, cinching the wading belt even tighter.

"We cannot stay here all night," he said.

"True," I whispered.

Talbot shouted, "I said we cannot stay here all night!"

"The cat knows we're here," I whispered. "He smells us. Look toward the far bank on the ledge just beyond the rock face. You'll see him."

Just then the cat rose out of its crouch, sniffing the air. Its eyes searched the water until it located us.

Talbot grew excited when the cat leapt into the shallow riffle. "Just wait," he said as the cat trotted across to where we stood.

"I intend to wait," I said.

As the cat neared, I started splashing water at it with the paddle. The cat kept coming.

"A little water will not stop my friend," Talbot jeered. He tried to catch the paddle, but I knocked him back with an elbow.

The cat kept coming until it was fifteen feet away. Then it sank from view and came up thrashing. I kept splashing it and poking the paddle at its head. The cat swam back to the shallow water of the riffle and waited.

And we waited.

The moon set.

I put my mind elsewhere. Patience. This was the last water Val fished before going to Iraq, and it was the first piece of water we fished when he returned.

The day before he left for boot camp, Val and I stood knee-deep where the cat now stood. After our last casts, he asked me for a good luck charm. "Something to remind me of this river," he said. "Something to bring me back here."

"My best luck comes from a Betty," I said, handing him one from my fly box.

He laughed and put it in his wallet. The week he came back from Iraq, he wanted to fish the Second Falls. We walked in.

As we were suiting up, I told him that I was having luck with bead head nymphs. "Want to try one?"

Acting shocked, he said, "You're fishing a fly not made of feathers and hair?"

Sheepishly, I said, "Sometimes."

"I have my fly," he said, picking the squashed Betty out of his wallet. And he caught fish all day on it, more fish than he ever caught before.

I remember the walk out. I asked him, "What got you through your months in Iraq?" I was thinking about Falluja, where so many of his friends died. I did not know what to expect as an answer.

"My oath, Dad," he said simply.

"Your oath?" I said to make sure I had heard him correctly.

"Yes, my oath to uphold the Constitution," he said.

My son had grown up and come home. And I thought of all the men and women who fulfilled their oath and for that reason never came home. And I thought of all the parents who greeted their returning son or daughter by placing a loving hand on the lid of a flag-draped box.

"Little Fish, pay attention!" Talbot shouted. "Is this getting to be too much for you? You have tears in your eyes."

"Just spray from the river," I replied.

"Too ashamed to answer," he said, invigorated. "I want an answer to my question. Is the strain too much for you, Joe?"

"Calm down, Frank," I said.

"What do we do now?" he asked.

"We wait," I said firmly.

"Let's just walk into the shallows and get this over with," he said. "Let's see who is stronger. You or the cat. My money is on the cat. No matter how long we wait, we can't get by him."

I said nothing. I had no doubt the cat was stronger and faster.

"Do something!" he shouted. "I saw this in business all the time. People like you freeze. People like me act."

"We wait," I said again.

The night grew darker. Time passed. I heard a coyote calling from the ridges. The cat returned to the ledge beyond the overhang, shook itself dry, and gave us one last, deliberate look before climbing the bank and passing into the shadows.

"Talbot, we're leaving," I whispered. I grabbed his belt and felt my way over more of the beaver's popple and alder, edging toward the bank. The river bottom rose up steeply, and for the last few feet, we climbed up on our knees, clawing slippery clay muck with our hands. Talbot looked at me quizzically. I did not explain. Throwing him over my shoulders as I might a hundred pound sack of dog food, I found the trace of a familiar deer trail that paralleled the river for a hundred yards. It was littered with flaming branches and glowing embers, not easy walking barefoot. Worse running. The paddle flicked away the worst of the debris. But the going was slow.

Talbot caught on. "Here, cat!" he shouted.

"Shut up, Frank. We need to get below this riffle. There's a deep pool where we'll be safe," I said.

"I want to end it here!" he shouted.

It was about then I heard splashing behind us. I should have waited a few minutes longer. The cat had crept silently downstream to where the shallow riffle extended across the whole river, and it was splashing its way over to our bank. I started to run. The noise of the splashing stopped, replaced by the thud of cat's feet racing the deer trail. Looking back, I saw a tawny fury throwing off sparks with each footfall, snarling at us with each step.

I kept running, not caring about the burning pain in my feet, not caring about what lay ahead. I did not think of Talbot's odds. I did not think about the cat's speed. I ran flat out until the deer trail ended in a mass of burning tree trunks.

Jumping sideways into the river, I splashed into a shallow riffle no deeper than my knees. Not good enough to discourage the cat. The long deep pool I sought was yards ahead. As he jolted on my shoulders, Talbot was yelling, "Move it!" Once he tried shaking himself off, but I held on tightly and squeezed the breath out of him.

Immediately I heard the cat splashing behind us. I did not look back, bulling my way into deeper water. Knee deep, thigh deep. The rasp of the cat's breathing drove my legs forward. Waist deep. Then the water abruptly dropped off to a soft silt bottom. Slipping Talbot from my shoulders, I pulled him alongside and swam toward a beaver lodge resting on a lone rock set in the middle of the pool. And I heard thrashing when the cat went in too deep, and I heard it back out. Then all was quiet.

"It's not far, Talbot!" I shouted. "Kick."

Talbot lay limp. And silent.

At one point, I felt Talbot's hand in my pocket, searching for the knife. I caught his wrist and twisted it. He cried out in pain. The knife was safe for the time being.

RAVEN

"$\mathscr{I}$T IS AS I SAID. THE ABLE-BODIED MAN KNOWS THE river better than the cat," Pauguck said.

"The able-bodied man was lucky," I croaked.

"Lucky? I am relieved you are listening as closely to me as you always do," Pauguck said, laughing. "It was not luck. He fishes here often with a hazel-eyed young man and the green-eyed woman. All three know this part of the river well, but the able-bodied man knows it best."

"It was luck," I croaked again, this time vehemently. "It is true the able-bodied man knows the river. But it was the coyote close by who forced the cat to move. Who could have foreseen that?"

"Something would eventually have made the cat leave," Pauguck replied. "The cat knows it has better opportunities downriver. And the able-bodied man knew it would not take much to distract the cat."

I went silent.

"It is tiresome talking to you," Pauguck said. "I would rather be conversing with the green-eyed woman now instead."

I remained silent.

"Tonight, I offered the green-eyed woman passage to my world," Pauguck pressed on. "I believe I frightened her." Pauguck looked over at me.

I continued to remain silent.

"I have seen the green-eyed woman sitting by the beds of the dead and dying. When I went for the spirit of the able-bodied man's father, she and the able-bodied man were there together."

"You retrieved the spirit of his father?" I asked, incredulous.

"Yes, the spirit of the father greeted me cheerfully and limped in the direction of the Blessed Isles on his own," he said.

"You sound like you admire the green-eyed woman," I said.

"Yes, I admire her very much. She complements me," he said. "We share so much."

"Enough of this. Let us get back to the problem at hand," I said.

"You mean your problem, Kahgahgee. The white men's blue eyes," Pauguck said.

"Yes, if you insist," I said. "My problem."

"All right, Kahgahgee," Pauguck said. "The cat never walks in the river if it can avoid it. The cat has one idea . . . get above its prey. The able-bodied man knows this. So he avoids those stretches of riverbank that put the cat above him. And the fire has worked to the able-bodied man's advantage, because it burned off all the tree limbs overhanging the river."

"The cat must change his tactics," I suggested.

"No, Kahgahgee. The cat must keep trying. That is all. There are places downriver where it will be all high ground," Pauguck said.

"You mean the Third Falls?"

"That is the best place for the cat. But I was also thinking of the braids above the Third Falls. The cat will have an opportunity there. But if the cat fails to catch the white men in the braids, then the Third Falls will offer the cat the greatest advantage. There, the able-bodied man and the cat must fight one-on-one," he said. "Without question . . ."

"In a few hours, it will be light and harder for the cat," I said. "Once light, the Highway 480 road block will come alive with National Guard and US Forest Service firefighters. EMTs and search parties will crowd the woods."

"Nonetheless, the cat needs only a few hours more," Pauguck

said. "Long enough for him to catch and drag off the white men."

"Does the cat know this?" I asked.

Pauguck did not reply.

"We've all lost so far," I said.

"No, Kahgahgee. You and the cat have lost," he said. "It is all the same to me. Whether the white men die now or die later, I will meet them on their way to the Blessed Isles. It is the final hike all make."

"I am going downriver," I said, preening my glossy black flight feathers.

"I will be walking with the cat," Pauguck said, dismissing me. The cat was already on the move as Pauguck waved back.

I flapped my great black wings to gain altitude. Circling above the smoke, I caught a glimpse of the cat skirting the beaver pool. It scampered up the spine of a high ridge set back from the water. From there, the cat could see the white men and the whole twisting course of the Escanaba down to the braids and the Third Falls.

And I thought, *Perhaps the able-bodied man's good luck would make him overconfident. That was all it was, after all. Just good luck.*

JOE

"COME ON, FRANK! KICK!" I SHOUTED IN HIS EAR. I WAS tired and resented seeing his immobile stump and bloody leg trailing in the water as I swam us to the beaver lodge. The fire had not touched the lodge, and, for a short time, it would be a safe place for Talbot's legs to warm up.

"We'll be here a while, Frank," I said.

"Then what?" Talbot asked sarcastically.

"We swim downriver," I said, exhausted.

"Just like that, Little Fish," he said brightly.

"Yes, just like that," I said.

"It's not that simple," he replied.

I checked the wading belt, put my hand in my pocket for the reassuring touch of the Buck knife, and then lay back, groaning.

"Too much for you . . . Joe," he said, unwrapping another power bar. "You don't have the stamina of the cat. You don't even have my stamina. People like me work after everyone else drops. It is then I have my best ideas. By the time the others wake up, I've won."

My feet burned. I checked the new blisters raised by the run down the deer trail. The swim in the river was soothing, but once on the lodge, there was no help for my feet, and they throbbed.

"I must hand it to you, Little Fish," Talbot said. "You've outwitted the cat this time. But the cat is a stayer, and he'll catch on to you. Even I can see that you're avoiding the high ground."

"You catch on quickly," I said, vaguely hoping to end this talk. I needed to retrieve my mental pictures of the places downriver where the cat would have the advantage. I needed to call each picture up and study it.

"Because you've proven yourself worthy, I'll tell you a secret," he said, turning to look at me with newfound energy.

"Yes," I said, propping myself up on one elbow.

"You have thwarted not only the cat but you have also thwarted me for the time being," he said accusingly. "That does not happen often."

"You mean I've stopped you from killing yourself," I said.

Talbot drew back in mock surprise. "You're catching on, Joe. Yes, I came out here to kill myself," he said, raising his voice. "You don't believe I'm going to live out my days watching surgeons snip off pieces of my dying body every few months, do you?" He was growing louder.

"Of course not," I said to calm him.

"Right you are, Little Fish," he said. "And then there's the blindness. It will come, and I'm not waiting for it. I don't believe in waiting for things to happen. I make my own future. Always have."

"Sure," I said.

"The plan was simple," he said, eyeing me suspiciously. "All I had to do was drown below the First Falls and make it look like an accident. Meredith was on board with it."

"Meredith approved?" I repeated, shocked.

"You did not see that one coming, did you?"

"No," I said truthfully.

"I tried to shoot myself at home. The old 'cleaning a shotgun' routine. But Meredith caught me in the middle of it," he began. "She took away my guns and knives and forbade me to kill myself . . . at home. After that, she never left me alone."

I was silent.

"You don't believe me," he said, leaning into me, nose to nose.

"You have in your pocket a good-bye gift from Meredith. She told me to use it when all else failed. Just a puncture wound . . . a jab to the jugular. Something a jagged rock or stick might do. I practiced at home under her watchful eye."

I remained silent, fingering the Buck knife in my pocket.

"You see Meredith's concern. It wouldn't have been good for her reputation if I died at home. With all my money and her, the only heir, the media would suspect murder. Bloodsuckers. But worse, it would not be good for stock prices. My investors might smell despair and lose trust in my firm. There would be investigations, and the share price would drop. Put in the wrong light, one of my funds could be described as a Ponzi scheme. I have been able to keep it afloat with my own capital." He paused. "Just waiting for the market to turn around."

Talbot stopped. "Say something, Little Fish. Am I going too fast for you?"

"I think I'm getting it all," I said sarcastically.

"I bet you are," he shot back, plainly skeptical.

"Look. Meredith knows the SEC could charge me and the firm with fraud," he began again. "I'm not worried. I have lawyers and a few senators on retainer." He glanced at me again. "Are you sure you're grasping all this?"

"As much as I need to grasp," I replied. "As I told you, I don't like money."

"Everyone likes money, Little Fish," he said. "You don't like money because you have so little of it. Your competitors have defeated you once too often, and you have given up. Learn from me. I never allow myself to lose. My proudest achievements are turning Wall Street's wunderkinds into losers. They give up after being slapped down a few times. Who slapped you down?"

"No one," I said a little too quickly. The last thing I wanted was another argument. His circulation slowed at the Second Falls, and I was not sure if his upper legs would ever pink up again.

"Anyway, Meredith demanded I make my suicide look like an accident. Her ground rules temporarily delayed another attempt. But then your lovely, saintly wife gave me the opening I needed. She was trying to cheer me up one day by talking about trout fishing. She knew I was a fly fisherman. So she went on about how her husband, Joe, would be happy to take me out on the Escanaba when I healed. I'm never going to heal, for goodness' sake. How stupid does that woman think I am?" Talbot's voice was rising again.

"Carol is kind. Always has been," I said soothingly. "She meant no harm."

"She meant no harm . . . she meant no harm. You two are a matched pair," he said. "You just don't get it."

"So you decided to take Carol up on her offer," I said, moving him along.

"You're managing me again," he said hesitantly and then forged ahead. "Meredith had you investigated. The report was encouraging. You've very little money. As a business man, you're a failure. You've never guided before, and you are not certified to do so."

"All true," I said reluctantly.

"You were perfect for my accidental death," Talbot said vehemently. "But tonight you've been lucky . . . so far."

"I was unaware of your plan," I said agreeably to calm him down. He was cycling to another raging rant.

My acquiescence did not slow him. "I could not find a certified guide service to take me. Once they learned of my condition, they required at least two men," he shouted, waving his arms wildly. "And they use river boats. Too stable to fake an accident. And they would have never agreed to fish the Escanaba. No, a real guide was out."

"So that left me," I said.

"Yes, and you must help me through this. I must be dead before you get out of this river. Later, you can make up a story about how I drowned before you could get to me below one of these falls. Or how the cat was too fast for you. Something like that," he said.

I thought for a moment, more to find the right words than to come to a decision. "Sorry, Talbot," I said.

"You have no choice," he said. "It's just a matter of time before the cat catches us in the open," he said angrily. "Just leave me. It's me the cat wants."

"I can't do that. The only way this comes out right for me is if I get you down to the 480 bridge alive," I said, holding back my growing anger. "Otherwise . . . ," I hesitated. "Otherwise . . . ," I snarled, flinging the words at him, "I will help you prove to the world I'm the incompetent man you and Meredith peg me to be."

"It doesn't matter what Meredith and I think," Talbot said. "Your record proves it." He then added in triumph, "What is your credit score?"

"Credit scores don't matter out here," I said evenly. "There's no discussion, Frank. I'm not giving you and Meredith what you want. You can try again with another chump."

Talbot fell silent, rubbed his forehead, and said, "Actually, I'm not worried how this will come out. You've failed your whole life, and you'll fail again. I will be dead before we reach the 480 bridge. I just need to be patient." Talbot settled back, the power bar finished. "If you were smart, you would leave me here with the beaver. I like it out here. As I have said before, this is where I belong."

"You don't belong out here, Frank," I hissed. "Everything out here is fighting to stay alive."

Talbot went silent.

"Get some rest, Frank. We're halfway to the Highway 480 bridge," I said before he could respond.

"You'll never make it," he said. "The cat will kill you, and if it doesn't, I will." Talbot looked up into the dark night. "Do you know why I tell you all this, Little Fish?"

I refused to placate him any further. "Shut up, Frank."

He smiled. "Because you don't get it. You'll never get it."

I checked the belt again and felt for the knife. It was still there. I shifted it to the pocket away from Talbot and then lay back, watching what was left of the fire's glare light up the sky. The air had cooled. Tomorrow would be clear.

As I stared into the night sky, my pool of resentment stirred. Its shoreless cavern sounded a low, moaning breeze. Talbot's words found a crevice in the decades old seal, and through it, his words blew an unsettling draft. Talbot sensed the injustice I felt against him, his kind, and his world altogether. It was probably not the first time. He would keep talking and probing, blowing my resentment into a froth, peeling back the lid of the seal altogether. He wanted a cataclysm. And I knew once my pent-up rage erupted, he would manage them to his own ends. This was a battle he enjoyed, vanquishing the angry and their sense of injustice. He was dying to teach me the cruelty of his truth.

I feared the cat but I feared the old anger inside me more. It was my secret Talbot was circling. I thought back to the first time it announced itself to me. The last year of Tech, a few days following graduation. We seniors were packing up, leaving for the rest of our lives. No more tests and one last party. Everyone drank too much, me included.

A fraternity brother, Tech's outstanding graduate that year, began to ride me. "Was that your father I saw at graduation, Grinder?"

My guard down, I said, smiling, "Yes."

"He's a gimp!" Then he stood up and imitated by father's limping walk.

Slowed by the beer, I just stared.

"Did you hear me? Your Dad's a gimp."

Every wound born of failure, every loss, coursed through me. I was on him in an instant. My sinews tightened, anger rippling down my arms into my fingers. In an instant, rage threw off the anchoring cables of self-discipline and gripped his throat. I saw my thumbs sink into his windpipe and would have crushed it without a word or a thought were it not for my fraternity brothers pulling me off. I wrestled them to get at the favored one, the one blessed at birth, the one who mocked my father. But they held me until my rage passed. Fortunately, the fraternity brother lived, although, as I later learned, for a month he had trouble breathing and carried dark blue bruises in the shape of thumbs prints on his throat long after.

The next day, in the haze of a hangover, I drove home to Marquette alone. Again and again, the details of the evening came back.

The shame of it startled me, and I realized for the first time an ungovernable well of violence lived within me. By the time I arrived home, I was living in fear of it. I embarked on shackling against another such murderous moment. And so it was for years I ordered my life with the sole purpose of controlling the overwhelming urge to kill. No taverns, no alcohol, only family and sedate company . . . above all, I needed reflection. I came to distrust exuberance. I hesitated letting go. Denial became my first impulse. Thoughtfulness became a way of life. Interpreting schematics, felling a tree, fishing—all were done thoughtfully. In time, I became emotionally disengaged from much of life, throwing myself into work for which I felt no passion.

Fly-fishing made it bearable. Thought guided every step on the river, every fly chosen, every cast made. I lived in reason on the river. Whenever the seal over my rage threatened to split along its seams due to money worries or anger at some slight to me or my family, I went to the river to fish. And when I returned, the seal held. But, more important, I developed foresight. I read more, learned to cook, and preoccupied myself with family life. Years later, I began to trust myself again. After withdrawing all my emotional investments in life, I believed I had reached my goal: total detachment. I even began to believe I was cured, that I had doused the murderous fires within me.

I was wrong. Talbot was bringing it all back—the shame . . . the rage . . . and the fear. My old self-doubts returned, and I worried whether the old disciplines would hold. He was clever and intuitive, and he divined my inner turmoil. He may not have envisioned my subterranean pool of rage, but he guessed what resentments drove me. He had seen them before. I was at a disadvantage; I had no inkling of what would drop out of his mouth next. I only knew that whatever he said would hit the mark. Rummaging among my memories, I searched for the old disciplines of mind, the ones I learned the years after Tech. I must discount his talk. Put my mind elsewhere. *Keep thinking*, I told myself.

How many hours left? Two more falls. Nine . . . ten hours. His agile mind, more agile than mine, was searching for the trigger to my rage. He wanted to die, and if the river and the cat did not kill him, he wanted me to kill him. All he needed to do was provoke me. I had taken the man's measure, and I expected before this trip was over that he would find the trigger and pull it. As it turned out, it was not the trigger either of us expected.

For the moment, my strategy was to become deaf to him, to muffle the sound of his voice. If I arrived at the 480 bridge with Talbot dead, the whole world would want to know why. I must arrive there with him, without fault, blameless . . . and most of all . . . provably so. Talbot was my best evidence. I needed Talbot alive.

Looking over the blackness of the river, the image of my hands pressing the windpipe of my fraternity brother surfaced, chilling me. In an instant, his face reconfigured into Talbot's sneering, disdainful face—the face I hated. The pool of rage within me sloshed and came alive. I looked up away from the river and saw the faces of Carol and Val among the stars, and I calmed, filled with the placidity of the universe above the rampant fires.

PAUGUCK

*T*HE ONE-FOOTED MAN FINALLY STOPPED SCREAMING AT the able-bodied man.

The cat took it all in.

But now its eyelids close, and its head nods. It is asleep.

The one-footed man too will sleep now. He has no worries. The worst that can happen to him is the death for which he yearns.

Not so for the able-bodied man. He cannot afford to sleep tonight, for he stands in everyone's way. And he knows it.

He thinks about the green-eyed woman and his son.

I envy him.

Perhaps I should offer the green-eyed woman another chance to join me. She knew the entrance to my world was right there before her, but it frightened her. She was thinking of the able-bodied man. She wants to see him again.

Should the cat kill the able-bodied man, then she may accept my invitation. We three could all walk together to the Blessed Isles.

Kahgahgee is still upriver. He will be back when the first glow of sunrise lights up the horizon, for that is when the white men will move downriver.

The one-footed man will make sure they move slowly.

A light northern breeze swirls among the hundreds of columns of smoke ascending from the burned-out woods. They waver and drift south, blown by a wall of cold from Canada.

I see the stars for the first time tonight. The able-bodied man sees them too.

His eyes are fully open.

CAROL

LEEPLESS, MY MIND CAST ABOUT FOR REPOSE. BUT THE absence of Joe from his place in the bed beside me bound all my thoughts to the Escanaba and my fears. I have gone without sleep for a day and thrived by ignoring all doubts about my readiness. Joe's father taught me that. He pitched in the era where starting pitchers took the mound expecting to finish the game. One day while watching a Tigers' game, he told me that no matter how strong a pitcher was, his arm was tired by the seventh inning. After that, it was all guts and cunning.

Dawn was a few hours off. Today would be a day of river miles. The Escanaba offered no beaten paths, no level ways, and no inviting routine encouraging human purpose. Each footstep would be an innovation. Today, reliance on habit could bring injury, even death. So often I have fought the ebb and flow of pain in my dying patients. The struggle to ease their pain can go for days, and I have sat with them throughout, fighting sleep and the discouraging inferences that come from the certainty that at some hour, not far off, they will be taken. So often my narrow victory is that they die comfortably. I have schooled myself to be satisfied with that. And as they linger, before the end, I have had to tell myself over and over, "Your exhaustion means nothing. Your fears mean nothing. Only their pain is real." I heard the same message echoing in the silence about me. "Your fears mean nothing. Only Joe's struggles are real."

Surviving the rescue was my first thought. I decided to jettison strategy, a difficult concession. Staying attentive and exercising judgment each step became my plan. A twisted ankle, hitting my head in a fall, smoke and ash clogging my lungs—all were possible. And there was always the unexpected, the unimaginable. It was the way of the Escanaba to tire its trespassers, confuse them, and then deliver the bad news. Deliberate. I must stay deliberate today. It was my first thought wading the river. Today I would be striving against the worst the river could do. I thought of Mother McCartney and heard her singing, "I do not ask to see the distant scene . . . One step enough for me . . ." Then I felt her gentle hand on my forehead, and for two hours I dozed.

And I dreamed I was again beside the First Falls watching common mergansers, orange-headed fish ducks, diving into its plunge pool. Mergansers are gypsies, moving from river to river, diving for a quick meal of fish and then flying off to new water, not to be seen again for a year or two. They have no home; to fall in love with a place risks starvation. In my dream, I dove into the pool with them. The waters of the falls churning above me, I swam down past the mergansers and down past the silver flashes of fleeing trout. And with my left arm extended like a javelin, I went down, down, down past resting chubs, suckers, and darters, to the very bottom with shells of empty clams and dismembered crayfish, snails, and worms. The dead were all there. All that the river drowned and all that the land gave up were there. The river had washed them, and the rains on the land had washed them. And all were resting on the bottom, peaceful and somber, displayed as at a wake.

I rested and stretched out on the bottom, gathering the dead to me. Composed, I became one of them, giving myself up to death. And the fear of death left me, and the fear of Joe's death left me. And I waited, mind clear, for something to stir in my imagination. A pounding took hold of me, and I allowed my inflated lungs to gently lift me to the surface. Slowly, slowly, slowly I floated upward until my face broke the surface of the pool. I gasped and looked around. The mergansers were gone, seeking out another river reflecting the promise of plenty, a false promise that they were never to realize during their short lives.

And I told myself, "I love this place." There were better trout rivers and better hospitals, but I no longer cared. This was my place, a harsh place, neither fertile nor lush. It was a place where everything I had I had earned. It would always be my place—no matter the risks, no matter what happened today, no matter what happened to Joe.

I slept on with Mother McCartney's hand on my forehead and her voice singing, "For why in the valley of death should they weep or in the lone wilderness rove."

JOE

"LITTLE FISH." TALBOT WAS AWAKE.

"You should be resting," I said. I checked his pump display; his blood sugar was falling. So I broke off a piece of candy and handed it to Talbot. "Your legs need rest and warmth."

Talbot nibbled the candy bar. Between bites, he said, "Your father worked at Lundine, didn't he?"

Talbot's guess struck home, and my shocked expression told him he was right. "He worked there before you bought it," I mumbled reticently. "He was a retiree when you ended his health benefits and reduced his pension."

"Imprecise again, Joe. Your father never had health benefits. He had the promise of health benefits," Talbot said airily.

"For him, it was the same. He counted on Lundine's to keep its word," I said.

"You've lost me now, Little Fish." Talbot chuckled. "Keep its word . . . keep its word. I hope I am not talking over your head now, but when you talk like that, I think of another word, and that is the word *naive*."

"It was a written policy," I said angrily.

"Money is too valuable to tie up waiting for a doctor to present his bill," Talbot said, raising his voice. "Money can't be allowed to sit around. Do you understand me?"

Realizing he was starting another rant, I said simply, "Yes." But it was not enough to deflect him.

"I did not hear you, Little Fish!" Talbot said, shouting now.

Exhaling, I said more loudly, "Yes."

"Good. That is what I do. Liberate money. Like the money backing Lundine's benefit package."

"You mean you stole it," I said, now feeling the first heat of anger.

"The bankruptcy judge even complimented me on making the hard decisions to save the business," Talbot said. "I became a hero for looting Lundine. My shareholders were ecstatic."

"They did not need hip replacements," I hissed.

"Whatever my shareholders need they get because we've learned never to trade on promises. They have the cash," Talbot crowed.

"Both my father's hips grew arthritic from doing Lundine's business," I flung back at him angrily. "You could have left him money for that. In your world, it wasn't much."

"On that we agree. We sweep that kind of money off the trading floor at the end of a day. It's just about the cost of a Paris weekend," he said. "Which is probably how I spent the money for your father's hip replacements. Private jet, three nights with a lady friend—certainly not Meredith—in the Belle Etoile Suite of the Hotel Meurice, a dress or two from Chanel, a few dinners at La Tour d'Argent or Alain DuCasse would do it." He paused, looked down at his festering foot, and then, looking up with his eyes sparkling, asked, "What is your preference when you are in Paris? La Tour or DuCasse?"

"Toward the end, my father's diet was macaroni and cheese followed by four aspirin for dessert," I said, so angry my words came out like automatic gunfire. They did not hit their mark.

"You're not holding up your end of the conversation, Little Fish," Talbot said. "Where do you stay in Paris? Tell me. Does your hotel put a rose on your pillow? Chocolates?"

"I've never been to Paris," I said and then, remembering Carol's warnings, added, "You're playing with me."

"Yes, I am," Talbot said, relaxed now. "And you want to know why."

I was tired and took refuge in silence, turning my back on him. The talk of my father's last days upset me. I guessed it would be the first place he would go to enrage me. I wondered where he would go next.

"It's because I want to impress on you how small you are," Talbot said, refusing to let up. "You have forgotten your place." Then Talbot slapped the back of my head for attention and bellowed, "But the cat and I will remind you once and for all!"

"We need to get moving," I said. But when I went to get up, my foot slipped on some new mud the beaver left from a recent repair. I sat down hard, and the jar opened black emptiness within. Talbot was draining my resolve.

Taking it all in, Talbot said with a broad smile, "I'm thirsty."

I heard in the black emptiness my rage shouting to kill him. I looked into his eyes menacingly. But I saw the fever of death in their sparkle and was calmed with the knowledge that he was truly in the grip of death, and for one last time, my anger relented. I did not need to kill him. The impersonal forces at work in the universe that first favored him had turned against him and were killing him cruelly. Instead, I smiled and said, "You can't trust river water, especially water near beaver. I know a small creek a mile or so downriver that has sweet water and even now is probably running clear."

Talbot grunted. "Ordering me around again."

"No," I said. "Being a careful guide."

"You're no guide, Joe," Talbot said coyly. "I know your secret." He waited.

Curious and tired of the suspense, I asked, "Yes?"

"You're a killer," he said evenly. Another guess on the mark, and he waited. Stunned, I grappled with the truth of his words. I waited too long for a comeback. A denial would do no good. The silence lengthened. Finally, Talbot dispelled it. "This gets better and better. There need be no accident—just a murder." He waited before saying, "Well, are we going? I don't want to be late for the cat . . . or for you. Which of you will help me out first?"

This was no game I ever played before. Talbot was in charge, and he alone knew the rules. From now on, I thought, all his probing, all his gloating, all his insults had one goal: to ignite the murderous rage he perceived lay within me. I was overmatched.

Regrouping, I said, "Yes, we're going. But first I must tow that deer carcass back here." I pointed across the river where a dead ten-point buck jostled up against the bank. My hand was shaking as I pointed. Earlier, its horns had caught in the branches of a smoldering downed cedar. It was just beginning to bloat.

The tremors in my hand were not lost on Talbot. "O Careful Guide," he began sarcastically, "will you share with me why we need a dead deer?"

"It will keep your legs out of the water."

"Ridiculous," Talbot said.

"We have a ways to go yet. Your legs must stay dry, and there's nothing else handy," I said. During our rest, Talbot's fingers had pinked up, but his calves had not. Now both legs beneath his knees showed a dark shade of a grayish blue. His one foot was purple, almost black, and its skin was like gummy parchment. Keeping it out of the frigid river was unnecessary; it would never pink up. My worry now was gangrene.

As I pushed out into the river toward the deer carcass, I said, "This won't take long."

Talbot made a face. But he waited quietly, protesting only when I slid him onto the buck. "I can't stomach the smell." He dry heaved.

"Hold your nose," I said.

Talbot pinched his nose, and the heaves stopped. After lashing him to me with the wading belt, I picked up the buck's front legs and pushed downstream.

"Next time at La Tour, you'll have a new story to tell the maître d'," I said.

"There won't be a next time," he said, still holding his nose.

"Stop talking. I can't understand you," I said. The smell was noxious.

"How long?" Talbot managed in a high nasal voice.

"We're going into the braids," I said. "We have a little over two miles of them before we come to the Third Falls."

"Water," Talbot demanded.

"Yes, I haven't forgotten," I said. "We'll get to my sweet water creek in about half an hour."

PAUGUCK

I SAT FOR HOURS WATCHING THE BEAVER'S POOL FROM this high, gray ridge.

The cat slept through the white men's departure.

Kahgahgee will be angry with me for not waking it.

For now, the cat sleeps, comforted by the stench of the one-legged man sitting stagnant in its nostrils. It tastes him in its dreams.

All is calm now.

The whipping night wind, the wind that carried aloft the stench of the one-footed man, died. Only a laconic breeze whispers along the surface of the river.

And so the cat slumbers secure on this stony ridge.

It sleeps so soundly it did not hear the end of the white men's argument.

Nor did it hear the able-bodied man splashing through the river shallows as he dragged the buck carcass with the one-footed man into the braids.

The first dull glow of dawn begins to dim the stars.

Kahgahgee does not favor the braids and blames the beaver for them.

According to him, the beaver dammed the river in the time before the Anishinaabe first appeared on the Escanaba's banks. Gradually drifting trees, silt, gravel, and sand imbedded themselves in the dam, fortifying it. Every year, it withstood ice jams and spring floods, and today it stands firm.

Upstream, where a small lake and many beaver lodges once rooted, only the deep pool and the solitary lodge on which the white men rested survives.

Downstream of the dam, the river stutters. Its force nearly spent, it spreads out, lackadaisically coursing a host of narrow channels.

It is a maze.

Buffered by silt-bottomed swamp and dense stands of tag alder, this watery thicket admits no shoreline. Deer trails wander their way through the muck and double back on themselves once they reach the river's cool water. Few anglers fight through the brush to find the channels clear enough to cast. By August, even these few channels become leafy tunnels, so overgrown that the noon sun never dapples their surfaces.

The able-bodied man picked the first channel to the right. It is the channel farthest from this ridge and the cat.

A good choice keeping the river between us.

The confusion of the braids will confuse the cat.

But it is the able-bodied man's ruse that will put the cat off their trail. The smell of the rotting buck being drawn downstream cloaks the white men's flight as sure as a drawn theater curtain cloaks a scene change.

I expected no less from the able-bodied man.

Even should I wake the cat now, it will not have time to explore the braids thoroughly.

Dawn is minutes off.

A golden pink colors the horizon, softening the harsh desolation of the blackened woods.

A few fires still burn. Hundreds of smoky spindles span the horizon, marking the remains of the largest white pines, maples, and oaks. The fire crews will start once the sun shows itself.

I worry about the able-bodied man's resolve.

After the braids comes the Third Falls.

I need not think long about what will happen at the Third Falls because the future holds no magic for me.

Kahgahgee and the cat think hard on the Third Falls, trying to foresee what the able-bodied man will do there.

In the end, they can only guess. They know this.

And so they befriend the unexpected.

And they nickname it luck.

CAROL

*T*HE HOUR BEFORE FIRST LIGHT. THE UPPER BRANCHES of our white pines are still black against the night sky. When the dawn turns them glossy green, I will be on the Escanaba. Wearing heavy work pants, hiking boots, and a light cotton collared shirt, and pocketing a compass, I pulled a baseball hat out of the closet and found a bandana.

Now for the hard part: giving Val no choice. "Val, are you awake?" I whispered into the dark of his room.

"Yes, Mom," Val replied. "I couldn't sleep."

"Just a few hours for me," I said, standing inside the doorway. "I'm leaving for the Escanaba to find your father."

"You're not going alone," he said, a note of command in his voice.

"If you want to come with me, we need to leave in the next few minutes," I said.

"It would be best if you let me go alone, Mom. You'll slow me down."

"I'll be out on the river today with or without you," I said authoritatively. I expected Val to analyze the situation as the sergeant the army trained him to be. He would assume leadership and pick his team, preferring trained, capable, and fit young men and women. I did not match the profile. Being his mother would not be enough for him to choose me, and no maudlin arguments would win him over. I was proud of him for that.

"I don't think so, Mom," he said warily. "I don't want to hurt your feelings, but you're not up to the tangle of downed trees and smoky ravines we'll find out there. We'll need to move quickly."

"I've run the corridors of the hospital for years pulling gurneys and emptying ambulances. I'm fitter than you think," I said firmly.

"I'm responsible for you out there, Mom. What if you get hurt? I'd need to give up the search for Dad to pull you out. I'm sorry to say that would be wasted time."

"Val, Talbot's out there too. You don't have the training to deal with him. You're not even thinking about him."

"I know how to deal with diabetics."

"What about gangrene?"

Val fell silent. "He's that far gone?"

"Yes. Mayo was amputating because Talbot's leg is ripe for sepsis. Most likely he's slipped over into it by now with all that he and your father have had to endure."

"I still believe I should do it alone. You're not as strong as you used to be."

Val had studied us, and he was correct. "Val, remember when you were a teenager wanting so badly to grow up?"

"Of course."

"We misjudged your maturity, seeing you only as the little boy you once were. You are doing the reverse of that to me now. I'm not decrepit."

Val chuckled. "Okay. Okay, Mom." He thought briefly and then turned serious. "But the first time you slow me down, I'm leaving you behind."

"If that's the way you want it . . . "

"It's the only way, Mom. You know how important time is in emergencies. A second or two can make all the difference. I've seen it in Iraq."

"You're right, Val. I've seen it at the hospital. I won't slow you down. But if I find I do, I'll walk out on my own."

"Thanks, Mom." He iterated, "A few seconds can make the difference in saving Dad's life."

"I don't doubt you. It can make all the difference in saving Talbot's life also."

"I don't care about Talbot."

"He's my patient," I shot back.

"All right, Mom. It will be light soon."

"Let's not waste any more time arguing." I went down to the kitchen and rummaged through the refrigerator. I took six bottles of water and put them in a small knapsack with orange juice and some insulin I kept at home for emergencies. I heard Val walking around his room and shouted up, "What's keeping you?"

"Where are you?" I shouted up again.

The lid of Val's Marine footlocker creaked. "Let's move!" I shouted up.

"Looking for my boots and bandanas."

"I'll be in the shed getting a rope and an axe." Joe warned me there were many ways to die on the Escanaba, and lying awake last night, I ticked them all off. My worst fear was finding Joe dead, mutilated by predators. Nonetheless, if anyone was going to find Joe's body, I wanted it to be me and Val so we could honor him. I wanted to say good-bye in a blackened forest scraped clean of all human sign, an empty forest . . . without the distraction of official chatter from EMTs or sheriff's deputies who did not know Joe's worth as we knew it. And I wanted Val at my side when I did it.

I threw the axe and rope in the car and went back to the kitchen.

"All set, Mom." Val had his soldier's face on.

I shoved a cup of coffee in his hand. "We're taking the Jeep. You drive." I tossed him the keys.

RAVEN

"*Y*OU OLD FOOL!" I YELLED. "YOU LET THEM GET AWAY."
"They are your quarry, Kahgahgee," Pauguck said, unconcerned. "Quiet! You'll wake the cat."

"That is my intention." I croaked and croaked again. And the cat
awoke, sniffed, went rigid, sniffed again, and then rose up alert. It
was hungry . . . a day without meat. The wind had freshened, and he
did not smell his prize—the white man with the dead foot.

"Yes, they are gone," I said, speaking to the cat but staring at
Pauguck, who only chuckled.

The cat looked at me, hesitated, and then scampered down off
the ridge. It paced beside the river, nose in the air, sniffing. Growing
more frantic, it ran downstream along the base of the ridge, skirting
the muck of the braids and stopping every few yards to sniff the air.

Pauguck stood up to join the cat when I shouted at him, "How
could you let this happen?"

"I do not involve myself in the cat's hunts until they are over,"
Pauguck said. "You would be wise to do the same." Pauguck laughed.

I screamed my disgust and flew slowly downriver above the
braids, searching. The cat looked up as I passed over him. Not in
curiosity but in entreaty.

JOE

IN THE FIRE'S AFTERMATH, THE BRAIDS OPENED EASILY before us. When the fire jumped the river here, the low growing tag alders survived, shorn only of their leaves and catkins. It was the taller cedar and aspen that did not survive, many still smoking. A faint morning wind stretched out the clouds of smoke and dispersed them among the channels, flapping like white sheets hung out to dry.

The right channel was waist deep. But after a hundred yards, it dead-ended in an old log jam that I had fished many times. It held many trout but was impassable even for the wading angler. The slow-moving water of the braids percolated under the jam and through the surrounding tag alder roots, but the current was never strong enough to tear a path to the river below.

The log jam came up quickly. It was time to start looking for another route. The smoke and alder thickets lining the channels walled us off, but just before the jam, a narrow break in the screen beckoned. Using the paddle, I pushed back stray shoots and, pulling on the buck's horns, squeezed all three of us through into the adjacent channel. It was wider but shallower, mid thigh, and stretched for hundreds of yards. The cat could run us down here.

I checked Talbot's legs. They were no worse than when we left the beaver house. Below the knees, his skin remained a light grayish blue running to violet lower down. His one foot and all its toes were a deep blue black. Mayo would not need a second opinion before surgery. I pushed his pants up above the knees. The upper legs were still pink. I checked the pump display. It was low, so I handed him more candy.

With his left hand, Talbot reached down for his pant legs. I pulled them back down for him. He angrily pointed a finger at me and was about to say something when he dry heaved. His frustration complete, he beat the side of the buck again and again with his left hand, finally giving up and laying back to stare up through the lace-work of bare tag alder branches to the dimly lit sky above.

Eventually, he looked at the candy and began to eat it. He did not hear the raucous croaking of a raven, nor the tinkle of falling pebbles coming from the far shore. I fished out the knife and thrust it into the buck's stomach cavity once. The escaping gas further nau-seated me and gagged Talbot. His eyes flashed, but he clamped down harder with his jaws and held his nose even more tightly with his right hand. Again, he futilely beat the sides of the buck with his left hand.

Watching Talbot's beating hand, I thought of my father's death and my hand in it. I saw my father's beating left arm as he lay dying in a Marquette hospital bed. He was always in pain and often in a coma. His left arm, the great, strong arm that carried his University of Chicago ball team to so many victories, now beat futilely against his bed's railings for relief. He tore out his IVs and monitoring leads, so the hospital staff bound a board to his arm and reattached the leads. The relentless slap of the board put my mother and me on edge. Our vigils were exhausting.

My father's hospitalization was unexpected. Once he was retired from Lundine, his hips grew more and more arthritic, and it was painful for him even to sit. With his health benefits gone after Lun-dine's reorganization, he was waiting until he qualified for Medi-care. He had a year to go for the hip replacements he needed. To get through that year, he swallowed great quantities of aspirin tab-lets to dull the pain. What was unanticipated was that the aspirins masked an infection in his gall bladder, which grew necrotic and burst, thoroughly infecting his abdominal cavity. For short periods, heavy doses of antibiotics brought him back to consciousness.

One day, when his eyes opened and he saw the anxious faces of me and my mother, he said with difficulty, "Don't worry."

My mother began to weep. I rose to say something soothing in his ear. He looked up at me, terrified. I smiled, but the pain took hold again, and he lapsed back into a coma.

The next time he awoke, he said with a smile, "Joe, as I have said, you go to the hospital to die."

I was about to say something encouraging, but he waved the board and said, "Take care of your mother."

By the time I said, "Of course," he had lost consciousness, and the relentless beat of the slapping board started again.

Toward the end, his periods of consciousness grew less frequent. Carol Campbell visited my father's room often. Two years earlier, she returned to Marquette to care for her mother and took a nursing job at the same hospital where my father was now losing his hold on life. By then her father was dead, and three years later, her mother followed him. Carol was left alone.

After her shifts and on her days off, Carol sat with us. She warmly greeted my mother with a hug. She was cordial with me, but a cool distance and its questions hung between us. Nonetheless, day after day, Carol joined us, always giving my mother a hug and politely nodding to me.

At my father's bedside, I saw Carol's gift, the gift that Mrs. Campbell implored me not to hold against her. It was so simple. My father awakened, and all three of us were there. He smiled wanly and said, "My three favorite people."

"Feeling better?" Carol asked.

"Yes. Thank you for being here," he said to her.

"The Tigers have a day off," she said, chuckling.

My father smiled broadly but then sank into unconsciousness and again beat the bed railings. Carol went to his side and placed a hand on his forehead. His features relaxed, and the beating stopped . . . for a time.

Once when Carol was sitting with us, my mother motioned to me. She wanted a break. Carol said, "Take your time. I'll be here when you get back."

Sitting in the hospital cafeteria sipping coffee, my mother was the first to speak. "Well?" she asked sternly.

I looked up in dismay.

"Well?" she repeated.

"Well what?" I replied.

"You can be so dense," she said, irritated. "What happened between you and Carol?" she asked.

"I don't know—" I started to say.

"There's a good man dying upstairs, and he's had the same question for years," she said, raising her voice. "At least one of us should hear the answer."

I could not put her off. My thoughts were a jumble. "It was the dinners at the Campbells'," I started but then hesitated.

"Go on. What happened at the Campbells'?" she demanded.

"Many nights when Dr. Campbell was called out, he asked Carol to go with him," I said. "She always went."

"What's wrong with that?" my mother shot back.

"Nothing . . . nothing," I said hurriedly. "She went with him to help with his patients. The Campbells believed Carol had a special gift for helping the sick."

"Yes. Carol has that gift. You can see the way she comforts Dad," my mother replied as if saying "so what?" and "get on with it."

"It frightened me," I said. "It seemed so morbid."

"Morbid?" my mother said, shocked. "Morbid? You can be such a fool."

"It's morbid, Mother," I said.

"No . . . no," she said firmly. "There you are mistaken. Her special gift is nothing other than kindness."

I sat back, looked down at my coffee, and asked, "What strange pleasure does she get from it?"

"Joe, you've always been suspicious of people. What strange pleasure do you get from that?" she asked softly.

I was silent. "Carol is just kind," my mother said firmly. "She can't be any other way. Don't hold it against her."

I had heard these same words so many years earlier and had lied. This time I decided not to lie, a decision that left me wordless. I sipped my coffee. It was cold.

"Joe, most of us, especially the old among us, wake up every morning waiting on kindness. We are waiting for . . . a hug, a personally prepared lunch, a conversation, someone to listen—really listen. There is no currency for purchasing kindness. Nonetheless, without kindness, most of us would give up," my mother said. "Someone like Carol who shows kindness in her every action, in her every word, gives us the hope we need to carry on. Without it, we feel worthless."

She paused, wiped tears from her eyes, and said, "Just look at me." And then she said emphatically, "The promise of her kindness keeps people like me alive, and when we see our own death coming, her kindness helps us embrace it, confidently, for we are confident we will meet kindness again when we pass beyond this world."

I waited, overwhelmed.

"I have one more question," she said.

"Yes?" I said, waiting.

"Her kindness, her dedication, was not the only reason you dropped her, was it?" she asked.

"No," I said, slowly shaking my head.

"Tell me what the real reason was," she commanded.

Surprised by her intensity, I recalled the shameful truth, the one that I sensed my mother had already guessed. I needed only to confess its name, and she waited while I worked up enough courage to say the word.

As when shoving a canoe into a swift river, the leap into the stern calls on one's trust in the balanced load. And so I leapt, saying, "It was jealousy."

"That's what I thought," she said painfully.

"I'm sorry to disappoint you, Mother."

"It was understandable. You tried so hard to please your father," she said soothingly.

"I so wanted to be the athlete he was. You know, a pitcher."

"What's so sad, Joe, is that Dad never cared how good a pitcher you were," she replied. "It was you who made so much of it."

"Yes," I said. "I wanted so much to impress him." We both sat silently for a time, and then I added, "He was my hero."

"I understand now, Joe," she said and sat back, surveying me.

"I envied Carol, her love of baseball, and her joy in watching a game with Dad. My jealousy killed both for me," I said slowly. "It just got worse. I wanted her out of the house."

"You got your wish," she said sadly.

"I'm so sorry," I choked out.

My mother stared at me and said with a lilt, "And when straying may I meet thee, ere I join a silent band . . ."

"I have joined too many silent bands," I said without looking into her eyes. "Mom, I'll try to make it up to you."

"It's too late for your father."

"I know," I said.

My mother reached out. I took her hands and bowed my head. There was nothing more to be said.

Carol was sitting next to Dad, stroking his forehead when we returned. He was tranquil. When she looked up, she sensed a change in us and searched our faces. We both smiled, and Mom gave her a hug. And before she could sit down, I gave her a hug . . . tentatively. Carol was startled and then smiled and hugged me. It was then I first felt pierced by her kindness. And that long frozen part of me, that part of me that so long ago loved and admired her, began to thaw. Her kindness had always been there. And I wondered whether my rage, the rage that distanced me from so much of life, would have died stillborn if she and I had been seeing each other during college. It was a useless thought, coming too late.

RAVEN

I WILL FIND THE WHITE MEN FOR THE CAT.

A quick beat of my wings brought me to the head of the braids. Flying low down each channel, I searched through the smoke for them.

It was futile.

The smoke hung everywhere, trapped by the tag alder thickets.

As I flew back and forth, the cat plodded downstream with Pauguck at his side. From time to time, it looked up, comforted by my sweeps through the braids.

After many passes, the morning breeze stiffened, allowing me to stand in place on my tail feathers.

I would have them shortly.

One more pass over the right hand channel.

JOE

*M*OVING SWIFTLY, I DRAGGED THE BUCK FARTHER AND farther down the shallow braid, about a mile in all. The drink I promised Talbot was just off to the right where the sweet water creek faintly gurgled. Hemmed in by a wall of tag alders, I looked for openings into the channel the creek fed. Just as we passed into the smoke of a great leaning cedar, I felt the shadow of a raven pass overhead. Once we were through, I looked up into a grayish yellow sky, and it was gone.

A few more yards and a narrow defile in the thicket opened to our right. The water was deeper and the current stronger. I swam with the buck through the opening, pushing off the alder roots with my feet when the carcass legs hung up. Once through, I saw the creek mouth shrouded in smoke a hundred feet downstream.

The thoughts of my father's last days still hung on my mind. Just before the end, after a day of spiking temperatures and flushed skin, Carol asked me to have coffee with her in the cafeteria. I looked over at my mother, and she said, "Go ahead. I'll be fine."

Sitting opposite each other, Carol said, "We're nearing the end, Joe."

"I understand," I replied. "The charts show a steady decline. Longer and longer periods of fever with higher and higher temperatures."

"We must prepare for his last hour," she said.

"Of course," I said, anxious.

"Just before the end, his breathing will become labored. He will sound hoarse, and he will be gasping for breath. Mucus will begin to block his windpipe," she said matter-of-factly.

"Yes," I said.

"About then, if a nurse is present, she'll leave the room," Carol said, pausing. "She'll leave so that your family can be alone with your father's death. Do you understand?"

"I understand."

"Good, Joe." Then she leaned forward. "Your father does not deserve to suffer during his last hours. It will be up to you to see that he does not."

"What do you mean?" I asked, confused.

"One of the IV lines carries a pain killer . . . morphine. It is metered," she said, watching me carefully.

"What do I do?" I asked.

"During his last minutes, he may suffer intense pain. I have seen severe pain cause the dying to spasm. And I have seen them become so agitated they try to climb out of bed."

Apprehension gripped me. "I don't want Mom to see that," I said. "That should not be her last memory of Dad."

"I agree. And I'm sure your father would not want it either. That's why I'm talking with you now, Joe," Carol said earnestly. "You'll need to take responsibility for your father's last minutes. Your mother will be too distracted by then. Her memories of your father will paralyze her. It is you who'll need to allay the intense pain that may take over his body at the very end."

"I'll do what I can," I said. Thinking of the pain I had caused him, how I steered Carol away from him, and worst of all, how I had lied, I said even more emphatically, "Yes, I'll do what I must."

"What you must do is push more morphine into him," Carol said, hesitating. "Just enough to stay ahead of his pain."

"I can do that for him," I said.

"But, Joe, you must also be aware that the morphine will interfere

with his breathing," she said. "And this is the point. You will be dulling the pain, but at some point, you may be hastening his death. It
is a difficult balance. You could be shortening his life a few minutes
nonetheless."

Her words struck me. I sat back and reflected on them and the
alternatives. "There's no other way," I replied slowly and took Carol's
hands and squeezed them.

"I wish you and your mother could be spared these last hours,"
she said. "But I know your father, and I know he's prepared to
leave us."

Many times I have played over in my mind my father's last minutes. His breathing grew more and more labored. The nurse left,
and my mother stood composed by his bed, holding his right hand.
Carol was at the head of the bed with a hand on his forehead, whispering in his ear. I heard her say over and over, "Just let go . . . You
have done everything you could in this life . . . Joe will take care of
his mother . . . Don't worry . . . Just let go . . ." I stood near the IVs
and, hesitantly at first, started to push more morphine down the
clear tube when my father showed distress.

I looked on his face listening to his breathing, and sadness took
hold of me. I realized I would never again talk with my father. His
left arm and the beating board fell to his side. His breathing stopped
and the monitors keened like a siren. There was no longer any need
for morphine. My father's face relaxed, and the happy, energetic man
I knew returned briefly. My mother began to weep quietly. Carol
moved over to her side, putting an arm around her. Looking over at
me, she said in a whisper, "Thank you, Joe." It was then that I knew
how much she loved my father.

And so I may have had a hand in my father's death. I will never
know. Often, I have looked back and tried to count the seconds I
may have taken from him. Nonetheless, I would do it all over again
if I had to because my father did not deserve the pain. I just wish I
knew for certain that I did not shorten his life. It was this feeling of
uncertain guilt I submerged with all my other defeats. But this defeat
was like no other. In my cavern of rage, it glowed as brightly as the

lights at the bottom of a nuclear cooling pool, reminding me every day of Talbot's toxic genius.

Talbot and I reached the creek to find debris from the fire choking its mouth. With the paddle, I pushed it out into the channel and watched it bob downstream. Wading a few yards into the creek, I dragged the buck and Talbot up onto an exposed sand bank flanking the creek entrance. I dropped the paddle, and undoing the belt, I carried Talbot farther up, away from the stench. We were in a cul-de-sac. If the cat found us here, it would have the advantage.

The water was cold and clear. Talbot drew in a deep breath, smiled, and cupped his hands. He drank and drank until he had his fill, water spilling down the front of his shirt. Once he was finished, I turned away and splashed water into my mouth and over my face and neck. I heard a scuffling behind me, but tired, I paid no attention.

RAVEN

*O*N MY LAST PASS OVER THE RIGHT CHANNEL, I SPIED THE white men resting on a creek bank off the right hand channel.

They were drinking water.

I should have followed the odor of the dead buck. It too was there, filling the air with its decadent, sweet smell.

The fire had cooked its insides, and the smell gagged even me.

I flew back upstream for the cat. Hovering over it, I began to croak, feigning flight in the direction of the white men. The cat came alive and moved into the braids.

I circled back to keep the cat on track, but I need not have, for the cat always stayed below me.

Three channels and several hundred yards away from the white men, the cat threw up clods of muck, dodging this way and that, before crashing through the thicket to stand on the edge of the first of the slow-moving channels. It stared into the water for an instant, then leapt into the current and swam to the next alder screen. The smoke had thinned considerably by then.

Poking here and there as it drifted downstream, the cat struggled to find purchase in the bordering thicket. The water in the channel was deep, and it was slow going for the cat. Finally, it found an opening and snaked through.

The next channel, the middle channel, was shallow. The cat

splashed downstream, sniffing the air, again looking for an opening to the right, to the third channel, but the tag alders bordering this channel were thicker, and the cat found no easy passage through. Frustrated, it leapt into the thicket wall, trying to bull its way through. Hanging up on a mass of branches instead, it was completely pinned. Struggling frantically, its efforts only wedged it deeper into the tag alder trunks.

Squawking, I encouraged it but without avail.

The cat became quiet.

It began to gnaw at the branches binding it.

One after another, it gnawed them off until it could drop to the ground and pick its way back to the middle channel.

Subdued, the cat swam downstream carefully, exploring the thicket wall to its right, looking for a crevice in the tag alder wall.

Once it made the right hand channel, the white men would be dead.

Pauguck took all this in patiently. He glided through the braids unhampered. Watching the cat struggle, he stood by unconcerned.

At one point, he looked up at me hovering above and asked, "Do you hear me, Kahgahgee?"

"Yes, I hear you," I said, peeved.

"You are a meddler!" he shouted and then waited with crossed arms for the cat to make its way downstream.

Pauguck was not looking for an argument, so I did not give him one.

CAROL

ET ME DEAL WITH THE PEOPLE AT THE ROADBLOCK, Val," I said. "There's a good chance I've nursed one of their relatives."

"Sure," Val said, taking in the collection of cars and trucks blocking the 480 bridge.

"Let's go," I said as Val parked the Jeep on the shoulder.

Two officers walked toward us as we stepped out. One of them smiled. "Morning, Val."

"You know why I'm here, Pete," Val said abruptly. It was Pete Christianson. He and Val had served together in Iraq. "I would like you to meet my mother."

"Nice to meet you, ma'am. This is Sergeant Ketunen, Val," Pete said. We all shook hands.

Pete turned to the sergeant. "Val was my sergeant in Iraq. His father's missing. He was on the river with Mr. Talbot when the fire hit."

"Mr. Talbot, huh?" Sergeant Ketunen said coldly.

"Didn't I tend your mother once when she was hospitalized?" I interrupted, sensing the sergeant was one frustration away from ordering us to the emergency center.

"Yes, now that you mention it. We spoke more than once at the hospital," he said, looking over at the Jeep. The sergeant turned and smiled broadly at me. He relaxed. "I'm sorry about Joe, ma'am. I understand your worry."

"How's your mother doing?"

"Fine, but you're not here to ask about my mother."

"It's light. Shouldn't you be moving into the woods?" I asked.

"That was my plan," the sergeant said, stiffening again. "But then the sheriff received a call from the governor ordering us to cooperate with Talbot's security director. A guy by the name of Donahue. Flew in from D.C. last night. Donahue says we wait for his team. So we wait."

I narrowed my eyes. "What about your men?"

"What we want doesn't matter, ma'am. We're under orders. I am being polite with you because Joe's out there. Don't push."

"What if we waited before tending people in the ER? You know, waiting on some administrator to tell us to go ahead."

"There are others with missing relatives, and they're at the emergency center. Patience—"

Before the sergeant could finish, Val interrupted, "When will Donahue's men arrive?"

"Probably in an hour. Maybe a little longer. It's up to Donahue to make the call," he replied.

"This makes no sense," I said, raising my voice.

"Val, I'm ordering you and your mother to leave now," the sergeant said, his frustration unfolding.

"There's no time to lose," Val said, his voice rising.

A short man standing on the bridge looked over at Val and the two officers. He was dressed like a SWAT team member . . . black baseball cap, black protective vest, and a black Glock. His polished black boots flashed in the dawn as he made his way over to us and the officers.

"That's Donahue," Pete whispered.

"Why aren't you moving?" Val asked as Donahue came up.

Donahue bristled. "I don't need to explain my actions to you," he said, crowding in on Val until they were nose to nose.

"My husband's out there, and every minute counts!" I shouted at him.

149

Donahue looked over at me. "You're out of line," he responded. "I'm going in when I'm ready to go in."

"You're wasting time," Val said.

"Officer, arrest this man," Donahue said, grabbing Val's arm.

Val pulled away. And the sergeant stepped in. "Let's both of you cool down." Turning, he said, "It's time to leave."

"Okay," I said.

"Arrest this man!" Donahue insisted.

"For what, Mr. Donahue? Being worried about his father?" Sergeant Ketunen said firmly. "He's on the river with your boss."

"Donahue, if you're not going in, then my son and I will do your job for you," I said, staring into Donahue's eyes. Donahue stared back.

"You're amateurs," he hissed.

"We know these woods, and we know this river," I said.

Turning to Sergeant Ketunen, Donahue said, "Sergeant, we can't have unsupervised people roaming these woods." Donahue then added under his breath, "Do you want your sheriff to get another call from the governor?"

"Mr. Donahue's right," the sergeant said. "I think it best you two leave now. Wait at the emergency center."

Donahue shrugged and crunched back to the bridge. Once Donahue was out of earshot, the sergeant turned back to Val. "Don't make me arrest you, Val. You see my problem. The sheriff doesn't need any more guff from the governor."

"We don't want to cause you any trouble," I said. "But—"

Interrupting, the sergeant said, "I know, I know, but officially I'm ordering you to wait at the emergency center. That is an order. You've followed orders before, haven't you?"

Val and I went silent.

The sergeant relented, "We have your telephone number."

"Pete, walk Mrs. McCartney and Val back to their car and fill them in on the way."

As the sergeant turned to go, Pete took Val's arm. "He's a good guy."

"Yes. So fill me in," Val said impatiently.

"We haven't seen your father or Talbot. Our spotter planes will be up shortly. My guess is if they stayed on the river, they should be at Larson's camp by now. Yesterday afternoon, the spotters reported the road into Larson's was clear right down to the Third Falls."

I pictured Larson's camp road. Most of it ran through sand waste. "That would be the best way in," I said. Val looked over at me. "Once we're at the Third Falls, Mom, we face the really hard question. Should we search upstream or down? A wrong guess could kill Dad."

Coming up on the Jeep, Pete stood with Val by the driver door. "Val, I need to warn you. I've spent the last two hours listening to Donahue boasting about his exploits as a private contractor in Iraq. You know the type. A 'shoot first and ask questions later' kind of guy. I don't know what he would do if he found the two of you out alone in the woods."

"I do know the type."

"Then you know to stay out of his way."

"Thanks for everything, Pete," Val said, climbing into the Jeep.

Pete looked in at me. "I'm sorry about Joe," he said. "If it means anything, I'm worried about him too."

"It means the world, Pete."

Then Pete turned back to Val, smiled, and said, "Good luck. And I mean it. You have about an hour and a half before Donahue will be out there committing who knows what."

After Pete left, I said to Val, "We're on our own, Val." Closing the Jeep driver door, Val said dolefully, "We've been wasting our time here."

JOE

*T*HE SCRAPING SOUND WAS TALBOT. I SAW THE FLASH OF the wading belt looping over my head and felt one of his knees slam into my back. The noose tightened around my neck, and I could not breathe. It began cutting skin, and I could feel blood oozing down my neck.

Talbot had picked a good spot. He was above and behind me on the sand bank.

"No more rides on stinking carcasses," he grunted, pulling harder on the belt. "The cat'll be here shortly. It'll all be over by then."

Surprised, I flailed my arms and twisted about, trying to get a hold of the belt. But as with so many of those who lose the use of their legs, Talbot had built up the strength of his arms. He kept the noose so tight I could not work my fingers under it. I scraped at the webbing without finding a finger hold.

"In a minute, you'll black out, Little Fish," Talbot whispered in my ear. "Then I can finish what I came out here to do."

Talbot expected my flailing. So I quickly leaned back, hoping to put some slack in the noose. Talbot just pushed harder with his knee until my back was fully arched. My head began to pound, and I felt the first stirrings of panic.

"Who's the better man now, Joe?" Talbot whispered. "As I have been trying to teach you, you're a loser. Always have been. Always will be. Chalk this up as your last lesson."

I continued to flail.

"You'll lose consciousness, and I'll hang on until your bowels burst. That will be a welcome smell for once. Only then will I let you loose."

Talbot was being thorough. Afterward, the cat would find him, or he would try for the Third Falls and fake his accidental death. My obituary would be short, leaving the questions about my part in Talbot's accidental death unanswered.

I decided to do what Talbot could not. I rolled and staggered upright. The knee dropped from my back, the loop slackened, and I pivoted about, swinging him in front of me. We were face-to-face now, and I could breathe.

"Drop the belt, Talbot," I said, coughing and sucking in breath.

"When I'm ready," he said, pulling harder with his arms to tighten the loop.

I looked down at him, snaked my arm through the belt at my neck, and pushed. The wading belt went slack. I grabbed it and buckled it around my waist.

Talbot fell back and chuckled. "No harm, no foul, Little Fish."

I gave him a hard look and then looked up at the sky, breathing long and slow. "Is that what you told yourself about my father's money?"

"I never think about your father's money." Then he said heatedly, "I'm sure he was just as big a fool as you."

He was goading me again. "You had a hand in his death," I said accusingly.

"I've had a hand in many deaths," he said triumphantly.

I looked at him blankly.

"I take being a predator seriously. To be good at it, you need to stay in practice. A few deaths are part of the hunt," he said. "Your father wasn't quick enough or strong enough. He got what he deserved. Extinction."

I tensed.

"That's all there is to it," he said. "Your father and his friends made it easy for me. They didn't even know I had their money in my sights. So trusting . . . like newly dropped lambs."

My hands came up, flexing. I was too angry to answer and began to shake. My murderous rage flared up. I looked down at him and could almost feel his soft neck in my grip.

He saw my mood. "Go ahead," he said. "Kill me."

The spell was broken. Talbot recoiled immediately, knowing he uttered one word too many.

I exhaled. "I need you alive."

"I'm counting on being dead before we make the 480 bridge."

"Everybody's entitled to their own dreams, Talbot," I said.

"The odds are I will be dead."

"Have it your own way . . . Frank."

"We're back to that," and he began to recite in a singsong voice, "Have it your own way, Frank . . . Have it your own way, Frank." Then he went quiet.

"We're going," I said.

"I'm not done drinking." He started to crawl on all fours toward the water.

I caught one of his arms and dragged him toward the buck carcass.

"You know, Joe, if you really believe I had a part in killing your father, you should leave me out here to die. Just simple, straightforward revenge. Right? Something a truly loving son would do."

"It was all of you, your shareholders, your lawyers, the bankruptcy court . . . " I said.

"But here and now, you can take your revenge on the instigator," he said. I dropped his arm, and he looked hopeful. "It's the least you could do for your father."

"Talbot, for a lot of reasons, I need you alive. The sweetest of all is to know that every time you look down at your puss-soaked bandages, and every time a surgeon slices away another part of your decaying body, and every time the urge to walk reminds you that you have no feet, you'll wonder why you are alive," I said, smiling.

"And—this is the good part, Talbot—you'll think of me . . . and curse me."

Pausing, I took hold of his jaw and, wagging his head from side to side, said, "You'll curse me because you will never forget this moment. You'll see my face, the face now before you, when you despair, and you'll know that I kept you alive solely so you would think on what you did to my father. And I promise you that you'll come to regret what you did to him."

"Never!" he shouted, twisting his head to break my hold on his jaw. And then, in a more conciliatory voice, said, "Come now, Joe. You're just confused." Talbot readied himself to make one last argument.

"Shut up, Talbot!" I barked. Looking into his blue eyes, I whispered, "You'll endure the suffering my father endured in his last days." And I started in a singsong voice, "Big Fish, Big Fish, that is my revenge . . . Big Fish, Big Fish, that is my revenge." My mocking tone was too much even for me. It was not the tone Carol would have used. Nor was it the tone my father would have used. I stopped.

Talbot was angry. "Go ahead. Gloat about beating up a cripple. If I had full use of both my legs, you'd be dead by now."

"Self-pity is not your way, Talbot," I replied.

"I'm just stating a fact," he said. "Sometime you should think about what it's like to live with part of one leg gone."

"I lived most of my life thinking about that," I said with disgust. "My father lost part of a leg in a car accident."

"So you're the son of a gimp," Talbot said coldly.

Talbot had found the trigger. And he had pulled it, but the gun misfired. He must have felt some faint resonance from my cavern of rage, however, for he kept pulling the trigger. "The son of a gimp. Do you hear me? The son of a gimp." But the hammer fell on empty chambers.

My rage slackened. The memory of the fraternity party and the face of my fraternity brother turning blue in my grip came back. Time to say what I should have said then, "Never thought of it that way," I said. "My father was the strongest man I ever knew."

Talbot stared.

"Years of walking on his artificial leg inflamed his arthritis, yet he went out every morning in pain to Lundine . . . to work," I said proudly. "That's why he needed hip replacements." Confidence surged through me. The cure had taken; the years of fearing the rage that lay within me were over. Or so I believed at that moment. A few hours later, I would learn my error, my prideful smugness.

"So what's your point? That as a fellow gimp, I should have left him money for his operations?" Talbot said. "Is that your point?"

"I know you well enough by now to know that it would not have made any difference to you whether my father had one leg or two," I said and picked up one of his arms and started dragging him across the spit of sand again.

When we neared the water, I dropped his arm and stood over him to shift him to the floating buck. Talbot looked up and said, "I'm more fortunate than you. I never knew my father."

"Fortunate?"

"Yes. I'm invulnerable to feeling any shame for him."

I looked down on him, his face a mask. I saw his battered blue legs and saw the final course of his disease: a man without legs and hands, and blind. Then he became only a voice in my mind, the rest too pathetic for consideration. Rolling Talbot onto the buck, I tied the wading belt around him.

"Did you ever look for him?"

"My father? . . . Why? He did me a favor when he left before I knew him." Talbot stared down at his useless legs.

And I saw what Carol had seen all along. A shattered man. I reached down to touch his forehead, for his cheeks appeared feverish. He drew his head back, afraid. "I'm just checking your temperature."

"You're not qualified."

I put my hand on his forehead, and it was as I feared. "You're beginning to run a fever."

Talbot looked away and muttered, "Just leave me. I want this over with."

"No," I said without compassion.

As we worked our way down the sweet water creek, I touched my pocket, checking for the knife. It was still there. Pushing off into the right hand channel, I saw the smoke had cleared. It was a mile to the Third Falls, and this channel would take us all the way there. Five feet in most places, it was deep enough to discourage the cat.

I knew every detail of the Third Falls, having fished it often. Tired, so tired. All I could think of now was my regret. Every detail of the days after my father's funeral was washed with regret. Even as we lazily floated downriver, I remembered that I had never fished the Escanaba with my father. Together, we fished lakes. At first, in the years following World War II, my father fly-fished their shorelines collecting bass and pan fish. He was a superb fly caster, the best I ever saw, long and accurate, using the strength of his left arm to cast hour after hour. In those days, fly rods were heavy, made of bamboo. And fly lines were made of silk. He had two. I remembered how every night he strung them between chairs to dry and every morning he ritually greased them with Mucilin. Two lines made a full day. When the second line began to sink, he would reel up and say, "Let's head for home."

Most evenings on vacation, he chatted with my mother and me while sorting through his fly boxes. And that was why when spin fishing took hold, I was surprised my father was one of the first converts. He never fly-fished again, giving me his fly rod and fly boxes. Instead of arguing the merits of the Royal Coachman, Professor, Adams, and Pass Lake, he started talking about Daredevil spoons, Mepps spinners, Hula Poppers, rubber worms, and Flatfish. And he started fishing deeper water, exploring weed beds and drop-offs. It was exciting, and I was caught between two worlds. I spin fished lakes with him, but because I took pleasure in the intricacies of fly-fishing, I fished rivers where the water was better suited to fly-fishing. Even promising to take him to stretches of river where he would have the advantage spin fishing, I could never interest him in trying it. He had one love: fishing in lakes and ponds.

So many attending his wake were anglers. Hundreds of people came, and Carol and I flanked my mother to greet them all. Soft words and sniffles. Over and over the words, "I am so sorry for your loss." Often I heard my mother introduce Carol, telling mourners, "I don't know what I would do without her. She's like a daughter." Carol would smile at the words, shake hands, and say, "The McCartneys are my second family. Mrs. McCartney became a mother to me after my own mother died."

After greeting the visitors, my mother led the singing. I joined in on one song. Carol was singing beside me, and when I lifted my voice, my mother looked over, nodded, and smiled.

I sing because I'm happy,
I sing because I'm free,
For his eye is on the sparrow . . .

It was one of my father's favorites. After he retired, I saw him with his cup of morning coffee, watching for hours out our kitchen window at the backyard bird feeders. By late fall, all our summer migrants had flown south and only our permanent residents visited the feeders— the chickadees, juncos, and woodpeckers. And when the temperature dropped below freezing and the winds reached thirty and forty miles per hour, he worried about his birds. Many froze, but when the winter weather broke and the spring migrations started, with joy he reported sightings of song sparrows, his favorites, resurrected at the feeders.

Numb from the emotions of the wake, I hardly remembered the funeral service. One distinct memory stayed with me. It was the thud of dirt clods on the lid of my father's coffin. The sound played over and over in my thoughts during those bleak moments of the day when my father and I usually chatted. For several days, my mother and I sat wordless at meals. A few evenings I found her weeping quietly when I came home from work. Sleep brought monstrous dreams and drove me to root in the refrigerator late at night for leftover hot dishes from solicitous neighbors. But the sound of the microwave did not cue happier memories.

A week passed, and one day, I telephoned Carol at the hospital. "Mom needs company," I said.

Carol apologized for not looking in on her. "A shift change," she said. "I'll come this evening."

"Come for dinner," I suggested. "I'll play chef."

"How can I refuse?" She laughed. "In the meantime, give your mother a kiss for me."

That evening, the person missing at the table entertained us all. Mom and Carol started telling Dad stories. I joined in, and we were living back in the years before the words "I'm so sorry for your loss" and the thud of falling dirt clods. At dinner that night, we imagined the whack of a hard ball hitting a catcher's glove, the tinkle of a full stringer of bass, and the splash of summers at Blue Lake. There were so many stories, and all three of us laughed and cried into the night.

Finally, my mother rose. "Thank you for coming, Carol, but I'm tired and have so much to do tomorrow. So many things I've been neglecting."

Carol was smiling. "I'll look in again tomorrow, Mrs. McCartney."

"When are you going to start calling me Mother?" my mother said.

"Starting right now," Carol said, laughing. "But I need to get home. Early day for me tomorrow . . . Mother McCartney."

My mother laughed and then, looking at me, said in mock sternness, "Joe, make sure Carol gets home safely."

"You mean, 'Make sure that Sis gets home safely,' " I said.

My mother searched for words and then said, "I hope she's more to you than a sister."

I should not have brought it up. But Carol jumped in, "Don't worry, Mother. I think of Joe as an adopted brother."

We made small talk on the way to the Campbell house. I could not dispel the feeling that Carol was a sister. My only sister. She had been as good to my father as any daughter could have been. And when I leaned down to kiss her neck as she turned to go, she turned back and met my lips. They were full and moist, the lips of a mature woman. I lingered too long and, embarrassed, stepped back with a lurch.

Carol giggled. "Joe McCartney, you are full of surprises."

But she did not push me away, and I liked the promise of that. I knew that night I would dream of her and her red hair and shapely figure instead of my father's burial.

Carol then winked and, turning, said, "See you tomorrow, my Joe."

"See you tomorrow," I said and skipped down her front steps, knowing there would be no microwaving tonight.

I blinked as I felt water splash on my face. It was Talbot. "I'd love to drown you," he said menacingly.

It was then I heard the sound of a raven clearing its throat and looked up to see it hovering overhead.

RAVEN

*T*HE WHITE MEN HAVE CAUGHT THE CURRENT.

They will ride it down to the Third Falls. As they approach the falls, the current will pick up speed. They will be there in twenty minutes.

Too late for the cat as it paddled tentatively into the creek mouth.

Its disappointment was bitter, for the sand bank gave off the unmistakable stench of the white man's dead foot. The cat paced back and forth with its nose to the ground, sniffing. Following the scent trail back to the river, it drank, sat back on its haunches, and looked downriver with slumped shoulders.

And as I passed over, it looked up at me forlornly.

The cat must make the falls before the white men.

I croaked and led the cat away from the river to a deer trail that skirted the creek. The trail dead-ended in a moldering logging road that turned and ran directly to the Third Falls.

The road was clear.

Raising spurts of ash as it ran, the cat scampered ahead, passing in and out of vagrant smoke plumes, which stalked like ghosts through the forest of burned trunks.

It looked neither left nor right.

It will make the Third Falls in ten minutes.

And I croaked exultantly because I was now certain the able-bodied man and the cat would meet.

But before then, I must plan.

I took one last look at the running cat and saw Pauguck loping beside it.

He looked up, so I shouted, "Now I will get my blue eyes!"

Pauguck laughed, happy, but not for me. Hardly looking at me, he waved me on, as if to say, "You are deluded."

JOE

SWIMMING JUST HARD ENOUGH TO KEEP PACE WITH THE current, I towed the buck with Talbot downstream. The anger I felt about my father's last days gave me purpose, and the regular stroking in the moderate current of the braids steadied my mind.

I owed my father the truth of my break with Carol, and he never heard it. After his funeral, I wanted a new start with Carol. It was what my father would have wanted. Our kiss led me to believe we could make that start without confronting the hurt I caused her. I wanted—I needed—to believe that she had forgiven me. I glowed with the prospect when I went to bed that night.

My dream died the next evening. Carol and Mom sorted through Dad's clothes, packing up most for Goodwill. I kept a few sweaters and his fishing hats and later made sandwiches. Mom was grateful to have someone to share her memories as we bagged up each piece.

That evening, walking Carol home again, our conversation grew more stilted the closer we came to the Campbell house. There was no good night kiss. Instead, Carol invited me in. "Take a seat in the living room, Joe. I'll get coffee."

Shouting from the kitchen, she asked, "Sugar? Cream?"

"Both," I said.

Cups and saucers. I remember the clinking as Carol set one in my hands and then sat down in a wing chair opposite me. The formality of cups and saucers warned me that this was not the conversation I expected after last night's kiss.

"I have thought a lot about last night, Joe. We like each other . . . We like each other very much," she began. "But that will not be enough to begin all over. And that is what you want, isn't it, Joe? To begin all over again as if nothing happened."

"Yes," I said, unsure what more to say to her.

She did not expect me to say more, for she continued, "It cannot be, Joe—"

"I'll make it up to you," I interrupted. "My thoughtlessness . . ." No other words came to mind, so I repeated, "I will make it up to you." So there would be an apology.

"Was it thoughtlessness, Joe? Are you being honest with me?" She waited, but I just stared, my mind churning. "I believe, Joe, that we can never make up for what we have done in the past," she said deliberately.

"What should I do to show you that I can be trusted again?" I pleaded.

"It doesn't matter," she replied. "We cannot go back." Then she said, "Feelings are so fleeting."

"But my feelings have changed," I protested. "The last few weeks near you have opened my eyes."

"Yes, one thing we've shared is love for your father," she said, sitting back and taking a sip of coffee. "But we can't base a new relationship on what we feel about your father."

"We shared so much in high school," I blurted out. "We could begin there."

"True, but our time together back then was not enough to stop you from cutting me out of your life," she said tonelessly.

"I want to start over again," I pleaded.

"I don't want to start over," she said. "Joe, as I look at the man across from me, I believe the same thing will happen again. You'll form grievances against me now as you did then. After a few weeks or months together, your grievances will dominate our relationship." She paused. "My days are full, Joe. I've no time for arguing with you."

"I've changed," I said, raising my voice, irritated.

Startled, she looked sharply at me and said slowly, "You're afraid you won't get your way with me."

I was about to deny her words when she said, "Before long, Joe, you'll begin to hold my work against me as you did before. And you'll see my absences as slights against you."

I tried to interject, but she held her hand up to stop me. "It's inevitable, and then you'll leave me again."

"But I love you," I said.

"I'm sure you do," she said. "But that's not enough."

"Just give it a try," I said.

"Something else I don't believe in," she said.

"How can you be so sure?" I asked.

"My life has little regularity. You believe in schedules and evening meals. You'll want to know where I am every minute. And you would question me about whom I saw every day and what was said."

Her words struck me deeply, and I looked to the door.

"I could never reassure you," she said gently. "And the truth is, Joe, I wouldn't even try. I've hardly enough time in my day for what I believe I should be doing. Spending my time reassuring you, or anyone else for that matter, isn't on my schedule. You would need that, and I couldn't take your need seriously."

"If that's what you want, I won't ask about your work," I said.

She just stared at me skeptically. Finally she said, "You don't understand, Joe. Remember the meals at my parents' when my father and I were called away? You were upset. My life today is even more chaotic. Every day, you'd be adding another slight to your store of grievances against me. And you would give them a name, a name like *morbid*. I couldn't respect someone who denigrates my deepest convictions."

Hearing the word *morbid* shook me. I gathered my thoughts together, reassembled them, and went on. "I didn't mean what I said," I told her. "You'll see. It will be different now. You have your hospital schedules. We could plan around them," I argued.

"No, Joe, my hospital work is the easy part," she said. "The hard part is my helping those who are dying. Dying knows no schedule."

"I promise you I'll curb my suspicions," I pled, for I felt my hope, my need, for a new relationship with Carol slipping away.

"Joe, as you saw with your father, death can come at any time. My work puts me beside the dying in their last moments. Any plans I have for an evening or a weekend take second place to my patients and their needs. Often you'd be alone, unexpectedly alone, and holding my absence against me."

"But . . . ," I tried to interrupt.

"Joe, listen to me," she said.

I tried to talk over her. She just sat patiently, crossing her legs and sipping coffee until I ran out of arguments.

"Let me help you understand," she started. "My nursing is a career and can be organized up to a point, leaving time for a personal life. My desire to help the dying is different. It's a calling, a calling my parents fostered in me. It's who I am. You cannot organize that."

"I could try to understand how important it is to you," I said.

"It doesn't matter whether you understand its importance to me or not. I don't want to take the time to explain what to me is as natural as breathing," she said. "Inevitably you'll take offense and then it will gnaw at you until you shut me out again."

"What am I to do?" I asked morosely, fully defeated. "I believe we belong together."

"Perhaps we do," she said. "But not now. I've a long day tomorrow, Joe."

As I left that night, I turned back at the door and asked, "Can I call you?"

"Any time," she said. There was no good night kiss.

I did not know then that the "not now" would stretch out for months. A year later, I began to believe she meant "maybe never." I did not foresee that then, for if I had, I would have doubted my patience, which was the slim, wavering straw I clung to in the end. But it was not patience with Carol. It was patience with myself.

Talbot growled, "Little Fish." The buck was beginning to spin. Its front legs caught on a downed cedar resting just beneath the surface of the river. Straddling the log, I wrenched the buck back on course.

Talbot was holding his nose but was elated. Occasionally he turned his head and looked at me. "You've been elsewhere."

"Yes," I said. About ready to add more, I then thought better of it and continued to swim.

"That's good," Talbot whispered. "You're daydreaming when you should be thinking of the cat."

"Time enough for that," I replied.

Before turning back, he said gravely, "You're a dead man."

We both knew the cat would be at the Third Falls. I called up pictures of the high ground ringing the falls. Too much of it. I needed to decide on a course of action, one that would limit the cat's options. A course of action where, if I guessed wrong, I could make adjustments in the moment. I told myself to concentrate on a plan and, once I had the plan clearly in mind, told myself to picture what likely actions were left to the cat.

So tired. The pictures of the terrain around the Third Falls slipped from my mind. I wondered if there would be enough of me left for a wake. At least my father had a wake with an open casket.

We were at the end of the braids. All its channels emptied into a gentle rapid, hurried on when the river dropped six feet over the last hundred yards before the falls. I pulled the buck and Talbot up against the last of the tag alder thickets just above the rapids.

Lifting Talbot off the buck, I said, "We don't need the buck anymore." I shoved it off and watched it speed toward the falls and then drop from sight. The river was running full. A break for us.

"Talbot, I don't expect you to help me, but I'm warning you that if you interfere, I'll make it uncomfortable for you," I said, looking directly into his eyes. His eyes met mine and they did not flicker. He was excited.

"Going to kill me?" he asked. "Please say you are. Give me something to look forward to."

I didn't entertain the question.

"Worried about my friend, Little Fish?" he asked, laughing.

"Yes," I replied.

Talbot was collecting loose rocks from the rapid's edge.

"Put those down, Talbot," I commanded.

"No one tells me what to do," he replied and raised his arm to throw one at my head. I lunged and slapped it out of his hand.

"You've heard of picadors, Joe," Talbot said slyly.

"Yes," I said, my hand still stinging.

"I am playing the cat's picador," he said.

I hesitated and then told the truth. "You've been doing a good job." It was as I had guessed. "But I will not be charging any caped swords."

"The cat won't wait for you to charge," he said grimly. "He knows what it means to be a predator."

Again Talbot was right.

THE
Third Falls

RAVEN

*T*HE THIRD FALLS IS ALL SMOOTH SURFACES.
A granite apron precedes it.

Millennia before the braids formed, before my black shadow ever fell over it, the apron was a granite plug that, over time, sliding glaciers wore down. When the last glacier melted, the Escanaba, its offspring, shallowed the apron out in its center, leaving sloping folds of smooth granite that reach forty feet upward into the hillsides, mimicking the upraised front and back of a saddle.

The Escanaba runs straight through the middle of the apron, over the center of the saddle, and in time the river made a geometrically precise cut in it. So regular, the cut is mistaken by casual visitors as the work of chisels and human toil.

It is four feet deep throughout, and its water feeds the Third Falls at a constant rate for most of the year, a metered flow in the midst of a chaos of rapids and leaping foam above and below.

Altogether, the falls are thirty feet high.

But this is no precipitate drop of water into the turmoil below.

Rather, the water slides down a single sloping rust-colored granite wall.

In wintertime, it is my playground.

Once the cold sets in, ice and snow coat the walls of the falls. And I turn myself into a sled and skid to the bottom of the ice field.

Again and again. A black dart sailing down a glazed world, gleaming white and smooth as porcelain.

In late summer, in the days before the white men, the Anishinaabe picnicked here with their children. The children swam the cut, vaulted over the lip, and slid down the falls into the shallow rapids below where their parents caught them. In those days, the Third Falls rang with laughter.

That will not be the case today.

There will be angry shouts.

There will be screams and roars.

It is not an even match, but then again, in the forest, there are so few even matches.

I strut the apron across the river from where the cat now hides. Preening my great black flight feathers, shaking off the gray ash which collected on my feet, I practice my dance.

When the white men arrive, I will be to the left of the cut and the cat will be to the right of it. Even now, the cat slumps down behind a fallen pine tree, twenty feet up from where the white men will enter the apron.

The white men will not chance the cut. The slog through four feet of water will slow them down, and the cat need only strike from behind and snag them at its leisure.

No, the white men will make their run across the dry apron.

The cat's success all depends on whether the white men come out of the river to the left or to the right of the cut. If to their left, near me, the cat will need to jump the cut. The able-bodied man will see it and have time to prepare for its charge. Or he may even try for the lip of the falls and slide down, clutching the one-footed man.

The cat will not follow.

But I do not believe this will happen.

I believe the cat and the able-bodied man will confront each other to the right of the cut.

I will make sure of that.

There is no better time for a fight. The able-bodied man is tired, and the cat is pent up with its hunger and frustration. I believe the cat will press its advantage, here and now, forcing the able-bodied man to defend himself.

It is time I took on a new character.

A clown.

Yes, a clown.

I will become a clown and distract the able-bodied man.

What is taking so long? He and the one-footed man are late.

CAROL

*T*HIS IS AS FAR AS THE JEEP WILL GO, MOM," VAL SAID. Gently braking, he stopped on a rise in the road leading to Larson's camp. Looking ahead, Val worked the wipers for a clearer view. We saw a landscape of gray and black: gray ash and smoking black tree trunks to the horizon. Some blocked the road. Beyond the horizon lay the Larson camp and the Third Falls. Probably a mile of unpleasant hiking altogether, I guessed.

Gingerly, Val dismounted, checking for hot spots near the car. He found none. "It's safe to leave the Jeep here."

I adjusted my baseball cap, slung the knapsack off the backseat, and started sorting through it, double checking. "We have everything, Val," I said, anxious to start toward the Escanaba.

"Let me carry the pack," he said as he slung a coil of rope over his head.

I handed it to him.

"Here, Mom, take a bandana," Val said, handing me a neatly folded square of camo-colored cotton.

"I have one of my own," I said.

I shook mine out, doubled it over into a triangle, and drew it over my nose, tying it behind my head. Val did the same with his.

"Make sure it's tight, Val. This stuff will clog your nose and throat before we've gone two steps."

Val took the lead and said, "Try to keep up."

"Val, I'm going to say this once. I wouldn't be here unless I believed I could take care of myself," I said. "Do you hear me?"

Ignoring my challenge, he said, "Okay, let's go." Staying in the lead, he loped down the road.

The ash on the road was three to four inches thick and stuck to our soles, hobbling us. Occasionally, a breeze kicked up whirlwinds of ash, blinding us. I pulled my cap lower. Shortly, the ash hung on us like plaster dust. We tasted it with every step.

I coughed. Val looked back sternly, but I waved him forward. He increased his pace, and I picked up mine to match his. A sip of water on the run and my mouth and breathing cleared. *No more coughing*, I told myself.

A quarter mile later, Val turned back again without losing a step. He heard me breathing hard. My lungs were burning. He was checking for weakness, for fatigue.

I resented it and angrily lifted the bandana flap. "Stop that! Leave it to me to decide when this gets to be too much for me. I'm fine." Val turned ahead, increasing his trot.

Ten minutes later, we came to Larson's fence line. The posts lay in charred fragments and loops of twisted barbed wire sprung up from between scorched, downed trees. "Just a half mile more!" Val shouted over his shoulder.

As we entered what little was left of the Larson's stand of red pine, the ash lay even thicker. Like snow, it drifted deeper where the road dipped.

"Another ten minutes," Val said.

Slowing only slightly, Val pulled out a water bottle, broke the seal, and drank from it.

I took a sip from my water bottle. "As I remember, it's a short hike from here down to the Third Falls," I said after swishing a mouthful of water and spitting it out. My lungs were still burning, but I smoothed out my breathing before I spoke.

"This is where it gets rough," he said pointedly.

I shouted to his back, "Find the trail and quit talking! You'll tire, and I'll have to do this by myself." He didn't laugh, and he didn't look back.

JOE

*T*ALBOT, WE'LL SWIM THE LAST HUNDRED YARDS AND come out on that granite apron fronting the falls," I said, pointing down river.

"No, Joe. You'll swim the last hundred yards dragging me all the way," Talbot replied.

"Is it too much to expect you to help?" I asked.

"You never give up, do you, Joe?" Talbot quickly replied.

I fell silent.

"Cat got your tongue, Joe?" Talbot asked sarcastically.

"The cat is an efficient killer, but you don't want to die its victim," I said.

"It's all the same to me," he said serenely. "Besides, Joe, it will start on me only after it is finished with you."

"You're talking madness, Talbot," I said.

"I'll have a front row seat watching it eviscerate you," he said with relish. "Is that too big a word for you? That will dull what little pain I may feel briefly afterward."

"You underestimate the pain you'll feel," I said.

"The cat is the only one out here worthy enough to kill me. We're two of a kind. As you so eloquently pointed out, it is better than having surgeons take years to snip me to death," he said, angry now. "I'm smarter than you are, Little Fish, and I have thought this

175

through carefully. I keep coming back to the fact that you're standing in my way. That's how simple it is. And you do so because—and
this is your great sin—you've forgotten how insignificant you are."

I was about to respond when Talbot interrupted, holding a finger
to his lips, "Uh-uh, Joe. I will have my way. The SEC and my shareholders will never even entertain the notion of my suicide if the cat
kills me."

"You could always change your mind," I argued. "Why not
rethink your decision and put it off until after Mayo?"

I waited for his response, but he just stared downriver as if I were
not there. I began again, "Why be so stubborn? After we get back,
you can set up other trips with other incompetents. It will be cleaner
for Meredith."

"You just don't get it, do you, Joe? I'm not stubborn. No, I've
decided to be stubborn. People like me never change our minds
because we decide not to change our minds." He swung around to
look at me. "For people like me to change our minds means we have
come to doubt our own strength. I never allow doubt to infect my
thinking. That's why, Little Fish, people like me run your world."

"If you go through with this, you won't be running any world,"
I shot back.

"Save your breath, Joe. I've already decided," he said.

"There's no dignity in this death," I argued.

"If I get my way, that's all the dignity I need," he said, and pointing downriver toward the apron, he intoned as if calling me to a
board meeting, "There. Right there. The big cat is waiting for us. We
should not keep it waiting."

Further argument was futile. "If that's your last word, we go."

"That's my last word," he said. When I tied him to me for the
swim, I caught his sense of relief that he had me back as his porter.

There was one important decision left. I pulled Talbot toward
the cut bisecting the apron. To the left of the cut or to the right of it?
And after that, a quick sprint across the apron to the lip of the falls.
Swimming the cut itself was not an option. It was too shallow and
would slow us down, making us vulnerable.

I felt so tired.

The choice . . . right or left? The apron was now just yards ahead. The rapids collected together here before entering the cut, and the bottom of the river rose up like flag, stone steps leading to a paved patio. It was just a matter of stepping up.

At the apron, I undid the wading belt, picked Talbot up, and shifted him to my shoulders.

"The moment has come, Little Fish," he whispered into my ear. "You're trembling."

"I'm tired, Talbot, and you haven't gotten any lighter," I said.

Right or left? I looked to the right. The hillside was clear except for an old downed pine. The cat might be behind it. But before I could inspect it closely, the antics of a raven drew my attention to the left of the cut. The raven limped, skipped, and hopped about as if favoring an injured leg. Once it flapped its wings to rise up and then just as quickly dropped down to strut and skip back and forth.

When I was last aware of the cat, it had been on the left side of the river. That was just before we entered the braids. And I did not hear any splashing behind us during our time in the braids. Chances were good, then, that the cat stayed on that side of the river and was hiding on the hillside just behind the raven. And the thought occurred to me that the raven was shadowing the cat. Had it joined up with the cat this time also? Perhaps, but I was too tired to consider this possibility for long.

In all likelihood, the safest course was entering the apron to the right of the cut. Using the paddle as a staff, I stepped onto the apron and hefted Talbot. I pictured us sprinting across the apron to the lip, where we would then slide down to the river below. That was my plan. It was time, and Talbot sensed it and tried to break my hold on him as I began my run. Shifting about, he threw my stride off, making my run more a stagger than a sprint.

I kept looking to my left across the cut to the raven and the rise behind it. The raven continued its antics, adding clucks and whistles. So far, so good. The lip was twenty feet ahead. No cat yet . . . that was odd. It was then I knew I had been fooled. Clamping down on Talbot, I squeezed the wind out of him just as he growled, "Too late."

I heard a snarl behind me. I turned and saw the cat twenty feet up from us. It was even bigger than I remembered. We would not make the lip before it was on us.

I dropped Talbot off my shoulders and straddled him. Pulling out the knife and hearing it click as it locked into place, I gripped it in my left hand, point up. In my right hand was the paddle, which I swung over my head like a propeller.

The cat charged, and just as it charged, Talbot kicked one of my legs out from under me. I went down on one knee.

The cat flew over me as I went down. Too high. But as it passed over me, it twisted about, reached down, and raked my left shoulder with its claws. I heard my shirt rip and felt sinew and muscle part and burn. The cat skidded to a stop just short of the cut. Turning back, it set itself carefully again. Its eyes never left me.

I kicked Talbot, freeing myself from his grip. I stood on his hand, and he screamed. The cat tensed and rocked back, setting itself for another lunge. I started the paddle going again and brought the knife out in front, lower this time. I was hoping the paddle would keep the cat upright so I could strike upward with the knife. The thrust would not kill the cat, but if I could start a trickle of blood, the cat might smell its own blood and retreat.

The cat took one bound and leapt. The paddle struck it, and it fell back, but not before it broke the paddle in half with a single swipe. I was left with three feet of handle.

The cat backed off and set itself to spring again. Without the full paddle, it would get closer this time. I poked the handle at its head as the cat came in waist high. As I struck at it, I thrust upward with the knife to catch the cat in its chest or neck. But the knife flashed in the yellow dawn. The cat saw the flash, and with its right front paw, it batted my knife hand. I heard a clattering on the rock apron.

The cat fell back a few yards. I could not feel my left hand. I looked down and saw it was still there. Empty, not bleeding, but I could not work the fingers.

We were done.

Done.

Talbot started to laugh and crowed, "It's all over!"

I started to swing the paddle handle. There was nothing left to do. The cat stepped back for one last hurtle. It would be on me this time. I thought of hugging it close, grappling with it, rolling to the lip of the falls, and going over. Perhaps it would release me during the drop to the rapids below before more serious damage could be done. I waited.

The cat rocked back and bounded forward, pushing off its front paws to meet me high up. I readied. But the cat missed to my left, snarling as it slewed sideways. Sitting back, it picked up its right paw tentatively and rotated it before its eyes. Then it put the paw back down gingerly. Blood seeped out from underneath as the cat put weight on it. Snarling again, the cat picked the paw up again and chewed at it. But when it took the paw out of its mouth, its tongue dripped blood.

Only then did I see the bloody knife point of the Buck poking up through the tawny fur of its right paw. The cat circled us, limping. And Talbot shouted to it, urging it on. "Come on! You have him!"

For a moment, the yellow eyes of the cat fixed on Talbot. Then it shrugged him off and fixed on me before circling once again. But with each step, its limping became worse, and with each step, more and more blood oozed out from under its right paw.

For a long minute the cat sat back on its haunches, facing us. A tawny menace, contemplating its prey. And that was the end. Slowly the big cat turned around and slunk back up the slope, now cantering on three legs. I looked around the apron tracked with blood and saw the knife handle. The blade was gone, broken off at the hilt.

Talbot lay back and screamed and screamed, "No! . . . No! . . . No!"

I said nothing and watched the cat go.

Gathering himself, Talbot said, "You were lucky."

"No, Talbot," I said angrily. "I was not lucky."

"You were lucky," he repeated.

"No. The cat broke the rules," I said. "And it paid for its mistake."

"There are no rules out here," Talbot said.

I shot back, "Out here, there are only rules."

"Lucky . . . lucky . . . lucky," Talbot repeated angrily.

"No predator jeopardizes itself for a single kill," I said. "The cat forgot that."

"You live in your own narrow little world, Joe. A narrow world choked with rules. But that's not the way it is in the real world," Talbot said, dismissing me. "There's only winning and losing. The winners fill their stomachs. The cat lost. He goes hungry tonight. That's all there is to it."

"No, Talbot. Out here there are only survivors, and the survivors are the ones who keep the rules," I said. Then looking down at him, I said slowly, "When predators do their best, they merely survive."

"I don't want to tax your limited powers of reasoning, Little Fish, but the cat is stronger and faster than you will ever be. He is fitter," Talbot said on his back, looking up at a cloudless golden morning sky. "He lost this round, but he'll be back to prove it."

"You're wrong. The cat may be stronger and faster than I am, but the cat forgot what's kept it alive 'til now," I said.

"Nonsense," Talbot said.

"It knew better," I said. "The cat went all in. That was its sin. The only shooting stars on this river are in the night sky. To survive, predators must stay healthy."

"No wonder you have nothing," Talbot said scornfully.

"Now you know," I said. Then looking directly into his eyes, I said, "It's too late for you to learn that lesson."

"You have nothing to teach me. I'm a survivor."

"Really?" I said, looking down on him. "Let's go. We have only two miles of river before the 480 bridge."

As I bent to lift Talbot, I staggered. He laughed. "You won't make one."

Feeling dizzy, I straightened up. It was then I realized I was in trouble. I felt the blood dripping down my back, the raging pain in my left shoulder, and my utter exhaustion. I felt the adrenaline drain from me when I stood for a minute to catch my balance. Talbot looked up at me, grinning. "You're not going to make it, Joe. This is the end of the line."

"Not yet, Talbot. I'm going downriver, and you're going with me," I said.

"You try the river. I'm staying here," he said. "You don't have the strength to lift me to your shoulders."

"Perhaps," I said, conceding the point. "But I can drag you to the falls, and the river will carry us the rest of the way," I said.

It was then I noticed blood spray over Talbot's face. I went down on my knees to examine him. No wounds.

I sat back when Talbot said, "It's yours, and you're losing it fast."

I reached back with one hand and felt my left shoulder blade. It was furrowed, and my hand came back smeared with blood. I was about to ask Talbot to take my shirt and staunch the flow, but he had anticipated my request and barked, "No! The cat was a disappointment, but in the end he gave me what I wanted. It's just going to take another half hour. You're dying, Little Fish."

I just stared and thought about leaving him. Talbot laughed as if crazed. But then a ray of sunshine fell on my back like a soothing hand. Encouraged, I realized I was thirsty and, crawling on all fours to the cut, drank my fill of cold water and splashed more on my face and back. My head cleared, and feeling started returning to my left hand.

I stood and said, "Time to go, Talbot." Standing over him, I grabbed his left wrist and started pulling him. He winced.

"Your face is turning gray, Little Fish," he said. "It won't be long."

"This could still be your lucky day, Talbot. Even if I don't bleed to death, the worst of the river is yet to come," I said cheerfully.

"My money's on you bleeding to death," he replied.

As I pulled him toward the lip of the Third Falls, I looked to my left. The raven was gone. It did not matter, for the real killer was ahead of us . . . the Fourth Falls.

RAVEN

"IS THE CAT LICKING ITS WOUNDS, PAUGUCK?" I ASKED, spiraling down to sit next to him on an exposed sand bank just below the Third Falls.

"It dare not, Kahgahgee," Pauguck said. "The knife point is very sharp, and it cuts the cat's mouth whenever it tries to grasp the point between its teeth. It gags on its own blood."

"Will it return to the river today?" I asked. "There is still the Fourth Falls."

"I doubt it. The blade drove through bone," Pauguck said, shaking his head. "It needs help to free it. And as you know there is none . . . that is . . . unless you decide to become its surgeon." Pauguck looked over at me.

"I do not trust the cat enough to get that close," I croaked.

"That is the first time today you've made sense," he said, smiling.

Frustrated with Pauguck's lack of concern, I blurted out, "Are you just going to sit here?"

"That's what I do best," he said, smiling. He was enjoying himself. "Besides, how has not waiting helped you? For all your efforts, you have still not breakfasted on the white men's blue eyes."

"The morning is not over yet," I said angrily. Pauguck's taunting was beginning to irritate me.

"It's over for you," he said, gloating. "The woods will be filling up with people soon."

Ignoring him, I said, "The one-footed man was right when he said the able-bodied man was lucky."

Pauguck surveyed me. "So we will not be talking anymore about the white men's blue eyes."

"Not for the moment," I said.

"Okay, we will now be talking about luck," Pauguck said.

"Yes," I replied.

"When you say the able-bodied man was lucky, all you are telling me is that you have no explanation for what happened between him and the cat," Pauguck said. "You're just telling me that you are ignorant."

"Go ahead. Be cryptic!" I screamed at him. "I am just trying to carry on a civilized conversation."

Pauguck stared at me, his eyes serious. "I am sorry, Kahgahgee, for my rudeness. Please forgive me," he said.

"That's better," I said.

"Then, is what you mean by luck the outcome of numerous forces with so many possible variants in behavior that it is impossible to predict the outcome? Is that what you mean?" Pauguck asked.

"Now we are getting somewhere," I said.

"And to carry it one step farther, are you also saying that the able-bodied man unknowingly stumbled into guiding the most favorable forces which then set off a helpful chain reaction to ultimately defeat the cat?"

"Yes, exactly," I said.

"But you cannot tell me which forces he pushed, if any, nor how the chain reaction sequenced," Pauguck said with great intensity.

"Exactly," I said.

"So am I to conclude that you do not know anything about the defeat of the cat, and that when you do not know the reason for such an outcome, you call it luck," Pauguck said innocently.

"Why do you taunt me?" I asked, feigning defeat.

"I am just reasoning with you, old friend," he said in a conciliatory voice.

"You think too much," I said.

"Perhaps," he replied.

We both sat together silent for a time, looking at the river. "I see that you have stopped following the cat. Whom have you decided to follow now?" I asked.

"I have not made up my mind. There were voices above the Third Falls that I should investigate. But then again, both the white men are approaching death. They passed here minutes ago. Neither looked good. Their deaths are not far off. Either the Fourth Falls, blood poisoning, or loss of blood will end their lives," he said thoughtfully. "I should be there to gather their spirits."

"You need to make your choice," I said. "With luck, and I say with luck, you will make the right choice."

Pauguck smiled at me and said, "What would I do without you? You keep me on point. It is always your point, but it is still a point."

"So admit it. When I say you need luck, you agree with me," I said.

"No, you are only reminding me that I have not thought deeply enough," he said. "So please leave me now. I wish to think."

"One more question."

"Go ahead—ask it."

"How could the cat lose?"

"It became obsessed with the one-footed man," he said. "The able-bodied man believes that it was the cat's obsession with the one-footed man that clouded the cat's judgment. And so the cat risked everything," he said. "That is what the able-bodied man believes, but I do not believe that to be the case."

"So where did the cat go wrong?"

"It listened to you. That's where its obsession began," Pauguck said, deadly serious and fixing me with his colorless eyes. "When you became the cat's ally, it became overconfident." Then Pauguck stood up. "Yes, no doubt it was you that brought about the cat's end." Then he laughed and said, "Or to put it in words you will understand . . . you brought the cat bad luck."

I flew off, croaking wildly into the dawn.

Pauguck turned downstream, hiking after the white men. He shouted up at me, "You have embarked on a dangerous course, Kahgahgee!"

He walked slowly downstream, giggling to himself as he went and muttering. "Perhaps it will not be long when you and I will make the journey to the Blessed Isles."

I shouted down to him, "The cat should not have snarled before setting on the white men! That was where it went wrong."

"It is all the same!" Pauguck shouted back.

I resolved to prove him wrong.

And the Escanaba would help me.

So often it set a feast for me in the past.

CAROL

Aʙᴏᴜᴛ ᴛᴇɴ ᴍɪɴᴜᴛᴇs, Mᴏᴍ," Vᴀʟ sᴀɪᴅ ᴏᴠᴇʀ ʜɪs shoulder.

"Do you remember the last time we were here?" I asked, breathing hard through my bandana now black, caked with ash.

"It was just before I flew out for Iraq!" Val shouted back.

"Yes," I said. "In your honor, Mr. Larson invited us to fish the river and have dinner with him afterwards."

"I remember," Val said. "He was a World War II vet." He added after catching his breath, "We cooked him a trout dinner with new potatoes out of his garden."

"Probably the last trout he ate," I said. "He died a month later of a heart attack."

"Out here?"

"Yes, he was sitting in his rocker when they found him. It was the way he wanted to go."

Val fell silent as we started up the last ridge before the river. He too was breathing hard, but his pace did not slow. And I kept up with him as best I could. Once we were over the ridge, the camp road forked. The right fork swung in a wide arc down to Larson's yard and house, now a leveled jumble of burned timbers and water piping and a wood stove sitting in the middle. The left fork dead-ended in an old logging road, which led directly to the Third Falls.

Two minutes on the logging road and we would be at the falls.

"Left fork," Val shouted back.

"I'm behind you."

We were both puffing hard coming down the exposed granite ridge before the river. Once Val looked back as I took off my bandana, snapped it out, and flipped it over. I did it without losing a step. He did not comment, and we pushed ourselves into a run.

As we turned into the left fork, Val thought he heard screaming. It was high pitched, and a few minutes later, it was followed by crazed laughter.

"Do you hear voices, Mom?"

"Yes. Sounded like Dad and Talbot." I listened for more and added, "I'm not sure."

Val shouted, but there was no response. As we neared the river, only the splashing sound of the Third Falls filled the dawn. When Val saw running paw prints in the ash, he pulled out the ax and began to run faster.

"Cougar prints?"

"Could be. We'd better hurry," Val replied anxiously.

Sliding down the last fold of granite to the empty apron fronting the falls, Val slowly circled about, eyes intent on the ground. I joined him and went down on one knee, checking bloody paw tracks and an ominous spray of blood.

Catching my breath, I said, "Cougar prints. It's bleeding and left here alone . . . limping."

Val agreed. "Not long ago. Five minutes at most. Dad got away."

"Not cleanly. Bloody hand prints," I said, breathing hard. "They lead to the cut where someone, probably Dad, splashed in the water. It looks like he was crawling on all fours after the cougar attack. But once he drank, he was able to stand up and walked back to where you see the blood spray." I kept my voice clinical. Backtracking, I surveyed the blood spray more closely. "A body was dragged toward the falls smearing both the cougar prints and a trail of blood drops. Probably Dad dragging Talbot."

Following the drag marks to the lip of the falls, Val said, "They went down the falls and are in the river below."

"Yes, Joe's alive, but the blood drops are large. He can't bleed like that for long."

"What's your guess?" Val asked.

"Twenty minutes before he loses consciousness. Maybe less."

"Are you sure, Mom?" Val asked grimly.

"This is no time for optimism."

"The Fourth Falls is a little more than a mile away. The river's fast here on down."

"If you ride the current, it's not more than a twenty, twenty-five minute trip," Val said. "We need to get downriver fast."

"The Fourth Falls is no place for the weak," I muttered.

Val started to trot back up the apron to the logging road. "The old road joins up with deer trails running along the river. Passable except for a bit of swamp."

"I've been on them," I agreed. The trot became a run back to the road. There we struck out following the nearest deer trail skirting the river.

"The swamp is a little tricky; the deer trails wander around. Dad and I did it in the dark once and got lost," Val shouted over his shoulder.

"I've hiked them several closing days with your father."

We then heard a croaking raven downriver. It was angry, and its cries echoed for miles.

JOE

ᎦLIDING DOWN THE FALLS, I FELT LIGHT-HEADED. WE cleared the short rapid to where the river began a compact course of twists and turns. Mostly gravel, the Escanaba slips right and left in turn after turn, sculpting neatly forested curves as it slaloms down to the Fourth Falls. There are few straightaways. For the canoeists, those few give only temporary respite from swinging their paddles right and then left in the quickly shifting currents. Swing too soon and the shallows hang you up. Too late and you are bouncing off rocky banks.

My thirst told me I was bleeding badly. I had hoped the Escanaba's cold water would slow my circulation and allow time for coagulation. I would then have enough blood to crawl out of the river just before the Fourth Falls. That was my plan. Then I could rest and carry Talbot to the 480 bridge and the EMTs. Pulling up in the slower water of a shallow, I watched the threads of water drip off my back. Hoping for a faint pink, a bright scarlet showed instead. Too much fresh blood. The river may have slowed the bleeding, but not enough. I started looking around for something to staunch my wounds. Nothing, so I washed my bloody shirt out, carefully lowered it over my back, and pulled it tight about me like a corset. Too little, too late.

Pushing back into the main current, my thirst was still with me.

I drank more water, but even then I knew it was in a losing fight. And that thought tired me more than anything else. I looked at Talbot. He caught my glance and smiled through bared teeth. Blood in the water. Before the end, he would strangle me when I did not have enough strength to fight back.

"Have you guessed yet?" I asked.

"No need to guess," he said. "Soon you will be too weak to keep me in tow. I am debating whether, when that moment comes, I should just let myself loose and let the Fourth Falls kill me or whether I should kill you and make my way down to the Fourth Falls delighted. Right now I am of a mind to kill you. It would give me one last pleasure."

"Either way, the Fourth Falls will finish the job," I said. Scanning the shoreline, I looked for something to stop my bleeding.

Talbot followed my eyes. "There's no help out here. You need pressure bandages and a nurse."

Carol's expert hands would know how to end the bleeding. I tried to imagine that picture. But instead I saw her bending over me, mourning . . . my dead body, laid out, intact, bloodless, and white as a sugar sand beach.

"People like you are so predictable, Little Fish," Talbot said, disgusted. "You are thinking of your saintly Carol, aren't you?"

"Yes."

"She's home picking out her next husband," he said. "Someone who can support her."

"No," I said, more to myself than to Talbot.

I must have sounded defeated, for Talbot ignored my denial. "She's the practical type."

I fell silent again and scanned the shoreline, thinking of Carol. Talbot chattered away. I paid no attention until he slapped me on my bleeding shoulder. The pain jolted me. "You should be listening to me, Little Fish. You'll learn something."

"Whatever you say."

"We're back to that," Talbot said. "You have just made up my mind for me. I will kill you when you become too weak to swim."

With that, he took to humming the theme from *Jaws*. And to tire me, he began testing the buckles on the wading belt. I wrestled his hands away and wound a single knot with the loose end.

And I put my mind elsewhere. In those first months after my father's death, it was not persistence that won Carol over. I did call her. Often. Occasionally our schedules permitted a dinner or a movie. Just a few hours. And afterward I was left wondering when to call again. At first, the turndowns were humiliating, but I checked my pride because Carol had not led me to expect otherwise. I had been warned. I knew she liked me because she told me she did, and I trusted her word. I always trusted her word. Very early, I caught on to not going down the calendar looking for a date. She never planned to go out farther than a day ahead. If I pressed, she would say, "Joe, I don't know. Stop trying to pin me down." So when I called, I asked simply, "How does tonight look?" Sometimes I might push for more than a tonight if it were a weekend. When she had time, we met— sometimes just for coffee or a brief walk.

Carol did stop in to see my mother. But it was always the three of us. Afterward, Mom would say to me, "You should marry that girl. It would make Dad and me so happy."

"I don't think Dad cares at this point," I would reply.

"Hush," my mother would say. "You know so little."

The snatched moments went on for more than a year. Then one day while I was waiting for Carol at the hospital, I saw a mother and son enter the emergency room. They were downcast, and I could hear them talking about "Dad." They could have been me and my mother a year earlier. I thought about what our last days with my father would have been like if Carol had not been there. And with that realization, I thought of all the people to whom she was important, as important as she was to us. And I realized how in pressing Carol for her time I was denying others the solace she had brought us. I was working to deny those now suffering the touch of her kindness, and I came to the conclusion that her work was more important than the small joys I snatched from our few hours together.

When she appeared in the lobby of the hospital, I said with finality, "Carol, I need to let you go."

Surprised, she waited for more—perhaps a carefully drawn speech calling an end to our dating. But I had nothing else to say.

To end my discomfort, she said, "Perhaps we now have something to talk about." My eyes must have brightened because she repeated, "Something to *talk* about," emphasizing the word *talk*.

I do not remember much of what was said that day over coffee. I told her about the mother and son I had just seen at the hospital door and haltingly explained what I meant about letting her go. She took it in, and I do remember she smiled and stroked my hand afterward. More important she insisted I keep calling, and her voice developed a lilt when I did call her. I don't believe we met any more frequently, but I sensed she looked forward more avidly to our meetings. As did I.

But it was only after I discovered my life's calling that Carol and I became a couple. I cannot say I ever had a career as an engineer. I worked as an engineer when I could get the work. Occasionally, small companies hired me to read blueprints or do drafting. Not enough work for a steady income. I spent most of the year logging and doing home construction.

I discovered my calling one Sunday afternoon when Carol telephoned the house. She was ill and called to say she would not be able to come over for dinner.

"It sounds like you have not been taking care of yourself," I said.

"No time for that."

"What are you doing for dinner tonight?" I asked, concerned.

"A can of soup. Joe, I need to rest. I'll call in a few days when I am better."

"Leave the front door unlocked," I said. "My soup is better than any that comes out of a can."

"Don't bother, Joe," she said, although I heard gratitude in her voice.

"No bother," I said. "I'll be there in an hour."

It was whitefish chowder. And when I mounted the stairs to her bedroom, I carried a hot bowl with crackers and tea on a tray.

I knocked at a few upstairs doors but knew I found the right one when I heard her say, "Come in, Joe."

"Where shall I put it?" I asked.

She shifted to sit up. I plumped a pillow and put it behind her back. Placing the tray on her lap, I said, "You know you need someone to look after you."

Tears formed in the corners of her eyes. "You're taking advantage of my weak condition, Mr. Joseph McCartney."

"Would you have it any other way?"

She laughed, "I've been thinking about that lately."

I made light conversation and left when she finished her chowder, but not before I said, "I'll look in on you tomorrow. I think I have found my calling."

"Thanks, Joe." She smiled and slid down beneath her covers. "Please turn the light off as you go out." She coughed several times and then said, "The chowder was perfect."

Over our next coffee, Carol said, "The old house is lonely."

More as a jest, I said, "We could always get married."

"I think that's the perfect solution," she said.

I was stunned and fumbled out, "Are you sure?" Carol looked questioningly at me, and I hurriedly said, "Of course I'll marry you . . . I want to marry you. But I'm curious why you're asking now?"

"I spend so much time with the dying. Each death reminds me what a lonely act dying is." Then she stared off, her face sad. "Living does not have to be that way. Joe, I don't want to live alone anymore."

"I don't know if I'm the right person for you."

"I've always loved you, Joe."

Talbot shouted, "When are you going to stop thinking about your wife?"

"I never stop thinking about my wife."

Talbot had no reply.

RAVEN

"HAVE YOU SEEN THE GREAT CAT, KAHGAHGEE?" PAU-
guck shouted up to me. He was walking the riverbank, shadowing the white men while I was patrolling the river between the
Third Falls and the 480 bridge.

"Yes," I said, landing in the opening of a blackened tree. Still
warm, the tree smoked from a slow fire gutting its core.

"Where is it?"

"You want to be there when its spirit seeks Ponemah?" I asked,
cocking my head to look down at him.

"Yes," he said. "It will need me then."

"It has climbed the pinnacle overlooking the Fourth Falls," I
croaked.

"Did it leave a blood trail?"

"Unfortunately," I said, shaking my head. "It tried to climb a
tree, but the pain in its right paw prevented it. The only refuge left
for it is on the pinnacle."

"The cat will have hungry visitors if it does not hide soon."

"The cat keeps working his teeth over the knife tip trying to
dislodge it. It may get lucky and pull it out," I said.

"Luck. There's that word again," Pauguck said impatiently.

"Exactly," I croaked, pleased I had provoked Pauguck once
again. "And that could happen any minute, and when it does,

Raven's Fire

the cat will return to the river seeking the white men," I added cheerfully.

Pauguck did not share my enthusiasm. "For the time being, I will continue to follow the white men. The able-bodied man continues to weaken from the loss of blood, and the one-footed man grows feebler as his legs die," Pauguck said. "The one-footed man puts on a good show, but both white men are in a close race for my services."

"That is how I see it," I croaked in agreement. "I may not need the cat. Even if the white men stay alive, they will not have the strength to get past the Fourth Falls."

"True. So many spirits I have led away from the base of the falls. Sitting on the river bank or perched on boulders, they look about dazed, unsure of themselves after their death," Pauguck said thoughtfully. "Anishinaabe and white alike. The river surprised them."

"Yes, the rapid just above the falls sucks in the unwary and wrestles them to their death," I said, squatting to take off. "I've enjoyed a few picnics below the falls."

Pauguck interrupted me. "One last question, Kahgahgee. I heard voices coming from the Third Falls. Who are they?"

"You are becoming lazy, Pauguck," I said. "Find out for yourself."

"And leave the white men alone?" he said accusingly. "You would like that, wouldn't you?"

I shook out my wings in disdain. "How your mind is poisoned against me, Pauguck."

"All right, then tell me, O Great Kahgahgee, who are the people at the Third Falls?"

"Since you are showing the proper respect, I will tell you. It is the green-eyed woman and the hazel-eyed young man, and they are hiking in this direction. But they go slowly because they are lost," I said. "It will be a while before they get here."

"Truly?" Pauguck asked, surprised.

"Truly."

"Now I have a dilemma. Stay with the white men, or fall in beside the green-eyed woman."

"That is what I was hoping for. Always happy to make your life

195

difficult," I said, mounting into the air. "Any of their eyes would be a prize."

I heard a commotion from the 480 bridge. Flying closer, I saw three black vans arrive and a dozen men with duffel bags dismount and stand beside them. And I heard the short man dressed all in black command, "Suit up." He was handing out maps. "Then check your sector," he said. The flash of his shoes in the dawn light nearly blinded me.

CAROL

*I*F THE SUN IS IN FRONT OF US, THEN THE RIVER MUST BE to our left," I said. ·

We had come to the swamp guarding the Fourth Falls. This is where the Escanaba would do its worst. I saw a desolate landscape. Before the fire, it held green tag alder and grass hummocks on its borders and acres of stagnant open water with lily pads in its midst. As an unhappy painter might with a turpentine rag, the fire wiped all green from the canvas. Now it was blacks and grays with thick dark mists hanging over the open water and a dawn sun like a smear of honey dripping down burnt toast. Protected from the wind, the smoke and ash had not fully settled here, and the sun dimmed as we tramped down and down into the muck and half light.

Lighter than Val, I had the advantage. "Let me take the lead, Val."

Val understood. "Okay, Mom."

The swamp's large hummocks floated on a mobile shoreline of grass and silt deposits. They rippled outward as we jumped from one to the next. Missing a hummock left us thigh deep in clinging muck. More time wasted pulling out.

I picked a route between a tag alder thicket on one side and the quaking bog on the other. It wandered. There was no alternative— more wasted time. The swamp was silent except for our muffled footsteps and the rustling of blistered tag alders tugging at our clothes. "I keep hoping we'll hear the river."

Val muttered, "I'm not sure where we are. All we can do is hike toward the dawn. The river can't be far off."

I too was uncertain how close the river was. Joe and I had fought through this swamp more than once. But each time we hiked it, we fell back blindly on our intuitive sense of direction. There were no landmarks, and each time through, it seemed we took a different route. I remember Joe saying once, "Keep going left because that is where the river is." Thus this morning, whenever in doubt, I pressed left.

Our goal was a ridge bounding the swamp. A short two-minute hike across that ridge, one last left turn, a five-minute walk, and we would come out at the foot of the boulder slide just below the Fourth Falls. "I smell the river," I said, perspiring, my shirt caked with ash and sweat.

"Me too," Val said, sniffing.

Veering left again, we left the hummocks and open shore. We pushed hard through the clutter of black spruce, cedar, and tag alder blowdowns, and the tangled thickets slowed us. Often the only way through meant grappling with charred tree trunks and branches pulling us or crawling on our hands and knees. Our arms and chests were soon black with the soot.

I kept checking my watch. The risk of sprained ankles and fractured legs increased, but our window of twenty minutes was disappearing fast. The feeling we were losing the race drove me beyond safe judgment. The ash was not as deep here, so I pulled the bandana down from my mouth, took gulps of air, and kept a few yards' interval ahead of Val. I reminded myself of Joe's words: "Be deliberate." But there was no time to be deliberate. Head down and trotting along, I kept fixed on the nearest level, dry place to step.

So often wading the river, the changes in stream bottom and riverbank were obvious consequences of the laws of gravity and attraction. Simple physics and geology told you what to expect. Not so for the swamp. Its dangers lay underneath our feet, concealed, and each step trod a new danger, a new choice. Pressed on by fleeing time, every step became a hasty decision with no guidance for the step coming after. It was as if I were skating the irrational, making sense of it through my forward progress alone. I was sliding along the surface of chaos. Blind intuition decided my course, keeping me barely less than frantic. I gave up thinking, judging, because I knew that would interrupt my confident flow, my walking stick.

Val heard me breathing hard. He was measuring my endurance, wondering when I would give up, too tired and too out of breath. "Should I spell you, Mom?"

Resenting Val's inspection, I shouted, "Each time we talk, we lose a step!"

I guessed Val would leave me on the ridge when we found it. From the ridge to the falls was a five-minute hike through light forest and open ground. There was little time, and I knew we both pictured Joe caught in the powerful undertow of the Fourth Falls. The ridge should be right there in front of us. Instead, all about was only scorched tag alder, downed spruce, and swamp.

The ridge was farther to the left than I remembered. But just as we considered backtracking left again, the slope of the ridge appeared ahead. "We're at the ridge, Val!" I shouted. "See that finger of rock there? That's the pinnacle. The falls are maybe five minutes from here."

"I see it," he said.

We clawed our way through the last of the burnt tag alders and ran frantically upward. Through mostly sand and loose rock, we climbed, slipping to the summit.

Reaching the top first, Val pointed directly ahead. "We stay on this course 'til we reach the other side."

I was breathing heavily again, and Val opened his mouth to speak. I sensed this was where he would leave me. "Don't say it," I said. "I'm not slowing you up!"

"No, but you will. Your reserves are gone. This is the safest place to leave you. I can't predict what's ahead."

"We don't have time to argue, Val," I said, bluffing. Val was right.

I was out of breath and beyond my reserves. I bent over gasping with my hands on my knees, noisily sucking in air.

"It's on you," he said, then turned and started running across a flat expanse of sand and burnt-out scrub fir. The ground was even here, and he lengthened out his stride. I followed, but with shorter legs, I fell behind his sprint. Breathing even harder now, my legs felt wobbly. Perhaps I should have rested on the ridge. Val slowed only when he came to the down slope off the ridge. It was steep, and I followed him, stutter-stepping on down.

"We go left now!" Val shouted back. "Don't stray far from the ridge."

"I know."

"There was a trail here once," Val said. "It doesn't matter. We just keep the ridge hard on our left shoulder."

The sun was coming up. The honey golden dawn promised a bright day.

JOE

W E'LL BE PULLING OFF THE RIVER FOR A FEW MINUTES, Frank," I said. "We need to warm up your legs."

"I don't feel them anymore," he replied. "I say we keep going until you run out of blood."

I scanned the riverbank.

"Are you hallucinating? There's nothing out there," Talbot said angrily.

"You're probably right."

"Stop doing that," he replied, his anger mounting.

"Whatever you say, Frank," I said, smiling to myself.

Talbot composed himself and then hissed, "It will make my day to look down into your bulging eyes as I strangle you."

Ignoring him, I said, "I see our pullout, Big Fish."

It was a gravel beach dominated by a smoldering aspen. The aspen was large, almost two feet in diameter. The fire had consumed its branches, and now charred black, the tree's thick trunk was hidden.

Dragging Talbot up the beach, I settled him against a small boulder. His fingernails were violet and both his lower legs a grayish blue. I took the socks off his foot and stump, washed them, and left them to dry in the sun. The necrotic foot was a dark blue, almost black. The stump no better. I had lost the race to keep Talbot's lower legs. Kneeling down next to him, I pulled up his pant legs and inspected his upper legs. They were beginning to color. As I inspected them, Talbot threw a handful of gravel at me.

"Leave me alone!" he screamed.

"It won't be long now, Frank," I said. "The Fourth Falls is a few hundred yards downstream. You can hear them if you stop talking." Talbot refused to look at me, "Less than a mile below falls . . . ," I said.

"We'll not make it that far," he said. "Just leave me."

I stood up and walked down the beach toward the smoldering aspen. Just before reaching it, I looked back, checking the gravel for splashes of blood. They were there. Large and red. The size of quarters. Also I noticed Talbot close his eyes and smile to himself. His head lolled and his breathing became regular. He was exhausted.

Searching the beach, I found a rock shard about the size and shape of a machete. Kneeling at the base of the smoldering aspen, I worked the rock up and down the trunk, scraping away charred wood.

Beneath the charring, the tree glowed hot, the deep red of freshly butchered meat. I blew on it and saw a flame flicker and then die. I untied my shirt, turned, and sat with my back to the tree. Judging as best I could the location of my wounds, I placed the left side of my back gingerly against the glowing trunk. The pain was intense. After a count of three, I pulled away and stood up. My knees nearly gave way. The smell of burning flesh, my flesh, hung in the air and gagged me. Steadying my legs, I took a deep breath, walked down to the river, and splashed water on my face and over my back.

I turned and checked my tracks. A few small drips of blood. I reached behind and tenderly felt across my shoulder blade. My fingers walked the cauterized crust until they came to an open patch of wounds near my spine. Returning to the tree, I scraped it again, blew on it, and again sat with my back to it, this time shifting my position to make sure the patch of open wounds met up squarely with the red glow of the trunk. I leaned back into the tree again and silently ticked off another three count. Pulling away, I tried to stand. This time, I slumped to my knees. So I started for the river on all fours. I never made it.

My brain became a black void, sucking in all my fears. I believed I felt Talbot's hands around my throat. I believed I was coughing out my last breath as I drowned in a pool of blood. I believed I heard the crunch of the cat's feet on the gravel nearby. I believed I heard a yipping coyote running closer.

And in the night of my worst fears, I felt the pounding of my heart—a slow, sure thud, like the tread of a booted sentry. And in my pain, I looked up beseechingly into that sentry's face, and it was Carol, who looked down tenderly and said, "Sleep, Joe. I will guard you."

And I dreamed. First of the day I married Carol. It was a short two months after our decision to be married. My mother was helping me dress for church. She was smiling. "You two have made your father and me very happy."

I knew enough by then not to make light of her references to my father. I replied instead, "Good, Mom. You are always welcome, you know."

"Don't worry about me."

"You know I will," I said. "The nights Carol's out, I'll stop over. And of course the three of us will have our Sunday dinners together just as before."

There were tears in her eyes. "I'm so happy."

"There will be speculation on why our marriage was rushed," I said. "I'm sorry to bring that on you."

She looked up sharply and said with an edge in her voice, "What do those people know? For me, the day I long hoped for has come." And in a loud voice, she began to sing, "Ring in . . . the larger heart, the kindlier hand."

Carol and I shared a large four-poster bed. From the beginning, I was reticent about our love making. I felt our sleeping together broke a taboo. At first, I attributed my feelings of reluctance to me thinking of her as a sister. She had been a member of our family, a true daughter to my father and mother, a better daughter than I was a son. There were days, even of late, when I saw the problems between us as the problems an estranged brother and sister might have.

Carol noticed but did not say anything. We did make love, but it was often awkward. And afterward, I felt defeated and empty. There were the few moments when the sight of her fed my passions to the point they overrode my inhibitions. And on reflection I realized that these were the moments when breaking the taboo brought delicious arousal rather than a sense of guilt. On those occasions, I could not shake the feeling that we had stolen a pleasure. That we had tasted a forbidden love, thwarting an imaginary, suspicious husband or father. And I enjoyed those moments.

I brought this up with Carol one afternoon while we were cooking together in the kitchen. "Could you help me understand something?"

"Of course," she said.

I explained my feeling that our lovemaking was to my mind like breaking a taboo and concluded by saying, "I think I feel too close to you for us to be sharing the same bed."

Carol laughed. "Well, stop having those feelings."

"I'm serious," I said.

"I can see that," she replied. "You cannot engineer lovemaking."

"So you believe my education is against me," I said.

"No, Joe. What I mean to say is that you are not a simple person. You try to be simple, but you aren't. You struggle with yourself," she said thoughtfully. "It is too much to think that your struggles with your feelings wouldn't affect us."

"I'm just asking that my feelings for you carry the ardor of a new love," I said.

"You might want to rethink that, Joe," she said. "Ours is an old love."

It was something to think about, and I dropped the subject.

Carol was right. We had fallen in love as adolescents under the diving raft at Blue Lake, and the experiences of the years between those days and today matured that love until now, when the mutual respect of a lasting marriage indelibly marked it. For me, that respect was rooted in Carol's kindness, her unfailing kindness. It drove her out the door on snowy, cold mornings, and it called her away from family barbecues on summer weekends. What I had feared as the dinner guest at the Campbells' became the anchor of my love for her. And I felt privileged to live with her tender, kind heart.

Another dream bloomed in the black void. It was from our senior year, from a day I was watching Carol's baseball team. It was a home game, and she was dressed in her whites. The score was close, her team down a single run. It was the last inning, and she was the leadoff batter. She hit a low drive over second base. Misjudging the flight of the ball, the center fielder was a little slow charging it.

Carol rounded first base, her eyes fixed on the center fielder. The visitor bobbled the one hopper. Her spikes throwing up spurts of dust, Carol dug toward second base. There was the slide, and Carol was bouncing up, safe and standing on the bag.

She stood there, breathing hard, hands on hips, face aglow, flushed, and triumphant. The life and heat coursing through her awed me. Even then, I asked myself, "How could I ever presume I was worthy to share her love?" Yet after the game, I was the first person she found, and she took my hand, laughing about the win. That day, I felt I was in the presence of a deity. And that is the same feeling I have every day waking up next to her. It is so simple, but it is the most important truth of my life. The best moment of my day is the moment I wake up next to her.

Our so simple life together. Forever after, I saw the two of us as vanishing points in infinite space, dust motes dancing to the music of the spheres.

The black void that held me cleared, and Carol was leaning down and whispering, "Wake up, Joe."

I heard gravel rattle and a shrieking followed by a blow on my chest. Talbot was screaming, "That bird ate my toes!"

A feather traced my eyes sockets, as if measuring them. I blinked and looked up into the beak and black eyes of a raven. It was standing on my chest, greedily looking down into my eyes. Just as its heavy beak came down, I turned my head and felt it strike my right ear.

I rolled over, rose to my knees, scooped up some rocks, and started throwing them at the bird. The raven rose up, hovered in place before me, and feinted in and out, going for my head. I kept throwing rocks at it. When one hit home, the raven flew off downriver. My ear was bleeding.

"It ate my toes!" Talbot kept screaming.

"Be right there," I said groggily.

I reached behind and felt the tightness in my back and checked the ground where I had lain for bloodstains. There were none. I went to the river for a drink and then returned to Talbot. He had scuttled closer to me while I was passed out. And a large rock was near his outstretched hand. I kicked the rock away, knelt down, and gently picked up his foot. Only spikes of white bone showed. His five toes were picked clean.

"This is strange," I said.

"Is that all you have to say?" he said angrily. "Strange?"

"You didn't need them," I finally replied without sympathy.

"They were mine!"

"Next time I see the raven, I'll explain that to it."

Talbot lay back. "You're no longer losing blood," Talbot said. "You might make it to the Highway 480 bridge."

"You'll be with me," I said pointedly.

"Maybe," he said. "You get me back. What then? Put in for a reward?" Talbot's sentences were becoming more and more clipped. He was tired.

"I don't want your money," I said, an edge to my voice. "I've told you I don't like money. Especially your money. I don't know where you got it."

Talbot sat up. "What about the money you believe I cheated your father out of?" he asked slyly.

I faced him and said, "Too late for that. It won't do my father any good." Talbot ignored me, so I added, "My father's pain is not for sale."

"People like you always have your hand out," he said cynically.

"What did you say?" I growled, jarred to my very core.

"People like you always have your hand out," he repeated vehemently.

"I am not going to say this again, Frank. I don't want your money." My voice grew hard. "I don't like money." The pool of resentment buried deep within me stirred, a breeze moaning across its surface.

"Afraid of the truth?" Talbot asked innocently. "Everyone likes money."

I knew he was riding me, but that knowledge did not dampen the cataclysm of murderous rage forming within me. "You speak the truth only when it's convenient," I said.

"If you don't put your hand out, your little wife will put hers out," he said, studying my face.

"Okay, Frank, a short lesson," I said. "I'm going to put my hand out." Extending my hand palm up toward him, I asked, "What are you going to put in it should I appear at your front door?"

"What?" he said. This was not the response he expected. He was now playing my game.

The storm was upon me, and a bellow from my darkest recesses demanded I strangle his voice and end all conversation. I was shouting. "Don't play dumb, Frank! What are you going to put in my hand when I show up at your front door?" Shaking, my rage erupted, blinding me. Talbot's face became a distant blur and his voice hardly more than noise.

"I don't know," I heard him say.

I slapped him hard. "Wrong answer, Frank."

Talbot's face colored, and fear played across his features. I wanted to slap him again to break off his jaw and end his insults. Instead, I sneered, "Let's try this again," and extended my hand to him again. "What are you going to put in it?" I was hardly coherent. My words deafened me to his response.

All I heard was "I don't know." He said other things, but that was all I heard.

I slapped him again, harder this time. "Wrong answer again, Frank." I waited and then said, "Shall we keep playing this game?"

"No," he whimpered. "Just give me the answer."

"Frank, the answer is . . . *nothing*!" I screamed in his face. "Do you get that? Nothing! . . . nothing! . . . nothing!"

I extended my hand again palm up. Talbot recoiled in fear. I moved in close. "So what will you put in my hand?" My cavern of rage howled, *Slap him harder!*

Talbot looked up and said hurriedly, "Nothing."

Seeing the fear in his eyes, I relented, "Very good, Frank." But I was as shaken as he was, and I could not look into his eyes for long. Instead, I looked down at my shaking hands and then at his necrotic legs. I saw the white bone tips where his toes had been and flies circling his dead foot. I thought of how he had never spoken with his father. And I felt disgusted with my self-righteousness . . . disgusted with my jealousies . . . disgusted with my rage. And I felt shame.

"I'm sorry, Frank," I said.

Talbot began to weep. And I sat down beside him and wept with him. I wept some for what he would face when he returned. But I wept most for the destruction my anger always brought. I thought of my father and Carol and how my anger fueled my jealousy of their friendship. I had ridden my rage until I believed it had died under me. I was mistaken.

I took a deep breath, blew it out, and said contritely, "Forgive me, Frank." Then I calmed, because I accepted the truth that Talbot and people like him were shrewder and quicker than me, but once I acknowledged that fact, it no longer mattered. The chaos of my conception brought me Carol and Val. Vibrant love. And there was so much more. Whatever I touched by the Escanaba was seething with life. I looked out at the river and felt its eternal energy. Visions of my mother and father flooded my mind, and I saw Val with a trout on his line and Carol whooping at a strike. My mind went back, and I saw Carol standing on second base, the triumphant, glowing girl she still is to this day, the woman I dared never believe I deserved. The universe had favored me after all, but I had been blind to that truth. My secret had blinded me. I reached down to get a hold of my secret to study it, to examine its lethal energy, to understand how it warped me for so many years, and to slay it. But when I dug down, I could not find it. It was gone. With that knowledge, I felt a peace, as if I were a child again swimming one warm August afternoon at Blue Lake.

"Is this a confession?" he mumbled.

"I suppose."

"To me?"

"You're the only one handy."

"You're such a fool," he said, and his weeping ended abruptly.

I smiled. Talbot had recovered.

"So you're going to save me from myself," he said.

I did not answer right away. I thought of the EMTs at the road-block. I thought of Val's comrades dying in Iraq. I thought of all the men and women who served in Iraq and Afghanistan doing their part to make a better world. I thought of Carol and all those in home care and hospice work getting up early to drive dark roads to minister to their patients. And finally, I thought of all those I knew who served others without encouragement, without compensation—concerned neighbors, children and grandchildren, church ladies, caring class-mates, and friends. These were my people. I had no doubt of that.

And I said, "It's what people like me do." I handed him my last candy bar.

Talbot had not expected my answer nor the candy bar. Con-fused, he stared at the bar in his hand.

So I said, "In the end, it's always people like me who save people like you."

We both sat quietly and looked out at the river together. Talbot bit off chunks of chocolate.

Then I said, "It's not over yet. We still have the Fourth Falls." I paused, looked over at Talbot, and then laughed. "It's a killer."

Talbot came alive and said, "Then let's go."

I tied the wading belt around us and carried Talbot to the river. I saw that his lower legs had not pinked up. He was dying. A mile or so to go, maybe half an hour more on the river. If I delivered a corpse to the EMTs, the media circus would begin with me spotlighted in the center ring. The urgency of his precipitate decline spurred me to move quickly and with purpose. Talbot must live. I bent my mind to this goal and began my kick to run it in.

As I stepped into the river, I heard my mother sing the words of the doxology, " . . . from whom all blessings flow," and my heart swelled.

We were just above the rapid leading to the Fourth Falls.

RAVEN

*P*AUGUCK WAS LAUGHING.

"I could not help myself," I repeated.

Pauguck laughed all the harder until he cried and, through his tears, said, "You had their eyes for the taking. Instead, you chose the one-footed man's toes." He began to gasp for breath. "I never believed . . . " He could not finish the sentence because he was now doubled over with laughter.

"Keep it up, you old fool," I said. "I will take their eyes below the Fourth Falls and you will spend four days in the shades. I cannot wait to watch you answer the one-footed man's questions."

"Perhaps you will get his eyes. That's because the one-footed man does not have another set of toes to distract you," he said. And he laughed harder. When his laughter subsided, I shook myself out like a drenched dog and took to repairing my flight feathers.

"Now tell me, Kahgahgee, why did you eat the one-footed man's toes?"

"Ask me nicely," I said.

"O Mighty Kahgahgee, the Great Robber of the Forest, why did you eat the one-footed man's toes?" Pauguck intoned gravely and bowed.

"Is that the best you can do?"

"It will do for now, if you do not want me to start laughing again."

"If I must explain," I said, "they reminded me of corn smut. You have seen corn smut, haven't you? The blue and gray kernels that grew on the Anishinaabe corn in the old days."

"Corn smut," Pauguck said. "That actually makes sense. I understand it tastes good."

"Not as good as toes," I croaked contentedly.

THE
Fourth Falls

RAVEN

*I*N ASPECT, THE FOURTH FALLS IS BENIGN.

It has always seemed so.

From afar, it looks like a jumble of wooden blocks abandoned by children called in from play.

Brown and red granite and green basalt boulders carelessly thrown about as if by a giant hand not bound to any design. The boulders line the banks of the Escanaba and climb upward from the rapid below the falls to the lip of the falls itself. At the top, huge cedars once shaded the riverbank alongside the rapid, but they are now gone. All that remains of them are blackened stumps. The work of the fire.

The falls take the shape of the prow of a ship, a semicircle of vertical rock more than forty feet high.

And from that height, the river falls white and sheer as a bridal veil.

Hour after hour, it sounds the tranquility of a summer shower.

There are few pools at the base of the falls, and these are shallow, at most five feet deep.

Yet in the heart of this Arcadia waits a deadly trap.

The river has guarded this trap for as long as I can remember, burying it in the recesses of the rapid leading to the falls.

The rapid hides an undertow, a giant liquid screw that cranks on relentlessly.

This screw is panther quick.

It grabs the unwary, the ignorant canoeist, the foolish wading deer or raccoon, or the preoccupied angler, and whirls them about with such force that they no longer can tell top from bottom. In their panic, they swim hard, they believe, upward only to find themselves fighting the bottom of the river and gulping in water.

By the time they realize their mistake, it is too late. By then, the river has carried them to the brink of the falls and thrown them over. Their last memory.

I have often scavenged the bottom of the falls.

It is all coming together.

I look forward to the two white men. The river will drown them. Thus, I need only wait for their bodies below the falls. With luck, they will be crushed on one of the boulders at the base. Then I need not challenge the Escanaba to take their eyes.

The green-eyed woman and the hazel-eyed young man are close by. They will be in the ravine beside the boulder slide shortly.

I must delay them before they climb the slide so they do not catch the white men before the undertow does its work.

Just a few minutes are all I need. Then I will taste four blue eyes, and my morning will prove Pauguck wrong.

And the woman and young man will mourn, spending the rest of their life exploring "what ifs."

Ah, the last arrival.

"Will you be sitting with me, Pauguck?" I ask pleasantly.

"Yes," he said as he made his way down the boulder slide.

"Where are the white men now?" I asked, showing concern.

"They are above the falls . . . arguing," Pauguck said. "I thought I would come here, below the falls, and wait for them. No matter what, they will come here. Dead or alive."

"We think alike," I said, smiling.

"No. We do not. Have you seen the cat, Kahgahgee?"

"Resting on the pinnacle," I said, surprised.

"Did you hear the coyotes?" he asked, pressing me.

"Yes," I said. "But they are unimportant."

"Really?" Pauguck said as though shocked. Then shaking his head, he said, "It is plain, Kahgahgee, we do not think alike."

"You work at being abstruse," I said, irritated.

Pauguck just laughed and took a seat next to me. Then he deliberately turned his back on the river and looked off toward the rim of the ravine. "I should visit her again, Kahgahgee," he said.

"The green-eyed woman?"

"Yes."

CAROL

"Do you hear the falls, Val?"

"Yes, Mom. We're close."

"There's that ravine just before we get to the river," I said, gasping for breath. The smoke was thicker now.

"Could be bad. It depends on what the fire left," Val replied.

"That's my thought also," I replied, for the first time apprehensive.

"You should have waited on the ridge," he said.

"You're wasting time."

"The ravine opens onto the boulder slide below the falls. Once we're up the slide, we'll come out at the top of the falls."

"I know. I've made the climb with your father."

The ravine promised more delay. Its bottom steamed like newly poured oatmeal. The fire had gone underground, and all was cloaked in dense smoke. Every cedar and black spruce in the ravine was down, and a few were still burning. Throughout, hot spots flared and smoked.

"We need to move, Mom," he said. "It's safer off to the left."

I pulled my bandana up over my nose and took a swig of water as we skirted the rim.

Finally staring down into the smoke, Val said, "This looks like as good a place as any to cross. I'll be moving fast." Val clambered down the slope in the lead.

Coyotes yipped from behind us in the direction of the pinnacle, and a cat snarled. Val turned back to look. "Whatever is going on back there doesn't matter," I said, checking my watch. Loosing a clatter of stones, I slid down into the ravine. "We're out of time. Hurry!"

The smoke grew thicker as we went lower. By the time we reached the ravine bottom, I could see no more than three feet ahead and soon lost sight of Val. The last words I heard from him were, "We'll know we're through when we hit the upslope." Before he disappeared ahead into a wall of heat, I said, "Get to the top of the boulder slide, Val. Don't think about me. Don't let anything stop you." I thought I heard a faint, "Okay, Mom." And then Val disappeared.

The soles of my shoes burned. Smoke choked me, and my eyes teared. I could barely see the ground for all the downed trees. Careful where I stepped, I moved slowly so as not to vent a hot spot. Reaching the bottom of the ravine where the smoke was thickest, I hunched over, looking for patches of rock on which to step.

I heard a fall of dislodged rocks ahead. It was probably Val finding the upslope and crawling out. I began to cough. I thought I heard the falls and turned in that direction. But before I could take a step, a seam of underground fire split open and gushed before me. When I jumped back, another seam opened behind me, blocking any escape. I was trapped, surrounded by fire and suffocating heat. My breathing grew labored.

A new smell joined the smell of burning wood and overrode it. It was a familiar smell: the sweet, repellent smell of death. Faint, but there nonetheless. And instantly I realized that in the crackling fire was a voice. And it was asking me to step into the fire, to cross into another world, the world into which I had shepherded so many of my patients. I sensed the spirit that was calling me was a compassionate spirit, as dedicated to his mission as I was to mine. I saw no one, but I felt his presence begging me to look into the fiery seam that had opened wider at my feet. And as strange as it sounds, I felt tenderness in this fire before me. And I knew that all I needed to do was leap into it, into the arms of that tenderness, to the world beyond, a world awash in infinite tenderness.

Instead, I straightened up and looked into the smoke. "My place is here," I said.

In argument, the smoke swirled, and the crackling fire sang lovingly to me. I looked down into the fire as if through a glass-bottomed boat, to a cooler world—sunlit isles, placid lakes, and meadows of swaying wild flowers. I heard happy chatter, and I saw my parents and Joe's parents, happy, picnicking together. The forests were thick and the lakes burnished silver.

"I may not explain myself very well," I started. "But I want you to know I've always appreciated you. You are unfailingly benevolent to my patients, and for that I'm grateful. But for the present, I belong here. I love my family and my patients. I must stay for the time being."

The smoke swirled and took on the shape of a man dressed in deerskin leggings and breechclout. His hair was tied up, and he was muscular, about my height. He had strong features, handsome even, and his face was pleasant, smiling.

I addressed him, extending my hand as a supplicant. "Why not join me here?"

He drew back.

I whispered, "You understand."

His face grew sad.

"Yes," I said. "There's an abyss of time between us. But it is temporary. Your reasons for not joining me here are the same reasons I have for not joining you today. Our lives have meaning, here and now, where we both stand. But you and I know another day will come when we will meet again. On that day I will happily make the walk with you into your kindlier world."

The fire exhaled like a strong wind rushing through an open window, and the crackle went into a lower register.

I said in reply, "I too look forward to that day." I bowed, and my friend disappeared.

The seams of fire closed and the smoke lifted. I immediately heard the sound of the falls off to my left and fought my way up the side of the ravine to shouts and a pleading voice that sounded like

Joe's. As I scrambled to the top of the ravine, I saw the boulder slide and the lip of the Fourth Falls. Pulling my bandana down, I inhaled a great breath of spray-washed air and began to run.

There were more shouts above the falls. I saw Val halfway up the slide, and I ran for the bottom, where a great raven sat perched. It cocked its head, studying me. Then it took off flying toward Val.

JOE

"STROKE, TALBOT!" I DEMANDED.

He looked casually at me and, as if bored, uttered, "No."

"We're so close," I said. "Start planning for your next fishing trip."

"Nothing has changed, Joe," he replied hoarsely. "You say this fall's a killer." Talbot was having trouble breathing. "I want to give it a chance."

The rapid leading to the Fourth Falls was just ahead. I had fished it several times, always careful not to venture too far out into the current. The stories of wading anglers upended and carried over the falls were oft repeated in local legend. Chilling stories of a powerful undertow quick as a panther topped the list of horrifying ghost stories to tell wide-eyed children sitting round campfires at night. The fact was the Fourth Falls killed enough people to prove the truth of the tales to both children and adults.

My destination was the right side of the rapid where the current was slower and just beyond the reach of the undertow. Swimming hard, I kept us in close, even touching the bank from time to time. But the bank was steep and high, more than three feet. Forestland set back from the river. A verge of Marquette green rock, basalt—some say the earth's first dry land—formed its base with sand, gravel, silt, and detritus from the decaying forest floor covering it in layers.

221

From the river, the layers were obvious, exposed by spring freshets. The base of green basalt showed the color of weathered copper and clearly marked the boundary between the fury of the water and the safety of the land.

Before long, Talbot and I must crawl out onto the dry land. There was no other way to the 480 bridge. Then we could make our way down the boulder slide and walk the river, less than a mile. The climb down the boulder slide would not be easy but could be done in stages. Usually the sun was hotter on the slide and would warm Talbot enough for our last push. The dawn sun was full now, and its early heat promised a warm day.

I heard the howl and yips of coyotes followed by the roar of the great cat. The sounds came from the pinnacle, a short ten-minute run. I could not challenge either of them in my exhaustion and expect to live. All the hours on the river and all the chances I took, and now the impossible stood in our way. The thought crossed my mind that if we made it to the slide, we could fortify ourselves among the boulders and throw rocks down on whatever attacked. It would buy time until rescuers came. In truth, I did not believe Talbot would live that long.

Time to pull us out onto dry land. The fire destroyed the cedars that shaded the right riverbank. I had expected that. And when the blackened stumps came into view one after another in a line down to the falls, I surveyed the ones nearest the river and looked beneath the stumps to their exposed roots, the roots that clung to the green rock. It was the roots I needed. They were my handholds to pull us out.

By the first cedar stump, the river was four and five feet deep. Beyond that stump, closer to the falls, the river became deeper by degrees, six and seven feet by the time the last smoldering stump came up. Beyond was just green rock. No trees and no stumps. No handhold and no toehold. Beyond them was the lip of the falls. And just before the lip, the river bottom rose up as it sucked its prey out into the heaviest current of the rapid and catapulted them over the falls.

The chances of pulling us out were best with the first stump. Just before we came up on it, I started dragging my right hand on the exposed bank. Sand, gravel, and cinders came loose, and we slowed a little. The roots were black with fire damage. I took hold of some with both hands and pulled, but they were brittle and snapped off in my hand. And we were caught by the river again. The next stump was no different.

By the third stump, I started looking for roots farther under the bank, hoping to find living strands protected from the fire. The river did not give me much time for inspection, so I just dug my hands into the sand and gravel, hoping to meet up with the wiry spring of a healthy, green root. I found some, but they were not strong enough to hold us. My fingernails were bleeding, and pain shot through me every time I dug my hands into the bank.

The last stump came up. The last chance to thwart the impossible. More roots were exposed. I started slapping the smooth green rock to slow us up. The taproot was partially exposed, and I grabbed it with one hand. Then both hands. It held.

"Come on, Talbot. Grab a handful and pull with me!" I shouted. "We'll be out of this water if we pull hard enough together."

"Let's see what you're made of, Little Fish," he replied. "My money's on the river."

Talbot had drifted out into the current. "Get behind me! Otherwise, the undertow will sweep you out into the rapid!" I yelled.

"No, Little Fish!" he shouted back, drifting farther and farther out into the current. "This is where the river and I eat you."

Alone, I pulled on the taproot and scrambled with my feet to make it up the green rock and out of the river. But with each effort, the swirling river knocked my feet off the underwater rock wall and left me exhausted. I tucked Talbot in behind me and then pulled again, trying to lever myself up. No go. The powerful current drained me. I held us in place, summoning all my strength for one last powerful effort.

Talbot must have sensed it. "This is the end, Joe!" he shouted to dissuade me. "Just let go."

"No," I said, gritting my teeth.

"Just release the buckle on this belt!" he shouted. "Let me go. You can make it alone."

"We're in this together, Talbot!" I shouted back.

"Only in your mind," he replied.

This time, I tried to lever myself up the green rock wall on my knees. My knees held the rock bank, and gritting my teeth, I pulled with everything I had left. My knees made it up and up the wall, and I was half out of the water when I felt the drag from Talbot pulling me back down. I looked behind me and saw that Talbot had shifted out into the current, spreading his arms and legs out wide. The river boiled around him. The thought of releasing the wading belt crossed my mind, but I dismissed it and pulled harder.

Talbot was laughing now. "Give it up, Joe," he cheered. "I've won!"

I pulled harder on the taproot and tried to push off the rock wall. It didn't help. Talbot had the easier part of it. I could feel my strength draining away. I had nothing left to call on.

The only course left was going over the falls. If I slowed us down enough as the river drew us to the brink, perhaps I could swim a few yards across the lip to a point where we could line up above one of the few pools sitting at the base of the falls. I let go of the taproot.

"You've finally faced reason, Joe!" Talbot shouted. He was elated.

From the last stump on, it was all smooth, green rock both above and below the water. As we drifted with the river, I slowed us by slapping my palm on unforgiving stone. We held for a second or two. And then we were carried by the current again. Slap . . . slap . . . slap.

I thought of the blessed chaos of the Escanaba, the blessed chaos of my birth, the blessed chaos of my life, and, composed, I entrusted myself to its mercy. We had fifty feet to go. Slap . . . slap . . . slap. We were traveling too fast.

"It's futile, Little Fish," Talbot said, reading my mind.

Slap . . . slap . . . slap.

PAUGUCK

*R*UNNING FROM THE RAVINE TO THE FOOT OF THE BOUL-
der slide, the hazel-eyed young man hesitated, studying
the jumble of rocks for the fastest way up. But there is no direct
route in this winding, treacherous, forty-foot stairway to the
top of the falls.

Shouting came from just above the falls. Pulling himself up
onto the first tier of boulders, the young man made short hops from
boulder to boulder and was making quick progress when he turned
back, hearing his mother scramble out of the ravine behind him. He
turned to wave when Kahgahgee mounted and wheeled into the sky.
Kahgahgee flew over his head, banked, leveled off, and flew directly
at him. The young man ducked, but again Kahgahgee resumed its
climb and returned. The young man ducked again, losing more time,
setting himself for the next attack.

The next time Kahgahgee took a pass at him, the young man
removed the coiled rope slung over his shoulder and started waving it.
Kahgahgee darted around him, croaking, elated with the challenge.
Continuing to swing the rope overhead, the young man fought his
way up the slide. Jumping and hopping upward, sometimes pulling
himself up like a rock climber, he stood just below the slide's summit
when Kahgahgee made one last rush at him, coming in close. With a
satisfying dry click, the rope loop struck one of Kahgahgee's wings,

and he tumbled in mid-air and dropped, but recovered, pulling out of the dive. Then he flapped his wings, gained altitude, and circled above the hazel-eyed young man, disappointment sounding in each departing flap.

JOE

*S*LAP.

All I had to do was release the belt buckle and let Talbot float to his death. I still had enough riverbank left to save myself. The bottom would rise up shortly before the brink. I had fished the spot, and there was a chance I might be able drag myself out. But with Talbot in tow, there was no chance. My fingers felt for the buckle, but I hesitated. If I released Talbot, he would not survive the falls. The finality gave me pause. There would be no going back. I could never return to this moment and repair history.

Why not give Talbot what he wanted? He picked me for my incompetence. So what if he and Meredith believed I was an incompetent? Carol and I would never see them again. Meredith's report to their board would be a slander, but I did not know and would never know those people. Living so far from Talbot's world, I could crawl back into mine, immune from the reports of his death in the financial news. My neighbors did not care about what happened on Wall Street. In a month, the report blaming me for Talbot's death would be collecting dust in some corporate archive. There would be talk of legal actions but, in the end, those would die out because we owned very little, and when it was liquidated it would not cover the first day's fees for one of their lawyers.

Just let him go. My fingers played across the buckle.

Slap.

Yes, it was true that if I let Talbot go now, he would escape the pain my father suffered in his last days. He would not face the endless months when his every breath reminded him of his impending death. But revenge against Talbot was my vendetta . . . not my father's. And I no longer felt like stoking that conflagration.

I remembered the day my father received the letter informing him that his medical coverage was terminated. And I remembered the day he and my mother were hunched over the kitchen table with the letter informing him his pension benefits had been slashed. They were trying to plan a new budget. My mother had tears in her eyes, and my father's face was dark with rage. There were bitter words. But in the weeks that followed, the new budget was in place and the letters filed away. My father sometimes drifted off when sitting before the television. He would wake with a start, look about quickly, and then his eyes would retreat inward as he reminded himself of the new confines of his life.

If I was in the room on those occasions, he would ask, "How did your day go?" And I would tell him. He lived through my stories. I was able to help out with the budget and lived with them to lend a hand around the house. I became a good son, the son I should always have been. Would I be a better son keeping Talbot alive so I could revel in his pain? I did not believe that to be true.

I once asked my father, "How can you live with what the company did to you?"

"My life is full. I have all I ever wanted—you and your mother's love and respect," he said, and I believed him because I felt hot tears slipping down my cheeks.

I asked that question more than once. I could not let go of what Lundine had done. Once when I asked my father the same question again, he said, "You go with what you got."

I did not understand and asked him to explain.

"When I was a pitcher, there were days I had no fast ball. Without my fast ball, I learned not to expect strikeouts. So I just kept throwing what I had, inside and low. And I got out of innings with three up and three down because the batters beat the ball into the ground."

I have repeated those words to myself many times. "You go with what you got." My father never asked me to avenge him. So what had I "got"?

My hand was on the belt buckle. Pull it loose once and for all. What would taking revenge against Talbot mean to me now? My resentment of him no longer mattered. If my father never pronounced Talbot's name in bitterness, why should I care what happened to Talbot? And I thought, "Let him go."

Slap.

I had fifteen more feet before the river rose up and offered me alone a chance of escape. And there was nothing clearer in my mind than the need to make my decision now . . . now, before the river drove us down those last fifteen feet to the brink of the falls.

I thought of Carol and Val. I needed to report to them. It was to them, and them alone, that I needed to tell the truth of what happened out here. And that is what it all came down to. I needed to file an accurate report with those I loved and those who loved me. I was not as good as the man I planned to become, nor was I as bad as the man I was afraid I might become. As I grew into the man I am today, I came to loathe making excuses. My report to Val and Carol would contain no excuses. Nothing that smacked of "it was him or me."

Nothing I did over the last day on the river was irrevocable. But at this moment, the irrevocable stood at the brink of the falls. I had fought it off until now. I felt the belt buckle. And I began to word my report. It would be short because I was near exhaustion and the lip of the falls imminent.

Slap.

And so my report.

My wife and son had a right to expect that their husband, their father, would risk himself to save another. That is what I knew I must report to them. And that is what I would report to them. They lived that code. Carol endangered herself every winter night she drove icy winter roads, the same roads that killed her father. Val risked it every day he was in Iraq. It was second nature to them. They lived and breathed it. And every day of our lives together, they believed it was my code also.

It did not matter that Talbot wished to die. He had a right to die whenever he wanted. But he did not ask my permission to make me a witness to his suicide. He expected me to just stand aside and lie afterward. People like me were never more than props in his world. He assumed I would be flattered to accept the role of some bit player in his financial melodrama.

So I would keep the code Val and Carol lived even if it meant my death. And they would hear my report, even if it was not from my lips. For if Talbot and I were found drowned, the belt would tell the story. The belt would report to everyone that I stayed with Talbot until the end. That I risked my life to bring him home safely. That I risked all and lost. That I was worthy of my wife's and son's respect and love. For truly, my death did not matter. What mattered was that I had risked my life for another. That is what Val and Carol would remember about me in later years after the sting of death passed. They would think about me and what my life meant, and they would know that I lived up to that same code they lived by, the only code worth keeping.

There was nothing else to add. And so that would be my report.

I pulled my hand off the buckle, sought the loose end of the belt, and pulled it tighter, knotting it double to make sure it held when Talbot and I went over the falls . . . together.

Slap.

I had to be attentive now. There was one moment coming soon when the river would lift us as the bottom rose up. That was the moment I could swim to my left out into the rapid, pulling Talbot along as I looked to line us up with a deep pool below the falls. Most were hardly more than puddles. My goal was a few boulders on the lip of the falls off which I could push off, guiding our descent. I did not believe I had the strength to swim that far, and in my heart I knew I was planning the impossible. The river would take us, and for a moment, we would float in air. Then we would hit below.

A few more seconds.

Slap.

I watched the green rock slide by. I took one last look up along the bank. One last look at dry land. And then I saw a hand. It appeared palm side to me. A hand just above the surface of the river. I reached up and grabbed the wrist of that hand, and the hand grabbed my wrist back. It was a strong hand, and it held me and Talbot stock-still in the current.

I felt it pulling me up, and I looked up into the face of my son.

Talbot spooked. He started swinging his arms and legs into the current to create more drag. But the hand held firm and pulled me halfway onto dry land. I started crawling on my face farther up the green rock, gushing water. Then Val released me and caught Talbot under his arm and slung him out onto the bank neatly and effortlessly. Talbot flopped about for a second, trying to fall back into the water.

Val stomped a foot on Talbot's chest to stop his slithering. Then he looked at me quizzically. "What's going on, Dad?"

"Mr. Talbot doesn't want to be saved," I said as I undid the belt and tried to stand up. I could not and sat down, slumping over.

"This yours?" Talbot growled, looking up at Val.

"Give me a minute, Val," I said, breathing deeply.

"Dad, what happened to your back?" Looking more closely, he added, "And your neck? It looks like someone tried to strangle you."

"The back was the work of a cat. The neck was Mr. Talbot's work."

"Mom's here too," Val said. "She's coming up the slide."

Anxiously I looked over to the slide.

THE

Rescue

CAROL

I saw Val disappear, vaulting over the rim of the slide. Scrambling from boulder to boulder, I hesitated halfway up, unsure. The hovering raven dove for me. Waving my hat at it, I fought it off. Retreating a short distance, it dove in closer. I felt its wings sweep against my throat, chilling me. And I smelled the staleness of old nests and decaying carrion.

The raven then changed tactics. It staged behind me and dove at the back of my head. Each time, I was forced to turn and fight it off. The tumbled boulders were treacherous footing, and I teetered each time I twisted about.

Finally, diving in from the side, the raven scraped its claws across the back of my head. I shifted around too fast and lost my balance. I fell into a crevasse, striking my head. As I lost consciousness, my last memory was the raven beating its wings just above me as its massive beak reached down toward my eyes.

RAVEN

*T*HE HAZEL-EYED YOUNG MAN WAS TOO MUCH FOR ME.
A black moment.

Then it occurred to me that the woman's green eyes were an acceptable trophy.

True, her eyes were not blue. But green was close enough.

She was lagging behind, tired, and unsure of her footing.

I swooped in and out forcing her to turn around to fight me off. I unbalanced her and she fell, striking her head.

Dazed, she lay still for a moment,

Her green eyes opened.

A moment—time enough for me to dig them out.

Two downward hacks with my great beak. That was all.

I could not chance the young man and his rope coming back, so I flew, croaking in my joy, to where she fell.

But as luck would have it, she was too far down in the crevasse for me to find a roost.

I fluttered my great wings over her, descending into the crevasse, working my tail feathers, hanging in place.

She was vaguely aware of me but too dazed to fight me off.

Two green eyes there for the taking.

Fresh.

As I descended, I heard,

"Kahgahgee . . . "
"Kahgahgee . . . "
"Kahgahgee . . . "
I looked up.
Pauguck was standing on a nearby rock.
"Leave the woman alone!" he demanded angrily.
Drawing my wings up out of the crevasse, I hopped onto a boulder and said, "Don't interfere, old man."
"Leave the woman. She is the best of them," Pauguck said sternly. "Do you hear me, Kahgahgee? She is the best of them."
"Stay in your own world," I said quickly.
"You have not stayed in yours," he replied just as quickly.
"The white men and their blue eyes are safe above the falls," I said. "I will have the woman's eyes instead. Small recompense for all I suffered."
"No," Pauguck said.
I heard a scrambling in the crevasse. The woman had come back to herself, and she was collecting stones to throw at me.
"Uh, too late," Pauguck said, smiling.
"You sneak," I croaked, lifting off and climbing higher.
"There are other eyes!" Pauguck shouted up to me.
"Which eyes?" I asked, exasperated.
"Have you forgotten the cat and its yellow eyes?" Pauguck asked, laughing.
"No," I said. "But I dare not get close to them."
"The cat will not need its eyes. Coyotes have surrounded it on the pinnacle, and it is losing blood . . . too much blood."
"This is not like you, Pauguck," I said suspiciously.
"True. But, you see, I have always been curious about the cat's thinking. As you know, it never speaks."
"It has never spoken to me," I said, a little mystified now. "If I take its eyes, you will need to guide it on the four-day walk to Silver Lake."
"That is the way I see it," Pauguck said, waiting.
"You want to guide the cat to the Blessed Isles?"

"Yes," he said. "Then it will be forced to talk to me."

"You would let me have its eyes just so you can ask the cat questions?" I asked.

"Yes," Pauguck said.

"I do not understand you," I said.

"Yes," Pauguck said. With that, he stood up and started climbing to the top of the Fourth Falls.

JOE

CAROL WAS THROWING STONES AT A RAVEN CIRCLING above her. As I started down the slide, the raven cocked its head toward me and circled, croaking, as if in imaginary conversation, and then, *thwack, thwack*, beat its wings to fly toward the pinnacle. The wound in my ear burned, and I was glad to see the bird go.

"Joe! . . . Joe!" Carol shouted.

"I'm here." The trip down was awkward. I didn't want to break the cauterized crust on my back. "I'll be right there."

As I looked down, Carol started to laugh. "You're a sight!"

"I've been better." Stretching to pull her up, I felt the burnt crust on my back crack and a trickle of blood seep out, warming my skin.

"How's Talbot?" Carol asked.

"Dying."

We both started up the slide, climbing hand over hand, Carol following just behind me. "Let me look at your back." I felt her fingers playing over my wounds. She stanched the dripping blood temporarily with her bandana. "Not bad. You've lost a lot of blood, and you'll need a full course of antibiotics. There's a little imbedded gravel, but the hospital staff can pick that out." She passed a hand over my neck. "Talbot try to strangle you?"

"I'll live. It's Talbot I'm worried about," I said, turning to look at her. "We need him alive."

Reaching the top, she said in a low voice, "I'm so sorry for sending you out on this."

"Don't. It was . . . *good* . . . for me," I said, emphasizing *good* carefully.

Carol narrowed her eyes. "Joe . . . ," she began plaintively.

"Shush!" I slid an arm round her shoulders, wincing as I pulled her close. "No. You were right. It was good for me. Talbot's the problem now. We need to make the bridge with him alive."

PAUGUCK

KAHGAHGEE FLEW OFF TO THE PINNACLE, AND I JOINED the one-legged man and the hazel-eyed young man at the top of the falls.

They were arguing. "Just let me crawl over to the river and take one last swim," Talbot said.

"Talk to my father about it. He's bent on keeping you alive."

"I don't want to live."

"If it were up to me, I'd let you go." The hazel-eyed young man dragged the one-legged man farther up the bank and started looking for saplings to cut for a stretcher.

Sitting up, the one-legged man pulled his pants up past his knees. Both lower legs were black with blue shadowing above the knees. He lay back and looked up into the glare of the morning sky, expressionless. Twisting his head to check on the hazel-eyed young man, the one-legged man waited until the young man was busy chopping. Then he turned himself over and began crawling to the river.

"Rest, Mr. Talbot," the green-eyed woman commanded. She and the able-bodied man stepped off the slide onto the riverbank.

"Nursey's arrived just in time," Talbot said and fell on his side.

The able-bodied man pulled the one-legged man back up the bank and sat between him and the river.

The green-eyed woman gently inspected the one-legged man.

"Val, lay the stretcher alongside Mr. Talbot." While she read his insulin pump and examined his lower legs, the able-bodied man and his son shifted the one-legged man onto the stretcher. Anxiously, the green-eyed woman looked up and said, "Mr. Talbot, you have gangrene. It's serious." After giving Talbot an insulin shot, she looked toward the able-bodied man and mouthed, "Quickly." With that, she grasped a handle of the stretcher, and all three lifted and began the dangerous trip down the slide.

Gangrene puts many on the path to Ponemah. Parts of the body die and infect the blood stream. Raccoons, deer, and men linger briefly once the infection becomes general. In a few hours, they are standing on the shores of Silver Lake.

The struggle on the pinnacle ended several minutes ago, time enough for Raven to snatch the cat's eyes.

With that finished, Raven will return, for Raven is always hungry.

I do not care to make a four-day journey to the Blessed Isles with the one-legged man.

He will argue with me the whole way, telling me how to do my job.

So I am ready to meet his spirit immediately upon his death.

It is close.

And Kahgahgee knows it also.

Even now, his heavy wings announce his return.

CAROL

$\mathcal{I}$'LL SEE YOU IN JAIL, JOE," TALBOT SAID WITH GREAT effort as we carried him downstream. We were wading the last stretch of the Escanaba before the 480 bridge. From horizon to horizon, the riverbank was devastated—stark, blackened trunks of tree stripped of bark and limbs and the dense undergrowth reduced to ash. Below the Fourth Falls, the river was gentle, with sand and gravel as level as a sidewalk. The riffles were hardly more than a foot and the pools never more than three. It was the shortest and fastest way to the bridge, and we were making good time. Another five minutes at most.

"You're not talking, Joe!" Talbot yelled. Joe ignored him and his silence only prodded Talbot to begin one of his rants. He hissed, "You answer me, now."

"Whatever you say, Frank," Joe said, provoking him. Before Talbot could speak, I broke in and asked, "Mr. Talbot, do you have any feeling in your upper legs?"

"Don't interrupt me," Talbot said, his fevered eyes sparkling.

"I'll be blunt, Mr. Talbot," I said. "I don't know if there will be enough time for you to take a flight to Mayo. That's the first decision your doctors must make."

"I don't care what the doctors say," he said, slurring his words. "Just arrogant men in white coats."

"Mayo's will remove both your legs above the knees. Just how much else you'll lose depends on how quickly we deliver you to the EMTs."

"Nursey, what's it like being married to a criminal?" he asked, fidgeting on the stretcher.

"You're lucky to be alive, Mr. Talbot," I said. "You have Joe to thank for that."

Val had been silent since he rolled Talbot onto the stretcher. Talbot looked up at him and said belligerently, "These ropes are scratching me."

"That's the best I can do . . . *for you*," Val replied, emphasizing his last words.

Talbot turned to me and said, "You should teach your son some manners." He then added, "You're lucky I don't fire you."

"Meredith's already done that," I said neutrally. "You'll have all the nurses you need at Mayo."

"I'm not going to Mayo," Talbot said. I looked over at Joe, who shrugged his shoulders.

The river deepened a few feet, and the stretcher jostled. Talbot's left arm dropped off the stretcher, leaving his hand to trail in the water. He was having difficulty raising it. Motioning to Joe to take my handle, I picked up Talbot's hand and placed it on his chest. Then I put a hand on his forehead, rubbing it lightly.

Talbot smiled. "Meredith's wrong as usual. You're my nurse," Talbot said. "I'm buying you for the balance."

I looked at Joe, who grimaced. "Long story. Later."

"Let's talk about it now," Talbot said. "There won't be a later."

Val turned threateningly. "Talbot, my mother's not for sale."

"Oh, you frighten me," Talbot said, plainly trying to push Val into retaliating.

With that, Val balanced his end of the stretcher across his forearm, snatched Talbot's other hand, and began to twist.

In pain, Talbot cried out.

"Coward," Val said.

"Let him go, Val," I said anxiously. And when Val dropped

Talbot's hand, I picked it up and began to rub his wrist. Talbot was close to falling into a coma. He was running a fever, and his blood sugar was low. But the challenge to dominate Val and Joe roused him, keeping him awake. He would be conscious when we arrived at the bridge.

Talbot smiled up at me. "That boy needs a good lesson in manners."

"He had words with Meredith, Mr. Talbot," I said.

"Meredith's not speaking for me," Talbot said.

I saw the 480 bridge in the distance. Val was about to speak, when I put a finger to my lips. Talbot was about ready to unleash his invective on Meredith.

"We're almost there," I said, leaning close to Talbot.

"I'm not going to Mayo," Talbot said. "My mind's made up."

Just before the bridge, the river narrowed, and we passed through a hundred yards of blistered tag alders. The water bubbled cheerfully over a scattering of small rocks. Blue-winged olive mayflies began to hatch. They sputtered out onto the surface, dried their wings, and took off. So quickly. This was the Escanaba's regular morning hatch. Downstream under the 480 bridge, sipping trout caught the stragglers. At least five fish were working.

Talbot looked up at me and asked, "Is Meredith here?"

"I don't believe so," she said. "But your security people are. A Mr. Donahue."

Talbot became thoughtful. "Meredith should be here. A good wifey would be here."

"I'm sure she'll be coming."

"She won't." Talbot waved his hand vaguely. His face became confused. "I had something to say."

Joe and Val ignored him. "Go ahead, Mr. Talbot," I said.

"I don't remember what I wanted to say," he said. "Arrogant men in white coats."

"As soon as we're out of the river, I'll call your doctors."

"White coats. They're just white coats . . ."

244

JOE

THE FIRE NEVER JUMPED HIGHWAY 480'S TWO LANES OF dirt and sand. Through the quick work of tanker trucks and fire crews, the forest to the east remained untouched and deep green. As we neared the bridge, I looked downstream through the arch of the bridge and saw dense pines and dark shadows playing on the riffles as the morning sun climbed higher. The musky smell of damp, black river bottom dirt and the clean smell of cedar blew upriver. With a great intake of breath, I smelled better days ahead.

At the bridge, we heard faint voices droning. "Hey, someone, give us a hand!" Val shouted up.

Pete Christianson's head appeared over the steel guardrails. "Be right down, Val." Then he turned and shouted, "Donahue, they have your man!" Sergeant Ketunen appeared over the railing. He was not smiling.

"A good thing you went when you did. We're still stuck waiting for Donahue to give us the go-ahead," Pete said as he slid down the embankment to the river's edge.

Pete took the end of the stretcher that Carol and I were holding. The bank was steep. The fire left it black and slippery with burnt brush and grass.

By the time Carol and I climbed up to the road, Donahue was pointing at us and screaming, "Arrest these people! Look what they've done to Mr. Talbot!" Talbot was lying in the roadway with two EMTs crouching over him.

"Steady, Donahue," the sergeant said. "Joe doesn't look too good either."

"Is that a thank you, Donahue?" Val said sarcastically, standing to the side.

"I've had enough of you," he said, unsnapping his holster and reaching for his Glock.

Sergeant Ketunen gripped Donahue's arm and pushed him back. "There *will* be an arrest this morning," he barked, "if you don't take your hand off that weapon!"

"Look at Mr. Talbot's bruises. He's been beaten!" he shouted, going nose to nose with Ketunen.

"This river's brutal, Donahue," the sergeant said. "Of course you wouldn't know that because you never got out there."

"They should give statements right now," Donahue said.

"If Mr. Talbot files a complaint, I'll investigate it," Ketunen said. "That's how we do things up here."

"You give me no choice but to call the governor," Donahue said.

"Go ahead and call the governor," the sergeant said, angry now. He fixed his gaze on Donahue through narrowed eyes. "What are you going to tell him? Some civilians did your job and rescued Talbot? Sounds like negligence on your part."

Donahue pulled out his cell phone but hesitated. The sergeant frowned and said to him, "Attend your boss."

Donahue turned on his heel, scuffed up some dust in disgust, and walked over to where two EMTs had moved Talbot from our makeshift stretcher to a gurney. They were bending over him, snipping away his pant legs.

"Sergeant," Carol said, "Mr. Talbot should be medevacked out immediately. His legs have lost circulation. Septicemia is setting in."

"Right, Mrs. McCartney," the sergeant said. "Pete, call for a chopper."

"Joe needs to get to the hospital also," Carol said.

"Of course. Walk him to one of the ambulances, Pete," the sergeant said.

Talbot started screaming at the EMTs. "Stop pawing me!"

"Sir, you need medical help. We need to get you to a hospital," Donahue said, kneeling in the dust beside him.

"I'm going home, Donahue. I've a business to run," Talbot said.

"Sir, listen to me. Mrs. Talbot is running your business," Donahue whispered, cowering like a much-abused dog waiting for a beating. "Actually, she's now head of your business."

"You're an imbecile, Donahue. Carry me to one of the vans and drive me home," Talbot commanded.

"Those are not my orders," Donahue said.

"I don't care what your orders are. I'm now ordering you to pick me up and carry me to one of my vans," Talbot said.

"Sir, I take my orders from Mrs. Talbot," Donahue said softly.

Talbot looked away. The expression on his face was a new one. For the first time, I saw defeat. Then he turned back to Donahue and asked, "What are your orders?"

"To wait on this bridge until we get a call from Mrs. Talbot to begin the search," he said.

"Get Mrs. Talbot on the phone!"

"It won't help, sir," Donahue said respectfully. "The board has voted."

"Get her on the phone, Donahue!" Talbot shouted, angrier than ever.

"I will, sir," he replied, punching in a number. Checking to make sure the phone was ringing, he handed it to Talbot.

"Meredith, I'm coming home. Tell that to your goon!" Talbot shouted into the cell phone.

Meredith replied, but it was not the answer Talbot wanted to hear, "Don't contradict me," he said.

Talbot listened and said, "What are you talking about? I'm not a danger to anyone . . ."

Whatever Meredith said in response, Talbot yelled into the receiver, "You've botched this! You should have waited for word about me, and you should have sent Donahue out sooner. Now there will be an investigation."

Meredith's voice could now be heard because she began shouting also. Talbot took the cell phone away from his ear. "The board's voted me in! . . . The board's voted me in!" she screamed.

"The board can just vote you out," Talbot said.

Meredith said something, and Talbot's features colored a deep red, and his anger reached such a peak he could hardly speak. "Don't hang up on me. I'm coming home."

But Meredith did hang up. Donahue reached for his phone. Talbot held it away from him so that Donahue needed to reach across his chest. As he did so, Talbot pulled Donahue's Glock and stuck it into his chest. "Back off."

Donahue raised his hands. "Mr. Talbot, put the gun down."

"Back off," Talbot ordered and loosed a warning shot. "You're trying to kidnap me. I want to go home."

Donahue rose to his feet and stepped backward. "We need to get you to a hospital."

"I have had enough of hospitals," Talbot said, waving the pistol. "When I get my company back, you'll be the first person I fire."

Carol stepped forward and laid a hand on Sergeant Ketunen's arm. "If Mr. Talbot wants to go home, we should follow his wishes. I'll accompany him and have his doctors meet us there." Talbot placed the gun on his chest and looked over at Ketunen, who nodded his agreement. "It's urgent you get care now, Mr. Talbot," Carol said. "We're wasting time."

"Of course," Ketunen said.

"Just a minute. This is a trick," Talbot said, slurring his words again as he looked directly at Carol and Ketunen. "Trick . . ."

"You are the smartest man I know, Mr. Talbot. I'm trying to do what is best for you," she said. For a moment, Talbot relaxed and gained the confidence I had seen yesterday when I settled him in my Starcraft, the chairman of the board again.

"You people have been wrong all along," he said to Carol.

"Yes, we have," Carol replied. "Give us a chance to make it up to you. Just tell us what you want."

"I never want to see this river ever again," he said.

"You never will. Now let's get you ready for the helicopter," Carol offered.

"This is a trap," Talbot said. "My legs hurt . . ."

Concerned, Carol said quickly, "No . . . No . . . Mr. Talbot, we just want to help you."

"That's true, sir," Ketunen agreed.

"You all want something from me," Talbot moaned. "You want my money."

Exhaling slowly to compose herself, Carol said, "We just want you well."

Talbot threw the gun at Donahue. "Get me home." The beat of the helicopter ended all conversation, and as it settled, the sergeant signaled the EMTs to board Talbot. As they did, Talbot sat up and shouted in his most authoritative voice, "Nursey, you're coming with me!" Then he slumped back, exhausted.

I turned to go. "You can't leave Dad," Val said in dismay.

"Dad will be fine."

"I'll be fine, Val," I said. "You'll be looking after me."

"But, Dad . . . ," Val began.

"No, Mr. Talbot needs your mother more than I do," I said. "He's her patient."

Carol kissed me as she had done so often before going out the door to work. "I'll get to the hospital when I'm done."

Talbot overheard and shouted back, "There'll be no getting away."

Carol's eyes flashed as she looked up at me. "He's dying. I must prepare him."

"I understand." And she ran to join the EMTs and Talbot as the rotors quickened their beat. In a whirlwind of dust and ash, they were gone.

CAROL

*T*HE HELICOPTER LIFTED OFF, CLIMBING STRAIGHT UP. Looking out, I saw the Fourth Falls. As we gained altitude, one by one the first three falls came into view, creases in the Escanaba. I also saw the white froth of the rapids and the dark depths of the river's pools. All cold and uncaring, answerable to no one. I knew them well, and I knew that death never touched the Escanaba. Whatever happened on the river was meant to happen, the flux of creation working out its dreams regardless of consequence.

As the helicopter climbed higher and banked north, heading for Talbot's house, I saw the map of my life. I saw our house upriver from the First Falls and then the houses owned at one time by our parents. I saw the sprawling flat roof of our high school and the newer roof of the hospital. Then the shoreline of Lake Superior came into view. The helicopter banked again to follow Route 550, the road that killed my father, and I saw, finally, Talbot's house set on its point surrounded by Lake Superior. I thought of them all—Joe and Val, my parents, Joe's parents, my teachers and classmates, the doctors and patients with whom I worked. It was a life of grace, and I smiled to myself.

Talbot's eyes flickered open. Reaching over to the gurney, I put my hand in his. It was cold. He turned his head and looked directly into my eyes. He was anxious, and he had a question. "What's that smell in here?"

"It's your lower legs, Mr. Talbot," I said. "They're dead."

He blinked his eyes and turned back to stare at the ceiling of the flight cabin.

I knew he was grappling with the meaning of his own death. I would have liked to put his mind at ease by telling him the moment of his death, the moment he most dreaded, had little meaning. But I did not, because he would not have understood. At least not today.

As with so many searching for the meaning of their deaths, Talbot came to the search too late. He spent his life busy and distracted from the thought of death. If he had roomed with that thought as with a lifelong companion, he would not now be trying to understand its meaning. He would know that the moment of his death held little significance. So he is ill-prepared to die, and the time for him to catch up on this lesson grows shorter.

Death happens to us. That is what Talbot needed to learn. It stops the heart and folds up the lungs. That is all. I have sat by the dying the instant their breathing stops. I never saw their eyes light up with some startling new revelation. Their minds were no clearer in the moments preceding death, and their last words carry no more wisdom than any of the words they ever uttered during their lifetime.

In high school gym class, our instructors lined us up to perform, one by one, gymnastic moves: rolls, cartwheels, and the rings. The farther down the line I was, the greater my anxiety grew as my place in line drew closer and closer. Then it was my turn, and in a few minutes it was over, passing before I could even comprehend what my turn meant.

Talbot's death will come soon. It would be better if he was ready to take his turn at death without anxiety. But he is anxious, and I do not see that changing any time soon. I will have my turn at death. I'm not sure how long the line is before my turn approaches, but I see that line shrink every day. When the time comes, I, who have studied death . . . I, who have helped others meet it . . . I, yes I, will do my somersault into the next world, trusting my kindly guide will set me on the right path home.

Nothing I say can prepare patients to welcome their turn at

death. There are no magic words. My parents thought I comforted the dying by listening to them. I do listen to the dying and draw them out, following up on what they tell me. Others think it is my kindness that helps. And it is true that I do all I can for the dying. But listening is never enough; kindness is never enough. It will certainly not be enough for Talbot. He expects people to listen to him, and he misjudges the motives of the kind. No amount of listening and no amount of kindness will change his attitude.

No, I help the dying by letting them happen to me. I let them happen to me in the way death happens to them. Their deafness and blindness; their nights sleeping fitfully on sofas when they could not find their bedroom in the dark; their dirty diapers and urine-soaked sheets; their untouched meals sitting on crumb-littered counters; their forgotten pill boxes; their anger and impatience; their loneliness when children forget to call; their tears; their confusion reading the mail; their grief when they lose their last friend and have no one left with whom to share their earliest memories. This all happens to them and so to me. And for my part, I shower them matter-of-factly, check their vital signs matter-of-factly, comfort them matter-of-factly, relive their memories matter-of-factly, entice them to eat matter-of-factly, and remind their children to telephone and visit, and I do so matter-of-factly. Most of my patients die prepared. They wait their turn at death without whining, without drama, without anxiety. Matter-of-factly. They understand that there is no mystery in that final moment. They understand that when their turn comes, it just happens.

Talbot has not yet learned this truth. He wants to jump the line. I look over at him in the helicopter cabin. He is concentrated, thinking ahead to his confrontation with Meredith and to his confrontation with his doctors. He will call for a new vote of the board, and he will fight with his doctors to treat him at home.

The helicopter descended. "Thank you for back there," Talbot said, pointing toward the Escanaba.

"You're welcome," I said, surprised he took notice. Looking out as the helicopter settled down on the helipad, I saw his house staff assembled on the clipped green lawn. Meredith was not among them.

"Where's my wife?" was Talbot's first question when the rotors cut out.

"She just left for the club, Mr. Talbot," his chief of staff said reluctantly.

Talbot scowled.

"We need to get Mr. Talbot bathed and settled," I ordered. "His doctors will be here any minute. Prepare the examination room." The EMTs carried Talbot into the lodge, and the helicopter departed.

I looked out at Lake Superior and saw the morning mist hanging dense along the point. It was gray and cold to the touch. I shivered and, looking about, saw a raven on the lawn. Picking up stones, I began to throw them at it. One struck home, but the great bird shook it off, waddling beyond range. I walked toward it, throwing as I went. The black bird flew upward, circled in the mist above me, and then descended slowly, coming to roost on the peak of the house. And I shouted, "Leave him alone!"

Walking back past the helipad, I knelt down and ran my fingers over the white cross on the black asphalt circle. It was damp with mist, and I felt a singing vibration in my fingertips as I traced, "Help me . . . help him."

One of last winter's maple leaves cartwheeled across the asphalt, clicking. It came to rest by my fingertips, and above the crash of waves, I heard my kindly guide say, "I will keep watch."

Standing, I said aloud, "Thank you." Then the leaf fluttered off, and all was quiet.

From the house, I heard Talbot ordering his chief of staff to "Round up the board."

One of Talbot's doctors arrived. I waved and accompanied him into the house.

Nothing of consequence happened after that.

IN THE
Forest

RAVEN

*I*T WAS A GOOD FIRE.

I am back above the First Falls, perched on my considerably shortened old white pine.

Once as solid as the rock on which it grew, loggers bypassed it for decades for fear of dulling their saws. Now dead, it will disappear, cut down by woodpeckers and beetles. One spring the first strong wind will topple it into the Escanaba's great eddy.

And I will need to find a new roost by the First Falls.

Time enough for that.

As with my white pine, all around is black. So black I am lost in the landscape until my glossy wings flash in the sun. All else bears a dull charcoal hide.

The Escanaba is untouched.

Death is the life of the Escanaba. Verdant woods feed the river spoonful by spoonful. Windblown twigs and branches and fall's yellow and scarlet leaves ride the river like a rich carpet until they sink and molder.

Fire quickens the pace of decay, of death. It hastens the migration of the woods into the water. Instead of leaf by leaf, it is tree by tree. Now, after every storm, the rain will stain the river black, flushing ash and cinders into its currents. No need for decades of green growth and more decades of decay; the fire reduced the woods to an ingestible powder in a day. The river will be that much richer, that much sooner.

Below me is the great eddy. It will collect and store it all, for the great eddy digests leaf and log, cinder and ember, soaking them in its juices until they settle to its bottom like gold at the bottom of a prospector's pan. Nuggets of life-feeding worms, caddis flies, stone flies, and mayflies.

By fall, the Escanaba's banks will be washed clean. And next year, blueberries, strawberries, and popple shoots will flourish. Tamarack and cedars will take root in its swamps. Jackpine will spring up everywhere. Next year, bears will graze the berries; birds will flock for the insects; and deer, with their newly dropped fawns, will browse the green shoots.

Amnesia is the disease of the riverbank.

Blackened tree trunks will stand for a short time as memorials to the fire. And for a short time, they alone will poke against the far horizon and prick the memories of those who lived through the fire. But then these blackened monuments will fall and give birth to vine and flower. In a few years, green saplings and bushes reaching skyward will close off the horizon. And the next forest generation will forget the fire.

I will not forget.

Today as I roost here, I am alone.

Pauguck left with the cat for the Blessed Isles.

Just before leaving with the cat, Pauguck asked me, "Kahgahgee, what do you want from life?" He is always asking questions like that.

"I want to keep living . . . as I have done for millennia," I said. "I want nothing else."

"But you have not seen the Blessed Isles and the shimmering Silver Lake," Pauguck offered. "They are like nothing you have ever witnessed before. Believe me when I say they are marvelously beautiful."

"I believe you, Pauguck, but I am not interested."

"Make the trip with me. I will personally guide you, and after

I show them to you, you will stay," he said. "All day, the spirits are at their leisure, talking with each other, fishing and swimming. The shores of Silver Lake are white sand and its water the blue of sapphires—bluer than the sky. And the sun, reflecting off its surface, spreads a blinding silver sheen. Peace and harmony. Green pastures and green forests, spring green, the green of newly budding trees. All in flower, and every flower giving off its sweet fragrance. There is no hunger and always someone new to meet. You will never be alone again."

"An inviting picture, Pauguck, but I must say no."

"What do you want, Kahgahgee?" Pauguck asked thoughtfully. "And please do not dismiss my question with some offhand answer as you do so often. I really want to know."

"What do I want?" I repeated his question. I have thought about my future, but to spend time talking about it always seemed pointless. "What do I want? Pauguck, do not misjudge me. My answer must be short, not for want of thought, but because what I want is so very simple." I paused and then answered slowly, "In truth, I just want an eternity of what I am doing right now," I said. "I have endured from the time before man, well before the great glaciers and the grayling that swam in the waters dripping from their base, and I have enjoyed almost every minute of it. This life is all I know, and it is a life I enjoy."

"But in your world, you have worries and close calls. There is no telling when you may die accidentally, and you have your daily aches and pains," he argued.

"That is all true," I said. "And I will not deny that I have moments, especially in the dead of winter, when I dream of a day scavenging fish washed up along a warm beach. But my life here is so much more interesting. I love the triumph of evading mobbing crows. I love the first beakful of roadkill when my stomach has been empty for days. I love stealing an especially tasty sausage from a backyard grill and laughing as I am shooed away. There is so much of this life I love."

"But you are often in danger," Pauguck said. "One day, you may even be killed."

"That is exactly what makes it so interesting," I said. "Unlike you, I revel in risking my life. Besides, what is the worst that can happen? I die, and afterward I meet you in the flesh, so to speak, and then I journey to the Blessed Isles."

"You had better keep your eyes, Kahgahgee, if you want to enjoy the spirit world," Pauguck warned.

"Get to me before the ants and the crows," I said.

I believe I glimpsed a look of fondness on Pauguck's face. "I will, Kahgahgee. I will," he promised.

And Pauguck's word was always good.

Yes, it was a good fire.

And it was good to see Pauguck again.

In several months, I will see the able-bodied man on the river again, for brook trout still swim the river he loves. I dream of him slipping and hitting his head . . . unconscious for five minutes. That is all I need.

But he knows me now. He knows I am a threat, and he will be more careful when he sees me about.

And I will be about.

About the Author

*J*OHN GUBBINS LIVES WITH his wife, Carol, alongside the Escanaba River in the Upper Peninsula of Michigan. His historical novel, *Profound River*, was recently published and has received acclaim as a well-researched and compelling story of Britain's greatest sportswoman. Spending his teenage years as a seminarian studying traditional theology and philosophy, he later attended the University of Chicago, where he received a graduate degree in humanities, and Columbia University Law School, where he received a juris doctor degree. After pursuing a big city law career, he came to his senses and settled his family near some of the Midwest's greatest trout streams. He spends his free time with Carol and his son Alex, fishing, camping, and poetry reading. Alex, a published poet, attends and teaches in the MFA program at Northern Michigan University.